MW00414544

BEER & BROOMSTICKS

UNLUCKY CHARMS BOOK 3

T.M. CROMER

Beer & Broomsticks Copyright © 2022 T.M. Cromer

All rights reserved. No part of this publication may be reproduced, distributed, or transmitted in any form or by any means, including photocopying, recording, or other electronic or mechanical methods, without the prior written permission of the publisher, except in the case of brief quotations embodied in critical reviews and certain other noncommercial uses permitted by copyright law.

ISBN: 978-1-956941-00-5 (EPUB)
ISBN: 978-1-956941-13-5 (PAPERBACK)
ISBN: 978-1-956941-11-1 (HARDBACK)
ISBN: 978-1-956941-12-8 (LARGE PRINT)

Cover Design: Deranged Doctor Designs

This is a work of fiction. Names, characters, businesses, places, events, and incidents are either the products of the author's imagination or used in a fictitious manner. Any resemblance to actual persons, living or dead, or actual events is purely coincidental.

This one is for my beloved Tinkerbell. You will forever hold a special place in my heart, my dearest soul puppy. Writing this story was a greatest struggle without you, my muse.

To Dani, Tracey, and Marion:
Thank you for knowledge of all things Irish!

CHAPTER 1

$\mathcal{B}$ridget O'Malley loved Ruairí O'Connor. She had since the day they'd accidentally met by the garden gate dividing their properties. At the time, she was four years old and didn't understand she wasn't supposed to love him. She was *supposed* to hate him with every fiber of her being as every O'Malley had hated every O'Connor since the family feud started two hundred and fifty years before.

Despite his betrayal when they were only twenty—the one she still couldn't bear to think about some seventeen years later —she found it difficult to call up the hate. Oh, for sure she wasn't happy with him, and she'd spend every hour of every day making him aware of the fact if she could, but she didn't hate him. Not even a little.

"Good morning, *mo ghrá.*" Ruairí had a deep, raspy tone that never failed to reach in and tickle her girly parts.

Bridget cast an irritated glance toward the stone fence where that good-for-nothing O'Connor stood sipping his morning coffee. Her standard sneering response was done more out of habit these days. "I'm not your love, Ruairí. I'm not your anything."

1

"Oh, but you are. Have been since the day I first set my eyes on you thirty-three years ago."

They were of an age. Both bonded as children and spent their youth sneaking out to meet at the same time they were being taught to despise one another. They'd continually laughed at their parents' attempts to poison their hearts and minds.

Until the day Ruairí had poisoned hers against him.

He'd done what her parents and grandparents hadn't been able to.

Snorting her derision, she turned her attention back to the rosebush she was pruning.

"We aren't getting any younger, Bridg. When are you going to forgive me?"

Her heart flipped in her chest, and her mouth went dry. If she faced him, she knew what she'd see. Six feet of contrite male with shaggy blond hair and a knicker-melting smile. She didn't turn around because she couldn't afford to lose her only clean set of drawers. Which reminded her, she needed to get the laundry on before heading to work at the pub today.

Goddess, she needed a clone.

"You're not plannin' on answering, *mo ghrá*? Can you not see your way past a wee mistake?"

That asinine comment brought her head around. "Wee mistake? Are you mad, Ruairí?" She chucked her pruning shears at his head, and lucky enough for him, he had rabbit-fast reflexes. Oh, if only she had the magic of a normal witch, she'd blast him to hell and back. And wasn't that another blame she could lay at his door? If it hadn't been for his bloody family, they would *all* be enjoying a taste of the Goddess's gift right now, instead of just her brothers.

Sometimes she dreamed about having abilities. What wouldn't she do with a spot of magic? Where wouldn't she go if she could teleport from one place to another in the blink of an eye like her brothers were beginning to do?

Fecking prophecy.

And fecking O'Connors for causing all their woes!

"You got a temper on you, ya do!" Ruairí shouted as he tried to mop up the coffee he'd spilled down his shirt when he dodged the shears.

Bridget experienced a pang for the discomfort he must've felt from the hot liquid, but she couldn't stop herself from running an appreciative eye over the sculpted chest displayed so nicely by the wet material clinging to each and every muscle. The blimey bastard even had beautiful nipples, small, hard, and perfectly pebbled at the moment.

With a heartfelt sigh, she turned her back, but not before calling over her shoulder, "Then feck off and don't come back, why don't you? It's not like I've asked you to hang about like a damned wraith."

"One day I won't come back. What'll ya do then, you bloody shrew? You'll be sorry for the way you treated me. You won't have old Ruairí O'Connor to abuse."

"Promise?" She gave him a hope-filled look.

The flash of his wicked grin nearly did her in, and she knelt at the base of the bush on the pretense of fluffing the dirt.

Damned weak knees!

Nothing was finer than Ruairí's face when he was amused by her. His blue eyes twinkled. Paired with that dimpled smile and the mussed white-blond hair that always seemed to need a barber, those peepers of his had the ability to melt even the steeliest of hearts. Cold, hard determination was no match for his roguish charm. And didn't that beat all?

"What are you doing here, Ruairí? Don't you have a job to see to?"

"It's Saturday."

She frowned and ripped out a weed. Her days all ran

together now that her family had opened O'Malley's Black Cat Inn. Between the pub and their bed and breakfast, Bridget was run ragged. Soon enough, her brother Cian and his new bride, Piper, would return from their honeymoon and relieve her of the burden of running two places.

"What time do you want me at the pub tonight, *mo ghrá?*"

Ruairí had stepped in a few months back—despite Bridget's objections—and taken over bartending while she prepared the occasional meal and waited tables when her servers failed to show. He'd initially done it as a favor to Cian, but he'd never left.

She couldn't say Ruairí was a terrible worker; he'd actually turned out to be a godsend. But she didn't have to like it, and she sure as hell wouldn't praise or thank him for his timely help.

"Three-thirty should do." If she could stand to have him around, she'd have told him an hour earlier to help prep for the evening ahead. However, it was essential to her mental well-being that she avoid spending as much time with him as possible. "Now go away. I've things to do."

RUAIRÍ STARED AT THE RIGID BACK BRIDGET PRESENTED TO HIM. The woman was as stubborn as the day was long. She refused to listen to any apologies or explanations of the past, convinced he was in the wrong.

And maybe he had been, *once.* But now? Now he deserved to be heard. Having dealt with her frigid stares and scathing remarks for the better part of seventeen years, he was working up to a fine temper.

Her brothers, Cian and Carrick, were convinced she'd mellow if Ruairí remained in close proximity. They were wrong. If anything, Bridget had reinforced the walls of her heart and effectively barricaded it against him. Convincing her that he sincerely regretted his fool mistake was getting harder by the day.

She tossed back her shiny red hair with a simple flick of her wrist and cast him a withering glare. "Still here?"

For some odd reason, he found the gesture humorous, but he dare not laugh where she could see, or she'd skin him alive. He couldn't resist saying the one thing he knew would irk her. "Aye, *mo ghrá*. It's difficult to part ways with one so lovely."

"Sure, and you didn't have a problem movin' on when you decided to stick your lying tongue down Molly Mae's scrawny throat."

Ah, finally. Bridget was ready to address the ever-present issue.

"Molly Mae kissed *me*, Bridg. Not the other way 'round."

She snorted. "From my vantage point, the kiss went on for a good day, and you weren't shoving her away, now were you?"

"She used a spell on me."

Her severe frown rivaled the dark clouds of the fiercest winter storm. "Spell? What kind of spell?"

He almost felt bad for Molly Mae and was glad she wasn't standing here now. Bridget would eviscerate her, magic or no. "One designed to freeze me in place," he improvised. "I'm telling you now, Bridg, I never knew she had magic powerful enough to control me that way."

Bridget squinted as she weighed his words.

Ruairí did his best to look innocent.

Yes, he'd kissed Molly Mae down by the stream under the large oak where he and Bridget used to meet in secret. He'd employed a whole lot of stupid with a huge heaping of arrogance when he'd come up with the idea to make Bridget jealous and force her hand. The decidedly dumb plan to convince her she couldn't live without him had backfired on an epic level. Seventeen torturous years later, he was still dealing with the fallout.

"Do you know your left eyebrow twitches and you grimace slightly before you lie, Ruairí?"

His hand flew to his brow, but he dropped it just as quickly when he saw the smug satisfaction on her face. Goddess, he was still three steps behind Bridget on a good day.

She stood and threw the clump of weeds in his direction. "Get away, ya fool. I've no time for your lies."

"Fine, you want the truth? I'll give it to ya. I kissed her. There. I said it." He crossed his arms over his chest, scowling harder when the wet patch from the coffee soaked through his sleeves. He was done with lies and half-truths. The time had come to put the past to rest. "I wanted to make you jealous, Bridg. You refused to marry me and leave the pub. I thought to change your mind."

"By kissing another woman?"

He winced at the shriek. Yeah, well, it hadn't taken him but a minute to register and regret *that* folly. "I wasn't the smartest tool in the shed back then, and—"

"You still aren't," she assured him with her hands planted firmly on her hips.

Ruairí ignored the dig. *"And* I grossly miscalculated your reaction. I thought to provoke you into admitting you loved me. Figuring if you finally realized we were meant to be, you'd agree to run away with me. Away from feuding families and cursed relics. Away where we could be happy, *mo ghrá.*"

Her silence made him fearful. Bridget O'Malley was never quiet. That she now was thoroughly disconcerted him, and the nerves of his belly all attacked at once.

"Well, you were a fecking eejit then, and you're a fecking eejit now," she finally said. Her eyes were a dark forest green, and it killed Ruairí to see them so. Once, when the two of them were happy and carefree, those eyes had shone like brightly polished emeralds of the purest quality.

"It's the truth, Bridget," he said in a low, serious tone. One he rarely used with her.

Her lids dropped, but not before he saw the glimmer of tears.

He wanted to go to her, yet as sure as the sun rose in the east and set in the west, she'd reject him. The tension in the way she held her luscious body said as much.

"No matter the motivation, you betrayed what we had, Ruairí." She sighed and pressed two fingers to the area between her brows. "What do you expect from me? Forgiveness?"

"That's a start."

"Fine. I forgive you."

His heart stalled and resumed at triple time. "Truly?"

"Aye."

With a smile on his face and a song in his heart, Ruairí braced his hands on the low stone wall, ready to scale it and kiss her rosy lips until stars appeared in her brilliant eyes and the night sky grew jealous of the glow.

She held up a hand, effectively stopping him before he got started.

"Hold it right there. You're still not welcome to set one foot on this property."

"What's this then?" He wanted to smash the wall with his bare fists. "Either you forgive me or you don't."

"You were twenty years old, Ruairí, and stupid to boot. Of course I forgive you. But it doesn't mean I intend to take up where we left off."

"Why the hell not? I love you, Bridget."

She laughed in what appeared to be genuine amusement. Laughed hard enough to double over. Hard enough to have tears pour from her eyes.

Ruairí almost despised her in that moment.

"Your face!" she crowed. "You look as if I stole your favorite toy."

"Is this about paying me back? Tit for tat?"

Bridget sobered in the blink of an eye. "Oh, no. I haven't begun to pay you back. But I will."

His unease was back as soon as he saw the promise of retribution in her eye. "You can't forgive and still take revenge, Bridget O'Malley. Sure, and that's not the way it works."

Her smile was pure wicked intent. "Oh, but it does, Ruairí O'Connor. It most certainly does."

CHAPTER 2

*R*uairí showed up for work an hour early, and Bridget cursed her damned luck. Sure, the contrary man had to do the opposite of what he was told. Without a word of welcome, she jerked her chin toward the back room. "The front coolers need stocking since you're here."

He grinned, probably because he knew good and well he'd gotten the best of her by showing up before his shift, but he went to do her bidding without a word of complaint.

She heard the bottles rattle as Ruairí stacked cases on the hand truck, and her mind wandered back to his confession earlier in the day. Had he really only kissed that horrid minger, Molly Mae Murphy, to provoke her into a jealous response? Or was he lying to save face? It begged the question why he'd bother seventeen years after the fact.

He returned with the beer and began stocking. His presence was larger than she liked. Never before, when Bridget shared the space behind the bar with her brothers, had it felt so small. Ruairí hummed as he worked, and the lively tune grated on the last of her nerves. She'd favored the song when they were young lovers—and he fecking knew it.

"Shut your yap and turn on the radio if you must have music," she grumbled.

His mouth twitched, and a small knowing smile played on those full, kissable lips of his.

Kissable? Where the hell had that thought come from? She'd be buggered if she put her lips where Molly's had been—even if he'd scrubbed his mouth five times every day since. "You only kissed her the once?"

His body jerked, and his head whipped around to stare.

Bridget stared back, shocked the words had left her mouth.

"Aye." He placed a hand over his heart. His sincerity couldn't be mistaken.

She threw her towel on the dark bar. "Pfft. Get to work. I don't pay you to gawk about, now do I?"

"You don't pay me at all," he replied dryly. A few heartbeats later, he asked, "And what about you, Bridg?"

"What about me?"

His jaw tightened, and a muscle ticked. "I heard you flew right into the arms of Dermot."

Dermot Neary had been Ruairí's best friend when they were kids. Directly after Bridget broke off her relationship with Ruairí, he and Dermot had a falling out. She'd never learned why, but the sight of him, looking as if he wanted to crush the beer bottles with his bare hands, made her wonder if Ruairí was jealous of his ex-best friend.

"Not the way you think. We were friends and had a few drinks to talk about our woes. Nothing more."

He frowned down at the cooler and gave a single nod.

"Would it matter if I had?"

"Of course, *mo ghrá*. What kind of fool question is that?"

The hard clink of glass against glass made her wince. "I—"

The side door of the pub opened. The darkened entry combined with the sunlight behind the newcomer made it difficult to discern their identity. "May I help you?" she called out.

"It's me who'd like to help you, beautiful Bridget."

She knew that voice!

"Quentin Buchanan," she breathed.

Ruairí's head came up, and he glared in her direction before turning his ire on the virtual giant at the far side of the room. "Who's—"

She didn't wait for his question or bother to answer. Fleet-footing it across the pub, she met Quentin midway and dove into his embrace. He laughed and swung her up and around.

"You're tinier every time I see you," he teased. "You're almost small enough to put in my pocket."

"Pfft, go on with you, you scut."

Flashing an über-white grin, he set her back on her feet and absently tucked a strand of his coffee-colored hair behind his ear. His chocolatey bedroom eyes glowed with a playful light. Leaning in, as he was now, it had to appear as if his six-foot-six frame was hovering over her in a semi-protective, loving manner. As if he were mere seconds away from sweeping her into a full-body dip and claiming her lips for his own.

Bridget was human enough—and sex-starved enough—to wish he would, but she also knew he was a happily married man with eyes only for the woman he'd wed. But oh, a witch could dream.

Quentin asked in a low voice, "Who's the guy behind the bar ready to rip out my throat?"

"Just someone who owed my brother a favor. He works here when I'm short staffed." She didn't bother to lower her own voice.

Quentin's chuckle was rumbly and sent shivers the length of her spine.

Goddess, what a delicious sound!

"Hmm." His dark eyes assessed a scene somewhere behind her. "And how long has he been in love with you?"

"He's not," Bridget responded, her tone sharp. She inhaled deeply and infused calm into her voice. "He's not."

Quentin's mocking half smile made her want to spit nails. "Right. Should I kiss you to prove it to you both?"

"No, thank you. Your wife is Alastair Thorne's daughter, and I'm not a feckin' eejit."

"They share a temperament," he agreed with a light laugh. "My prickly pear is an acquired taste for many."

"Sure, and not for you, though. We all know you've always adored her."

"I've loved her from the first."

She hugged him again. How could she not?

He was beautiful outside, but inside, he was just as stunning. Quentin had never met a stranger and was quick to go out of his way for those he cared about. Case in point, a few years back, he'd helped his wife's aunt save her abducted husband and remove a dangerous enemy from the Thorne's playing field without any thought to his own life or possible punishment by the Witches' Council.

The top of the cooler thunked shut, and by the sound of it, cardboard was being pulverized by Ruairí's bare hands.

Bridget didn't turn around.

"Not that it's not my greatest pleasure, to be sure, but what are you doing here, Quentin?"

He gestured over his shoulder to the woman standing just inside the door. Bridget had failed to notice her in all the excitement of seeing her old friend. "I thought I'd bring my wife on a little vacation."

"Oh!" Bridget rushed to Holly. "Sure, and it's lovely to see you again."

Holly handed off the toddler she'd been holding to her husband and clasped Bridget's hands in hers. "You, too. It feels like it's been forever, and we wanted to introduce you to Francesca."

Quentin began blowing raspberries on his daughter's neck, eliciting breathless giggles from the child. The sound was the sweetest Bridget had ever heard, and it made her heart ache. She'd always wanted a child of her own. The odds were great against it happening this late in life.

"I'm assuming you're staying with us? Was Carrick at the Black Cat to see you settled?"

"He was," Holly said.

"He told us you were here and sent us to get a pint," Quentin added.

"Well I, for one, am glad you decided to visit." Bridget faced Holly again. "Would you care for a bite to eat or is it just a bit of Granny O'Malley's brew?"

"I'd love both." Quentin swung his daughter behind his back to hang sideways between his arms. The child's peals of laughter echoed in the enclosed space. "If you don't mind."

When Bridget turned toward the bar, Ruairí's face was void of the thundercloud he'd been sporting minutes before, and he was now all smiles.

Smug plonker.

She almost wished Holly hadn't come so she could irritate him further with Quentin's flirty presence.

"Welcome." Ruairí's dancing blue eyes locked on Bridget. "Any friend of Bridget's is a friend of mine. Isn't that right, *mo ghrá?*

She bared her teeth, barely managing to smother a growl.

RUAIRÍ HAD ALMOST BITTEN OFF HIS OWN TONGUE WHEN THE god-like creature walked in the door. Sure, he fancied himself a good-looking bloke, but the other man was the stuff of women's fantasies, and there was no way on this green earth Ruairí could compete with the likes of *him*.

Only for Bridget would he have tried.

Then Holly had entered with their small daughter, and Ruairí was able to feel solid ground under his feet again.

Quentin was a natural-born charmer, with eyes able to assess and provide what a woman desired at a single glance, but it had only taken one look to see the man's world revolved around Holly and Frankie, as the toddler was introduced.

Even more delightful was the fact Bridget lost her buffer against him, and Ruairí couldn't be more thrilled. He knew full well she'd planned to use Quentin to keep him at a distance the second the other guy walked through the door. Intent lurked in the calculating gleam of her eye when she'd checked for Ruairí's whereabouts over her shoulder after she hugged the man. Her disappointment had been keen, but only to someone who knew her well.

Ruairí wasn't going to let her run this time. He'd told her true by the gate earlier today; they weren't getting any younger. Seventeen years was long enough to dance around their feelings. Either she gave him a second chance, or he needed to leave for good. No longer could he live next to her, catching glimpses of her bright ginger head and her mouth-watering body without going mad. He wasn't into self-torture.

After he'd poured a pint, he passed it to Quentin with an attempt at a friendly smile. Forgiving the man for doing what Ruairí couldn't and bringing the sparkle back to Bridget's face, even for a brief time, was difficult.

Quentin's dark laughing gaze flicked to Bridget then back to him.

The fecker had the nerve to wink!

Ruairí leaned in under the guise of wiping the counter. "Making time with another man's woman is not a way to make friends in these parts."

"Is that what I'm doing?"

He narrowed his eyes on Quentin's handsome face. A face with flawless features that Ruairí so desperately wanted to rearrange.

Maintaining eye contact with him, Quentin raised his voice to ask, "Bridget, darling, when are you running away with me?"

Holly extended her arm and smacked the back of his dark head without turning in his direction or missing a beat in her conversation with Bridget.

Laughing, he winked at Ruairí a second time. "My prickly pear would murder me, in addition to cutting off my balls. As lovely as your woman is, I'm not interested."

"It seems safer for all involved," Ruairí acknowledged. "My beloved Bridget's voice rivals that of a raving-mad banshee when she's in a foul temper. The sound will make your puir ears bleed. She'd give your prickly pear a run for her money, sure she would."

"My sympathies, man. I've been on the receiving end of a foul temper and a sharp tongue a time or two myself."

The men tapped their glasses together in perfect accord under sour looks from the women.

Faster than Ruairí could blink, Bridget picked up the hose and squirted his crotch.

"*Ya mad—*"

Another spritz of water shut him up. He charged and ripped the nozzle from her hand. With a menacing grin, he soaked her shirt. "Two can play that game, *mo ghrá.*"

"But only one of us can be kicked in the bollocks, Ruairí O'Connor."

"And *that* is our cue to leave." Quentin scooped Frankie up in one arm and wrapped the other around Holly's shoulders. "We'll catch a bite in town. Have fun, lovebirds," he called over his shoulder with a laugh.

"Coward!" Ruairí hollered back.

"I'm a lover, not a fighter, man. You're on your own."

The other guy had given him an idea, and Ruairí scooped Bridget up into a fireman's hold then set her on the cooler by the register.

"I swear, I will rip your insides out and serve them up to you, if you ever touch me—"

He stopped her threat the only way he knew how—with his lips.

The wild beating of his heart was like a long lost relative returning home for a visit. Only Bridget had ever caused his pulse to gallop out of control as it now was. Lifting his hands to cup her jaw, he deepened the kiss, shocked she let him. He was even more surprised when she grabbed fistfuls of his shirt to draw him closer.

The sound of the outer door slamming jerked them apart. For a long moment, their gazes locked, and the rawness in her stunning eyes ate at him. Apology was on the tip of his tongue, but he'd done enough of that in the past, and he was damned if he'd say he was sorry for what they'd just shared. Especially if it woke her up to how much he still loved and wanted her.

"Give me another chance, Bridget. *Please*," he begged huskily.

Real regret clung to her words when she said, "I can't."

CHAPTER 3

The next morning Bridget was scrambling eggs to serve the inn's residents when Carrick's wife, Roisin, strolled into the kitchen and stopped short with her hands on her hips.

"I told you I'd cook and serve this morning, Bridget. Do you not trust anyone else to do your chores?"

Bridget nodded to the full coffee pot. "Pour us both a cup, why don't ya?"

"You didn't answer me."

"I trust you plenty. I couldn't sleep."

"Let me guess." Roisin handed her a mug of black coffee, containing a single teaspoon of sugar. "Six feet of blond hair and brawny muscles who worked with you at the pub last night."

After shooting Roisin a middle finger, Bridget dished up the eggs and handed them over. "Make yourself useful and set these on the table."

"Throw a lid on them. You've got time to tell me what happened."

"That fecking arse kissed me," she mumbled and hid behind the act of drinking her coffee.

Roisin's grin caused acid to churn in Bridget's belly. Sure, and her family all wanted her to find a mate, to be as happy as they all were, and they'd be chuffed as could be if that man was Ruairí, whom they all liked and respected. But Bridget was reticent, and she couldn't quite say why.

"What do you intend to do about it?"

Trust her best friend to go straight for the heart of the matter.

Bridget looked out the window toward his home. No lights burned this early, and she imagined he was fast asleep in his bed. *A bed she wouldn't mind occupying with him*, taunted the little voice inside her head. The man had learned technique in the intervening years since they'd been a couple. It stood to reason that skill would spill over into lovemaking. Had he kissed her like that when they were younger, she'd probably have forgiven him a lot quicker or maybe eloped like he'd begged her to do.

With a firm shake of her head to dispel the torrid thoughts brewing, she retrieved the platter of eggs. "Nothing. I intend to do nothing."

Bridget had to give Roisin credit for holding her comments. The compressed lips were a dead giveaway that she wanted to have a hearty go at changing Bridget's mind. After another few minutes of working side by side to set the table, Roisin gave into the urge.

"Have you ever thought about moving away? Of going somewhere else where you might meet another man you could fall in love with instead of remaining here, tangled up in conflicting feelings for Ruairí?" she asked gently.

Bridget couldn't take exception. Roisin was the sister of her heart and her sister-in-law by fact of marriage to Carrick. Their shared business interests kept them firmly entrenched in each other's lives. Unable to answer right away, Bridget spent an extra minute or two straightening the cutlery next to the plates.

"You have," Roisin guessed. "What's stopping you? This place? Carrick and I could run it, and Cian can manage the pub with Piper's help. Sure, and I bet Dubheasa would return if you asked her. She'd be able to work remotely for a while. You could take your share and go."

Tears blurred Bridget's vision, and she rapidly blinked. "I know, but it's not as simple as all that, Ro." Her friend's compassionate look was too much to bear, and Bridget busied herself retrieving the remainder of the morning's breakfast.

"As long as you live here, you'll weigh every man you meet against Ruairí. They'll come up wanting."

"You think I *should* leave?" Fear of the future unfurled in her chest. The pub and inn were all she'd ever known. Her responsibilities had never allowed for her to escape this narrow world. Never allowed her to venture out other than the occasional coven meetings GiGi Thorne-Gillespie hosted eons ago. "I don't know what I'd do," Bridget confessed.

"Between all of us, we could come up with the money for you to start anew. Or we'd ask Eoin. You know he'd not say no. Look, you could go anywhere on *Éire* or in the world. Enjoy your life."

The idea had merit, but Bridget loved her family, and she wouldn't hide from Ruairí. Not then, and certainly not now. She shook her head. "Thank you for the offer, but this is my home. He'll not run me out of it."

"Oh, Bridg, I just want you to be happy."

"I'm not *un*happy." She shrugged and arranged the place settings on the table. They had five guests through the weekend, not counting the Buchanans, and they'd receive the best hospitality the Black Cat Inn had to offer. Bridget prided herself with how she managed her bed & breakfast. "Perhaps a fine man, one perfect for me, will sail through the door someday soon." She forced a teasing grin.

Before Roisin could answer, the backdoor opened and Ruairí entered.

A shiver ran the length of Bridget's spine. It was as if the Fates had anticipated her words and sent him in at that precise moment.

"What are *you* doin' here?" she asked with a fierce scowl, irritated that the Fates were such fickle creatures. She noticed the duffel bag in his hand. "And what do you think you're doing with *that*?"

"The pump's gone out at my place, and I've no water." Dropping the bag by the door, he approached her. "I need a place to stay, and I've decided to stay at the Black Cat."

Ruairí O'Connor under the same roof as her? Not in this bleedin' lifetime! She wasn't functioning well as it was with him filling in at the pub. If he was constantly underfoot, she could kiss her sanity goodbye. "Forget it. Find another place or use your stolen magic to fix it, why don't you."

"Bridg…" His tone was wheedling, and damned if she wasn't tempted to set aside her grievances.

"No! We'll not be sharing a bed, and that's final!"

Roisin gasped, and Ruairí grinned.

"I'd not said anything about a bed, *mo ghrá*. But now I know where your head's at, and I have to say I like it."

"My head is not in the bedroom," she denied hotly, color flaming in her cheeks.

"Sure, and it's okay if you tell everyone that. You and I know the truth." The scut had the nerve to wink.

"I swear Ruairí O'Connor, I will gut you like a fish if you even think about setting one foot in my room. You'll stay across the hall in your own room, and that's final."

Both he and Roisin laughed.

Bridget replayed the conversation in her head and groaned

aloud. He'd neatly tricked her into saying he could stay, that silver-tongued devil.

Leaning in, he placed his lips close to her ear. "I'm more than willing to sleep in your room with you, *mo ghrá*, just say the word."

Because she wanted just that, she placed her palm over his face and shoved him away. "Get away with ya." She took three steps then turned back. "I suppose you'll be wanting breakfast?"

"If it's not too much trouble."

She shot a thumb over her shoulder at the table. "Have a seat, and let's say a prayer the Black Cat doesn't fall down around our ears. Goddess knows my ancestors will be rolling over in their graves at having a feckin' O'Connor set foot in our home."

As Ruairí covertly watched Bridget tidy up the kitchen from his seat, he mentally patted himself on the back for getting the best of her for once. He'd shamelessly made up the excuse about his home needing repairs, knowing she was a soft touch under her grumbly exterior.

Just this morning, he'd gotten word from his cousin Ronan that his uncle Loman had escaped the Witches' Council stronghold. The members of the high table had sent out a team on a worldwide manhunt, but wily ol' Uncle Loman was in the wind.

Ruairí wasn't taking any chances with the O'Malleys' safety, especially not Bridget's. As it was, she haunted him in his waking and sleeping hours. If anything happened to her as a result of their stupid family feud, he'd die a thousand deaths.

Also, he wasn't comfortable with someone who looked like Quentin Buchanan living in such close proximity. With a guy like him around, Bridget might get ideas she could do much better than Ruairí. It wasn't to say she couldn't, but he figured he should keep a watch on things, all the same.

Roisin caught his eye behind Bridget's turned back and winked.

He couldn't prevent an answering grin. Roisin had always been perceptive. She saw through most people down to their heart. And according to Ronan, she'd been fierce when she'd attacked his cousin Seamus after the man had attempted to murder her son. Luckily, little Aeden had survived, but alas, Seamus did not. None of them would lose sleep over his demise, though. His cousins had made their beds, and now they'd be forced to sleep in them.

"How's Aeden?" Ruairí asked her.

"Better every day. His nightmares still plague him, but he's physically back to normal, and he's found his appetite again. He acts like he's eating for four."

He laughed. "He's a growing boyo. No doubt you'll need to take out a loan to feed him until he's off to university."

Roisin snorted. "Aye. I've told Carrick to get to writing. He'll need an epic fantasy series like those Harry Potter novels to keep us out of debtor's prison, he will."

Bridget placed a hand on Ruairí's shoulder, then leaned in front of him to set another bowl of eggs on the table. It was all he could do not to pull her into his lap. "Mind you don't eat all of these," she scolded him. "The rest of the—"

Before the words left her mouth, Quentin stepped into the kitchen and gave an appreciative sniff of the air. "Ah, Bridget O'Malley, if I wasn't married—"

"But you are, you tool," his petite wife said with affection and an exaggerated eye roll as she followed him into the room. "And stop acting like you never get a well-prepared meal at home. I swear, it's from being adopted. You act like you're always starving to death." Holly handed off the baby to Ruairí like she'd known him all her life and sat beside him. "Next time I see your father, babe, the two of us are going to have words."

With a grin wide enough to split his face, Quentin leaned down, drew the hair from Holly's neck aside, and gave her a love bite. "No need to be salty, my prickly pear. I still appreciate your special skills. Can't blame me for starving after last night's—"

She clamped a hand over his mouth, blushing a fiery red. "Shut it!"

Ruairí looked at the toddler in his arms. He had quite a few family and friends who had children, and he'd changed a nappy or two in his time. But the second he gazed down at Frankie's enchanting face, he was a goner. She stared up at him with wide, inquisitive eyes that seemed far too trusting of a stranger. With a sudden grin, she slapped her hands together with his face between them, and gave his nose an open-mouth kiss. He did his best to remove the little suckerfish from his person, wincing when one sharp little tooth scraped his skin.

Bridget's laughter brought his head up. His heart went into high gear hearing it again and seeing it was directed at him. She wasn't laughing in derision as she once would've, but in genuine amusement, and it gladdened his heart to see it. Holding her arms out, she lifted Frankie away as the girl began gnawing on his chin and drooling.

"None of that now, love. Ruairí already has enough trouble being mauled by all the *álainn cailíns*." Bridget lifted the child high in the air, flaring her eyes wide and grinning as she brought the girl down until their noses touched. She laughed again as Frankie squealed her delight.

His heart stuttered, and he wished for nothing more than for it to be their child Bridget was playing with. Roisin kicked him under the table. As warning to close his gaping jaw, he was sure. But when Bridget's sparkling gaze locked with his over the top of Frankie's dark head, he couldn't look away, and all the love he felt was there for her to see.

A long moment passed, and neither looked away, but a flash of something—*sadness?*—crossed her face, and with a smile down at the child, she kissed Frankie's rosy cheek. "And what is it you'll be wanting to eat, my darlin' girl?" Bridget propped the toddler on her hip and walked to the counter filled with everything from fruit to scones. "We'll not tell your mam and da if you'd prefer sweets, yeah?"

Holly arched a brow. "Just remember, sugared-up children stay with the person who provided the sweets. No take-backs."

As Ruairí watched Bridget craic on with the Buchanans and a few of the other boarders over breakfast, it occurred to him that he'd be happy to be part of this routine every morning. To sit beside Bridget after helping prepare the meal, and laugh with visitors of the Black Cat Inn suddenly seemed like the perfect dream.

But the reality was Loman and Moira needed to be stopped first.

CHAPTER 4

*B*ridget didn't argue when Ruairí helped her clean up after the morning meal. It felt foreign yet comfortable with him beside her, drying the dishes she handed to him. Neither of them spoke other than for her to direct him where to put the occasional plate or cup, and he picked up the routine quickly enough.

"Why are you really here?" she asked. When he opened his mouth, she recognized the tall tale forming. "If it's a lie that's about to depart that mouth of yours, keep it. I've not the time nor the inclination to deal with such foolishness."

"And why would you believe I was lyin'?"

"Your lips are moving, aren't they?"

Those same lips twisted in amusement, and Bridget's heart beat faster for it.

Damn him.

Ruairí surprised her with the truth. "My uncle escaped from prison." A troubled look settled on his face and the furrow between his brows deepened. "Ronan told me early this morning. Though why the delay, I've no bleedin' clue."

"I remember the stories you told me about Loman O'Connor's cruelty. So, he's Ronan's father then?"

"Aye."

Bridget dried her hands, taking the time to properly form the question plaguing her. She didn't want him to believe she was being overly suspicious, so she needed to tread carefully. "Why did you never tell me Moira was your cousin back when Cian was dating her?"

"I didn't know he was, did I?" He placed a plate on the counter, set down the towel, and faced her. "You locked me out of your life. Remember, you only let me into the farthest corner of Lucky's two years past." Ruairí leaned in and met her questioning gaze. "I swear on me life, I didn't know Moira was the one he'd taken up with. If I had, you can be sure I'd have warned him that she was dangerous."

Oddly, she believed him. "And there's nothing wrong over at your place, is there?"

He rubbed his neck and crinkled his nose, an old habit he had when he knew he needed to confess but hated to give himself away.

She fought a grin and lost. "Ah, Ruairí, you never change. I suppose there's comfort in that."

A ghost of a smile played on his mouth, then he turned serious. "The truth is, you don't have magic enough to fight Loman, *mo ghrá*. Maybe all of you together, sure, but I'll not stand by and let you be hurt when he makes an attempt on your family." He brushed a thumb over her cheek. "And he will. He's an evil man and wants the O'Malley power. Knowing him as I do, he won't stop until one of your lot is dead."

"You think, with you here, you can stop him?"

"I can try."

His sincerity tugged at her heartstrings. Despite the kiss with Molly Mae, he'd never wavered in his devotion. He'd always treated Bridget's brothers well, too. Ruairí watched her with cautious eyes, and she felt terrible that he feared her reaction as much as he did. Had she truly been such a bitch to him? Probably, but she didn't know any other way to guard her heart against his easy charm. He made her want things she was better off ignoring.

Nodding, she gestured to his bag in the corner. "Grab that and come with me. I'll show you where you'll be sleeping."

"Sure, and it won't be where I want, but beggars can't be choosers now, can they?"

Laughter bubbled up inside her, and she ruthlessly tamped it down. If she gave Ruairí one bleedin' inch, he'd damned well take a mile. In their younger years, he'd always gotten around her moods with humor, his quick quips never failing to make her smile.

"How long has Loman been on the loose?" she asked him, mostly to divert herself from the tempting heat of his body next to her.

"According to Ronan, a few weeks now."

"Why do you suppose he's not shown himself?"

"He's a thinker, he is. The opposite of Seamus and Moira. Loman will have a plan before he attacks, but don't be lettin' your guard down, yeah? He won't make the mistakes my cousins have. He desires power at any cost."

"That sounds ominous, doesn't it?" she muttered.

He stopped her with a hand on her arm. "I mean it, Bridg. If you go anywhere, you need to go with another. Preferably someone with magic."

She lifted a brow and planted a hand on her hip. "And that someone, should it be you?" she challenged.

He dropped his bag and stepped into her, caging her with his palms pressed to the landing's wall. "Is that an invitation to be your constant companion, *mo ghrá*? Because if it is, I'll be takin' ya up on your offer faster than you can say, *yes please, Ruairí*."

Ignoring her pounding pulse, she placed a hand against his chest and felt the hard planes she'd noticed he was sporting beneath his coffee-splattered shirt yesterday. Ever so slowly, she trailed her fingers over those beautifully sculpted muscles until she reached the area above his heart. With a hard thump in warning, she narrowed her eyes. "You'll not get an invitation from me, Ruairí O'Connor. Not today, not any day. You'll mind your manners in my home and pub. And if I see you kissing the likes of Molly Mae, you'll be out on your feckin' ear, yeah?"

He grinned. "The only woman I'm interested in kissing is you, *mo ghrá*. Now and every day for the rest of our lives if you'll let me."

She was tempted. *Oh. So. Tempted.*

And for that reason, she didn't push him away. The heat from his hard body felt good against hers. Too good. Too perfect. As if they were made for each other. And maybe they were, because neither had been able to move on in seventeen years.

"Why did you never marry?"

He looked surprised by her question. Dropping his gaze to the top button of her blouse, with one hand, he toyed with the fastening, neither buttoning nor unbuttoning. "You need to ask?"

"Aye."

He lifted candid eyes to meet hers. "It's always been you, Bridget. From the moment we met until this very second, it's always been you."

She nodded slowly, because she felt the same way. Oh, she'd had other lovers along the way, just as she was positive Ruairí had, but never had her heart engaged. That worthless organ was reserved for him alone—even when she didn't want it to be.

"What about you?" he asked softly.

Unable to give him the power of her truth, she shrugged.

"I've been busy with Lucky's and the Black Cat. What time did I have to share?"

"And is that the only reason?"

She was positive his penetrating stare saw all the way to her soul. She answered the affirmative with a jerky nod.

"You really are a terrible liar, *mo ghrá*." He rested his forearm against the wall and leaned closer. When he was just a hair's breadth away, he said, "A terrible, terrible liar."

Then he kissed her.

She moaned at the contact. Ruairí had a firm handle on the art of seduction, and Bridget was quickly falling under his spell. She hated he hadn't learned it with her and had developed those skills on his own, but she happily benefited from his expertise now.

It took a good minute and a half for the sound of another person clearing their throat to penetrate her sexual haze. Ruairí was the first to react, and he drew back, but only enough to rest his forehead against hers and groan his frustration.

"If you're going to be snogging my sister like that, I'll be wanting to know your intentions, boyo."

Bridget pushed Ruairí away and met Carrick's laughing eyes. "As if I'm not an adult who knows her own mind. Be off with ya both!"

She'd made it halfway up the stairs before her brother stopped her.

"From the looks of it, he needs a room. Are you plannin' to let him wander the halls opening doors till he finds an empty one?"

She heard Ruairí chuckle behind her, and her face flamed in response to her forgetfulness. Never had she wanted to wipe a grin off someone's face as much as she did Carrick's at that moment. "Are you tryin' to say you don't know how to check the chart to see what rooms have been reserved or not?" she snapped.

"I'd put him in your room and be done with it," Carrick said with a short laugh. "It might sweeten your temperament, it might."

She slapped his stomach and stormed up the stairs, calling over her shoulder, "Get your feckin' bag and come with me."

RUAIRÍ SNATCHED UP HIS DUFFEL AND TOOK THE STAIRS TWO AT A time, pausing only long enough to observe Carrick's disgruntled expression. "I'd have thought you'd have known not to poke the bear at this point in your life, man. She's *your* sister, so you should know how quick she is to retaliate."

"Feck off," Carrick mumbled with a sharp look up the stairs.

Ruairí followed his gaze.

Bridget waited at the top, as gorgeous as he'd ever seen her —and in a temper. He couldn't stop his wide grin as he noted her crossed arms, tapping toe, and scarlet cheeks. The fierce blush should've clashed with her pretty ginger hair, but it only enhanced her loveliness, and Ruairí was starstruck.

"You love her, then?" Carrick murmured. "Roisin thought you might."

"Aye. I never stopped loving her," he answered, never removing his gaze from Bridget. "She's always been the one for me, whether she cares to acknowledge it or not."

"Well, I'll be wishing you all the luck with that one."

"And I'll be accepting it with gladness in me old abused heart."

"I don't have all feckin' day, O'Connor!" Bridget snapped from the top of the stairs. "Either get your arse movin' or go back to your own home."

He laughed as he bound the rest of the way up the stairs. "Your bellow is my command, *mo ghrá.*"

Carrick's snort carried to him.

At least someone appreciated his humor.

When he reached the top landing, he noticed the twinkle of amusement in Bridget's eyes, too. She simply shook her head and turned away, but not before he caught the twitch of her lips. One of the best things about her was her ability to laugh at herself. Perhaps it was why he hadn't expected her to react as badly as she had over the Mollie Mae situation. He'd figured she'd put ol' Mol in her place, snatch him by the ear, and claim him as her own. However, his fool move wasted a large portion of their lives. With a sigh and a shake of his head, he followed her down the hallway.

The room she showed him was tastefully done. One he'd seen when he shamelessly stalked her on the internet and learned the layout of the inn. At the time, he'd firmly believed it was to protect her should the need arise, but the truth was, he had been looking for any scrap of knowledge, any insight on her life that made him feel as if he could belong.

"You're lookin' thoughtful of a sudden."

He glanced her way, registering her deep frown. "I was thinking about you if I'm to be honest."

Her features smoothed and gave nothing away as she waited for him to continue.

"During our conversation yesterday, you said you'd forgiven me, Bridg, but have you?"

"I'd like to think I have." She shrugged and turned her attention to the garden outside the window. "At the time, it was a knife to my chest. Now? Sure, and I've never paused to reexamine how I feel about you." The mossy-green eyes she turned to him were full of sadness, and Ruairí's heart flipped in his chest. "I couldn't spare you anything but a passing thought."

"And I've only ever thought of you," he said hoarsely. "Mornin', noon, and night. From the moment I woke to the time I placed my head on the pillow, my mind was consumed with you, *mo ghrá*. And in every dream, you came to me, a smile on your lovely mouth and adoration in your eyes. Just like when we were kids. Those dreams gave me hope, they did."

Tears shimmered in her hauntingly beautiful eyes. "Oh, Ruairí, you bloody fool." She compressed her lips and shook her head, and he wanted nothing more than to pull her close to comfort her. But he knew she'd reject him, as certain as the rain would fall at some point during the day.

"I'm sorry for breaking your heart, Bridget. But you should know, I broke my own that day, too. One bad decision designed to spark your fire, and I sentenced us both to hell."

"I've replayed that day a thousand times," she confessed. "I should've reacted differently."

His heart rate picked up. "What are you sayin'?"

"I don't know. For someone who's never short on words, I can't seem to find the ones I need to tell you what's in my heart."

"Do you love me? Tell me you do, and I'll spend the rest of my days making you glad you did."

"I don't know that either."

He got a sense she wasn't being honest with herself, and the disappointment was crushing. Shifting, he threw his bag on the bed. "I'm sure ya have guests to see to."

He sensed her movement a second before she touched his back. "I'm sorry I can't give you the answer you want. But I can tell you I'm over the hurt of the past. My problem is trust, Ruairí. You have to admit your timing is suspect, yeah?"

He spun and stared down at her, uncertain what she could possibly mean. "Suspect? In what way is my showing up to protect you suspect?"

"Is that what you're truly here for? Not to prevent the loss of your part of the O'Malley magic?"

Reeling back, he could only gape at her. A wave of anger crashed over him, and he did his damnedest to hold his temper in check when what he really wanted to do was verbally flay her alive. How dare she question his commitment after all these years! He'd stepped in to help keep her pub running without so much as a fecking thank you from her.

She had the presence of mind to look wary and take a step back.

"I need a bit, or I'm likely to say things I'll be regrettin'," he stated coldly.

"Ruairí—"

"It's best you go about your day, Bridget."

She dropped her gaze and turned to leave.

Because he had to know, he asked, "Why are you allowin' me to stay if you believe I'm out to hurt you?"

Pausing, she remained with her back to him and her hand on the doorknob. "'Keep your friends close, and your enemies closer.' If you're truly my enemy, I'll know soon enough, won't I?"

"Aye. I suppose you will."

CHAPTER 5

*A*fter Bridget left the room, Ruairí fought off the last of his irritation and unzipped his bag to stare down at the weapon contained within. What would the O'Malleys do if they knew the Sword of Goibhniu was under their roof and within their grasp? He smiled grimly. Nothing good would come of their learning about it. They'd hang him from his bollocks and take turns beating him with a stick—if Bridget didn't kill him first.

About a year ago, Ronan came to him and entrusted him with the weapon. Ruairí had spent every spare moment since painstakingly studying the O'Malley riddle and running it through his mind from every angle. The conclusion? He had to find a way to get Bridget to "welcome" him, whom he believed to be her Enemy at the Gate, before he handed it over. If she wanted to gain her powers, she had to willingly accept him. He had hoped by getting her to allow him to stay at the inn, it might've been enough to fulfill the prophecy.

Apparently not.

But he had a backup plan, and Bridget only need follow the script to restore the last of the O'Malley magic. With an unrepentant grin, he conjured an eight-by-ten inch map, adding vague notations to three different locations. With a quick check of the room, he spotted a live plant by the far window and scooped out half a handful of dirt. Taking the map into the bathroom, he sprinkled the dirt onto the page and used his fingers to rub it in and create smudges. Then he folded the paper this way and that, opening it to refold ten more times, effectively aging the parchment. Satisfied it looked like it had been torn from a book and worn enough to have survived a good number of years, he set it aside and cleaned the bathroom until no evidence of dirt could be found.

Finally, he washed his hands, careful to check under his fingernails for telltale dirt that hadn't been there before. It wouldn't do to raise Bridget's suspicions too soon. With a gleeful laugh, he grabbed the map and went back to the bedroom to conjure the remaining items he needed for a scavenger hunt. He was certain, if he could get her alone, he could remind her of what they once shared. He only need help heal her heart and deliver on a promise of the moon and stars to win her. But if in the time it took to figure out all the clues, she still hadn't fallen back in love with him, he'd hand her the sword and be done.

"Anu, if you are listenin' at all and if you're of the mind, please help me to secure Bridget's affections," he whispered. "She's all I've ever wanted."

Goosebumps lifted along his forearms seconds before the sensation of fingers caressing the back of his neck struck. He jumped and looked around, searching for the source—and finding none.

"If that's you, Anu, I don't mean to give offense, but scaring the devil out of a man is not the way to his heart. It's more like to shrivel his bollocks, it is."

He could've sworn he heard feminine laughter and smelled the bracing scent of the ocean on a rainy day, and from the corner of his eye, he caught a flash of yellow. When he looked down at the sword, snug in the duffel bag, resting atop it was a perfect yellow primrose.

"Sure, and I'll be takin' that as a good sign."

BRIDGET EASED THE DOOR CLOSED TO HER ROOM, LEANED BACK against it, and inhaled deeply.

Ruairí O'Conner.

In her home.

Across the hall.

She snorted, shook her head, and pushed off the door. Well, her life had never been short on irony and bad luck. But Ruairí had revealed Loman O'Connor—reported to be the worst of their line—was on the loose. Her family needed to be told.

Crossing to the window, she stared out over the landscape, not looking or seeing much of anything as she formulated a plan. First, she needed to call the twins in New York, perhaps get them to come home. Eoin and Dubheasa were stubborn enough to ignore a warning to seek safety, but if she could somehow convince them they were needed here, it might work. Either way, they should be caught up to speed on what had happened to date and alerted to the danger of Loman, whether they chose to act or not. Next, she'd gather her remaining family and give them the news. Her final course of action would be to solve the last line of that bleedin' prophecy.

When the Enemy at the Gate is welcomed by the Keeper of the Sword, all that is lost shall be restored.

Technically, Ruairí could be considered the Enemy at the Gate. Sure, and hadn't she allowed him into her home? Would that satisfy the god responsible for their curse?

She lifted her arms to stare in disgust at her palms. She'd not felt so much as a tingle since the first sign of their family's ancient magic had made itself known to Cian. And when Carrick began lobbing blue energy balls around, she worried she'd never have any true power of her own. But if she did, what might that gift be? She'd attended enough of GiGi Thorne-Gillespie's coven meetings to know that, while witches could sometimes channel all the elements if they were strong enough, most were usually granted one particular element all their own. For GiGi, her gift had been air magic. Piper's was the same. But for Bridget, nothing. Not one spark.

But would that change if she found the Sword of Goibhniu? Would she become the true Keeper of the Sword, and would her reluctant kindness to her enemy be enough to restore what was lost?

She didn't know for certain, but she was willing to try, if only to take from Loman what he could use to hurt her family. If they were all on a level field, they might prevent that wanker from destroying anyone else.

She hadn't forgotten the horror stories Ruairí had told her. And as annoying as he was, he wasn't one to exaggerate. Or at least she hadn't thought he was at the time. Once she'd believed he'd always tell the truth, but now? Aye, his words and eyes held a sincerity that had been hard to dismiss. However, it could all be an act. He'd conned her before, and she couldn't let herself forget it.

Firming her resolve, she turned from the window.

She intended to seek out the O'Malley grimoire with the hope that it might provide clues to the whereabouts of the sword. And if she had to seduce the information out of Ruairí, she would. It was well past time that she stop being passive and allowing the Fates to control her life. She'd seen how taking charge had helped Piper and Roisin in their quests. She intended to do no less to protect her family.

Removing her phone from her pocket, she dialed her

youngest brother, not surprised when his voice mail recording answered for him due to the early hour.

"You've reached Eoin. I'm workin'."

Bridget snorted a laugh. Blunt and to the point he was. Her brother, the artist. And a damned fine one at that. She and Cian had not bothered him with their worries over finances in the past, agreeing to only turn to Eoin and ask for a loan as a last resort. Her little brother had enough hangers-on and syco-phants trying to gain favor due to his fame.

"Call me, Brother. There's something you need to be know-ing, and soon."

She disconnected and scrolled to find Dubheasa's number in her favorites. If Eoin was truly working and not shagging some New York model or sleeping the morning away, she'd not hear from him for a time. But their sister might be able to stop by his studio on her way to work to warn him.

Dubheasa picked up on the third ring, annoyance heavy in her tone. "What ya have to say better be important at this hour. Is everything all right?"

"No one's dead if that's what you're askin'," Bridget replied dryly. "But I've a tale to tell, and I need your full attention."

She gave a brief explanation of the events surrounding Moira and Seamus's attack, their plan to steal the O'Malley power once and for all, and how their cousin Ronan had turned against them to help Roisin and Aeden in the end. "Ruairí tells me Loman O'Connor is on the loose. The man is vile," she said.

Dubheasa, being the perceptive person she was, picked up on the one thing Bridget had hoped she wouldn't. "Ruairí? As in your neighbor Ruairí who you refuse to speak to? That Ruairí?"

"Feck off. And yes, that Ruairí."

Dubheasa laughed. "He's fit. I'd shag him if you weren't so enamored with him."

"I'm not!"

"Pfft. Scarlet is your mam for all the lies that pour out of your mouth!" Silence followed the statement, and when she spoke again, she turned serious. "I miss you, Bridg. I miss this."

"We O'Malley women always had to stick together, if only to best our knucklehead brothers."

"What do you think I should do? Come home? Get Eoin and run?"

Bridget gave it a moment's thought. "I'd love to have you all here and safe, but I suppose if you are both alert and pay attention to your surroundings, it'll do. Don't trust anyone new and stick close to Eoin, yeah?"

"Sure, and I can do that. But it'll be harder to make him mind."

"I know. As soon as I discover anything, I'll pass it along. I'll also send along the number for GiGi, and you can call her if you have trouble."

They talked for a few more minutes, and Bridget listened in amusement to Dubheasa's horror stories about working in the IT department at Lamda Unlimited. "And now there's some new fecker I've got to show around. Full of himself, he is. He's some consultant or other."

"Sounds like he's gotten under your skin. What's he look like? Is he fit?"

"Tall, broad shoulders, and yeah, he's fit something fierce. He wears his hair a bit long, but I'll admit to liking it." Dubheasa sighed. "And his eyes... I've never seen their like. Silver in certain light, and I feel he can see through to my deepest desires—one of which is him." She laughed.

"You're halfway to fallin' in love, to be sure," Bridget teased.

"Ack! No! It's lust, all the same. I think part of the attraction is that he reminds me of home. His accent... It makes me homesick, Bridg."

"Accent?" The hairs on the back of Bridget's neck stood at attention. "He's from *Éire*?"

"Aye. But not our village. He's a Dubliner, or so he says."

People traveled to America from all over the world, and Bridget knew her siblings weren't the only two from Ireland to settle in New York. Still, she didn't like the coincidence or the timing. "If you can send me a picture of the man, do it. But be careful either way, yeah?"

"Promise."

They said their goodbyes, and Bridget experienced a deep wave of sadness. She missed her younger siblings. Since their da had disappeared and was presumed dead, their mam had turned useless, Bridget—their primary caregiver—had practically raised them. Her desire to hold them close was what mother's all over the world must feel when their children grew up and moved away. And ever since the initial attack against their brother Cian had happened a few months ago, she'd been worried in a way she'd never been. Continually fretting over everyone's safety. Goddess help anyone who hurt her family, though. They'd not live to see another day if she got ahold of them.

CHAPTER 6

"*I*'ve a plan."

Roisin glanced up from polishing the nightstand. "Sure, and you always do, Bridg. What's it to be this time?"

Bridget scowled. "What do you mean, 'you always do'?"

"Just that you like to have a plan," her friend hedged with another swipe of the dust cloth.

Giving Roisin a look to silence her, Bridget plumped a pillow. "I'm going to find the sword."

"What?"

"I said—"

"Yeah, I heard what you said," Roisin grumbled, planting her hands on her hips. "But are ya mad? Why would you run off to try and find it now? What good could come of it?"

"I could finally get my magic, that's what." Bridget avoided eye contact. "And maybe stop those mad O'Connors in the process."

"You've lost your fecking mind, woman."

"I've not!"

"Ya have!"

The two of them glared at one another. Bridget was the first to relent, and she sank down on the mattress. "I've got to do *something*. Standing around, waiting for life to happen, waiting for those damned O'Connors to strike... I can't do it anymore."

Roisin joined her on the bed and rested her head on Bridget's shoulder. "Look, I get it. After you blistered my ears at the cottage, I realized you were right. I couldn't continue the double life I'd been leadin'. You helped me mend my broken family." She kissed Bridget's cheek. "And while I may hate it, I'll support your choices."

"I think Ruairí knows more than he's saying."

"You always do. When are you going to give him a break, Bridg? The poor man's wasting away with a broken heart."

Bridget gave her friend a light shove and rose from the bed. "He's a scut and deserves what he gets."

"Will you never tell me why?"

"He kissed Molly Mae—all to stir my jealousy, the eejit."

Roisin snorted a laugh. "I'm surprised you didn't shove her into a lake and drag him home by his ear."

"He said much the same. The fool thought he could provoke me into running away with him. What would make me want a player?"

"But he's not, is he? He's loved you forever. And I know a repentant man when I see one. Ruairí's been repentant since the day he screwed up."

Knowing Roisin was right didn't make the situation any better. Hurt was still hurt, and Bridget had been crushed at the time. "Aye. But should I give him a second chance to batter my poor heart?"

"I don't think he will. I think he's wise enough to treasure it this time around," Roisin said softly.

Undecided and feeling slightly off balance from the topic, Bridget shooed her off the bed to straighten the coverlet.

"Bridget?"

She looked up from her chore.

"You didn't see his face when you held Frankie. The man was beyond smitten. He was a fecking puddle at your feet."

Stomach in knots from indecision, Bridget didn't comment. As she left the room, she encountered Ruairí coming out of his. He paused as if unsure of his reception, and the wary look he was sporting pricked her conscience. She *had* been too hard on him for the indiscretions of a boy.

"Sure, and you need to listen without interrupting," she said irritably. Nothing annoyed her more than being wrong, but she could at least acknowledge when she was.

He raised his brows, and his lips twitched as if he fought a smile. Wise enough to remain silent, he gestured for her to continue.

"I'm sorry for not forgiving you sooner than I did." Meeting his startled gaze, she shrugged, uncomfortable with the entire conversation, but determined to power through. "You didn't deserve my treatment for as long as it lasted. I allowed the hurt to fester until it infected my soul, killing any softer emotions—like love."

"And now?"

"I'm making no promises. I'm not the starry-eyed girl I was. But I'm willing to be friends if you've a mind."

He closed the short distance between them. His warm gaze swept her face, paused on her mouth, and lifted to meet her eyes. "No, Bridget O'Malley. I've no desire to be your friend. From here on out, it's either all or nothing."

Hands on hips, she glared. "You aren't the one to be deciding such things."

He laughed, and the ice encasing her heart melted a little at the stomach-flipping sound of his genuine delight.

"Yes, I am. Leaving it up to you will get me nowhere fast, *mo ghrá*," he said huskily.

"I've things to do," she muttered as she turned away.

He caught her hand and gently tugged her back around to face him. His brows were drawn together in a slight frown. "Don't fight it, Bridg. We could be happy together. Forever this time."

Her heart was pounding so loudly, she was sure Roisin could hear it behind the closed guest-room door. "You don't think too much time has passed us by? We're not children anymore, Ruairí. How would we blend our lives?"

The building concern eased from his features, lending to a boyish appearance when he grinned. "Sure, and I'll do whatever it takes to make you happy. If it means always working by your side here or at the pub, then that's what it will be for me. For us."

Because his hope was too intense for her when she wasn't ready to commit, she glanced down at their joined hands, startled to see her knuckles were white where she gripped his fingers. He'd not shown a moment's discomfort, although the strength she exerted had to be somewhat painful for him. Easing her hand from his, she sighed.

"I've a riddle to solve first, then we can talk, yeah?" She hadn't been aware of holding her breath until he nodded.

"I've something for you." From his back pocket he withdrew a folded parchment, and it crinkled as he opened it. "I think this could help you find what you're lookin' for, *mo ghrá.*"

His expression grew guarded as he handed the paper to her, and as she accepted it, she continued to watch him. Years of dealing with the local patrons had given her an ability to read others with little effort. If Ruairí was anxious, he was hiding something up his sleeve.

And wasn't this why she had trust issues? Men!

To hide her disappointment, she dropped her attention to the map she held. "What's this then?"

"Look at the margin here, here, and here—" he tapped the

spots as he spoke "—I think it's meant to help you solve the riddle. Clues to the whereabouts of the Sword of Goibhniu."

"How do you know about the prophecy?" Her suspicion flag was flying high, and she wondered, not for the first time, if he was somehow involved in his family's schemes. A lot of time had passed, as she'd said, since they were innocent children wrapped up in each other's happiness, oblivious to the battle around them. But she'd rejected him, and a man's pride was a queer thing. Did he now intend to lead her on a merry chase, diverting her from her true goal, all so his uncle could finish what Ronan, Moira, and Seamus had started?

"We've always known. It was all my uncle could talk about. He drummed that fecking thing into the heads of all the O'Connors, McLearys, and Doyles. Anyone who was unfortunate enough to be related to the man."

"But you *are* related, aren't ya? And I can't be forgetting that, Ruairí."

His disappointment with her was obvious in the way his mouth turned down and a shadow passed over his face. The color of his irises darkened marginally. "No, you should never be forgetting it, Bridget. I'm like to steal the silver while I'm under your roof, don't ya know." He flicked the parchment. "Do what you will with that."

Turning on his heel, he left her alone in the hall with her doubts and self-recriminations. She'd tried to be candid, but it had backfired—as any honest moments where she bared her soul usually did for her. She'd find a way to ease the tensions so they could talk again. Luckily, Ruairí wasn't one to hold grudges.

AS RUAIRÍ REACHED THE KITCHEN, HE SPOTTED CARRICK RAIDING the refrigerator. The other man grinned as he held up a plate.

"Brain food, needed for writing." He paused in taking a bite of his sandwich and narrowed his eyes. "You're looking irritated. Who or what's got you in a tizzy?"

"Who else? Bridget."

"Do I want to know what she's said or done to you this time?"

"She's determined to make my life a misery with her cool words and suspicious nature, 'tis all."

Carrick chewed slowly as he considered the problem. After swallowing and taking a sip of water, he nodded. "I doubt she's ever likely to trust a man completely, and especially not one called O'Connor."

"All from a stupid misunderstanding?" Ruairí asked in disbelief.

"Misunderstanding? Yeah, and I'd like to be enlightened, but I'm talking about our da disappearin' when the twins were just *weens*. She's had to be both mother and father to all of us. And ya should already know Bridget doesn't take her responsibilities lightly."

Ruairí removed a handful of crisps from the bag Carrick nudged his way. "I hadn't considered the disappointments she faced after your da was gone. But yeah, I broke her trust when we were barely out of nappies ourselves. Instead of thawing, her heart became firmly encased in ice after a time."

"If my sister is treating you with caution, she's a reason. I'll tell you true, be honest with her in everything. Don't give her another reason to doubt you, because if she catches you out in a lie, she'll wipe her hands of you."

Unease stirred in the pit of Ruairí's stomach. He'd created the scavenger hunt to spend more time in Bridget's company, but would she see it as another of his games? An unforgivable lie?

"What aren't ya tellin' me, man?" Carrick's steady stare was unnerving. As if he could see right into Ruairí's brain and had already detected the deception.

He glanced behind him toward the stairs to make sure they were alone, then laid out his plan of action to Bridget's brother. The amused gleam in Carrick's bright green eyes convinced Ruairí all his plotting was harmless enough.

"Yeah, you're a dead man, but only after she takes a pound of flesh. It'll be some craic to see how this plays out." Whistling, Carrick took his plate and headed for the door.

"Why don't you eat your *own* fecking food?" Ruairí called out. "I'll not save you if Bridget takes a piece of *your* hide."

As the words left his mouth, he felt Bridget's presence behind him. Her light laugh swept over him a second before she touched him, and he almost swallowed his tongue when she rubbed a small circle over his lower back. After their breakup, Bridget had never willingly touched him other than to flick his ear or tug his hair if she considered him unruly in her pub. That she was doing so now was shocking. Heaven and hell rolled into one because he doubted she meant it as more than a friendly gesture. Certainly not the affection he craved and read into.

"He's been raiding our kitchen since he moved out," she said with a shake of her head. "You'd think, with as much as he makes off those ridiculous books of his, he'd have enough to stock his own pantry."

"Your cooking is far better than mine, Bridg," Carrick said.

"Sure, and you're telling me your woman doesn't know how to cook? I'll say you're a fecking liar." She shook her head at her brother's retreating back and took down two plates. With an arch look at Ruairí, she said, "I suppose you'll be wanting me to make you lunch, too?"

"I can go scrounge up my own, if it's a bother."

"It's all in the price of your stay, but if you go next door and grab us a couple of pints, I'll apply the family rate."

With a chuckle, he left to go draw two pints of Granny O'Malley's specialty brew. From all the hours he'd spent nursing a drink and watching her from afar, he happened to know Bridget preferred her granny's beer to anything else.

Halfway down the alley to the pub, he experienced a bone-deep chill. The flesh on his arms formed goosebumps as the hair on his body shot straight up to attention. A tidal wave of cold intent slammed into him, and for a split second, he floundered. He turned in time to see his cousin Moira plunge a knife downward.

Acting on instinct, he jumped to the side and blasted her in the face with a gale-force wind. Her weapon clattered to the ground as she lifted her arms to protect herself from the icy sting of his counterattack. Moira's outraged cry was piercing enough to attract attention from the residents of the Black Cat Inn, and Bridget charged into the fray with a rolling pin and a severe look of determination. If he hadn't loved her before, he would definitely have fallen for her in that moment.

Ruairí quickly kicked the blade in Bridget's direction then waved a hand, producing a protective barrier between the two women. The second Bridget realized he'd effectively halted her progress, her cheeks reddened with temper. Had the threat of Moira not been so dire, he'd have laughed and enjoyed the scene, making sure to tease her. As it was, he couldn't remove his concentration from his cousin for longer than an instant or he'd receive a pick ax to his brain as a reward.

"Begone, Moira. You've no business with the O'Malleys anymore," he warned in a frosty tone.

"There you'd be wrong, Cousin. I've every business here. Not just with them, but with you as well. And if not me, then you should be expecting a visit from Uncle Loman for certain." She sneered her disgust. "You're a traitor to the name O'Connor, is what you are."

"And you're a mad cow without an ounce of sense," he

countered with a disdainful sneer of his own. "I'll not let you hurt Bridget or anyone else. Not again."

A sly smile curled her lips, and she cast a glance sideways, taking in Bridget, who was helpless on the other side of the barrier. "That's the way of it then," she said with a hard laugh. "It's thanks I'll be giving you for helping me solve the last of the riddle."

"I've not helped you with shite," he snapped.

"But you did, Cousin. You showed me exactly who the last line of that bloody prophecy was about. You and the bitch. I've only to remove one or the other, and the magic reverts back to us."

Ruairí's lungs locked up, making breathing difficult, and his blood turned to sludge in his veins, causing his pulse to throb in a fierce manner. Outwardly, he remained unmoved—a trick he learned early on in dealing with his evil-incarnate family. "You can play guessing games all day long, Moira, but you'll not solve the riddle, nor will you stop what is meant to be. And you're a fool if you believe you can halt a prophecy in motion."

A snarl formed on her lips, and her blue eyes turned stormy. Her hands curled into claws as if she were eager to use them to remove the flesh from his bones. "You may think you can, but you'll not stop Loman O'Connor. All of you combined are no match for him. And don't say I didn't warn ya."

In a blink, she was gone.

Ruairí met Bridget's wary gaze across the distance before snapping his fingers to dissolve the barrier. There was nothing to be said about the incident, not between them. Moira had said it all. "Go back to the inn, *mo ghrá*. I'll get our pints."

CHAPTER 7

*W*hen Ruairí returned to the kitchen, Bridget was sitting at the table, unnaturally silent. Wordlessly, he placed a pint in front of her and sat down where she'd set a place for him. He was eaten with curiosity as to why she was so quiet, but she'd tell him her thoughts when she was ready.

The moment came as soon as he took his first bite.

"Never do that again, Ruairí. I'm not a child to be protected."

He set down his sandwich and sipped his drink before replying. Choosing his words carefully, he said, "No, you're precious to me, and I'll not apologize for keeping you safe."

"But you can't, not always, and it's not your job."

Staring at her, he felt helpless, unable to tell her how essential she was to his wellbeing. To his very life. A world without Bridget didn't bear thinking about. "Don't ask me not to try, *mo ghrá*. Please."

She surprised him when she reached for his hand. "I understand the need to try, Ruairí, I've done it with my own siblings. But I also know they are bull-headed enough to do what they intend to without any interference from me." With a gentle squeeze, she released him. "You earned more of my trust today. And I had a chuckle when you called Moira a mad cow. Did you see how scarlet her face turned?" Bridget's grin was infectious. "I thought her bleedin' mind was going to explode. 'Twas grand, it was."

With a laugh and a toast to getting the best of his cousin, they ate their lunch, each taking the time to tease the other about their reaction to the threat.

"A rolling pin, Bridg?" He snorted. "Sure, and if her magic was gone, I'd have put my money on you in that fight."

"It was the first thing handy," she retorted with a smile. "And don't think I've not used it a time or two with our rowdy patrons."

"Oh, I've seen you have a go. It warmed me heart to have someone else be the target of your anger a time or two."

Her light laughter charmed him in a way no magic could do. She was a witch with no real ability but the one to draw him under her spell. For many years, he'd shoved down his hopelessness, refusing to believe she wouldn't love him again as he so desperately loved her. Before that exact moment, she'd barely cast a glance in his direction, and she certainly hadn't had a kind word for him. To see some of her hurt and anger over the past dissipate was encouraging.

"What are you thinking?" she asked softly.

"How much I'm enjoyin' this moment. How much I appreciate you settin' aside your grievance for a short while so we can laugh again, *together*." He said the words with all the sincerity he could muster, positive she'd wave him off, but praying she wouldn't.

"I was thinking much the same."

She swallowed hard, and Ruairí got the impression her next words would be a more difficult confession.

"It's not that I can't be myself with the others, but there are expectations with family. And probably I imagine those. But with you, there's nothing but the act of being me. Being us."

"Yeah, and I've missed this, I have," he said gruffly, coughing to clear his throat of the thick emotion trying to choke him. "I don't know how many times I can say I'm sorry—"

She stopped him with a touch to his forearm. "No more, Ruairí. You've no need to say it again. What's done is done, and we can't go back, but maybe we can let sleeping dogs lie."

"That's the point, *mo ghrá*, I don't want to. I want what we once had again. I want to spend the rest of our lives bickering and shagging afterward in apology." A sweep of color in her cheeks told him she wasn't immune to him or their memories. "I want you, Bridget."

"Give me time. I've a sword to find and a prophecy to solve first."

His guilt kept him silent as she pushed away from the table to take her dishes to the sink.

"I've had a look at the map you gave me," she said conversationally. "Did you see there are clues in the corners? It's like someone put their thoughts to paper as they tried to solve the riddle."

"Yeah?" He tried not to look like the con artist he was. "I can help you search."

She paused in scrubbing her dish. "You'd do that?"

Boy, would he.

"Aye, if it will stop Loman and Moira." *And secure your heart,* he wanted to add.

The excitement in her eyes shone bright as she dried her hands. "I'll get the map while you finish up here. We've an hour until I have to take over at the pub. Let's try to figure out the first challenge together."

He grinned. Her reaction was exactly what he'd anticipated. She was as good as his. "Go on with ya, I'll wash up and meet you in the salon."

Practically dancing in her eagerness, she breezed by him, stopping only long enough to brush a feather-light kiss on his cheek. "Thank you."

Again, he was overcome by an attack of conscience, but he ruthlessly suppressed it. Whatever underhanded trick he needed to use to sway Bridget back to his side, he'd do and be the happier for it.

BRIDGET FELT LIGHTER THAN SHE HAD IN AGES. SHE DIDN'T WANT to think too long or hard about it, or give credit to Ruairí's presence in her home. The fierce protectiveness he'd shown in the alley melted another block of ice encasing her heart. With his quick, instinctive action, he'd shown her he cared. Although she'd hated being effectively halted in her tracks, she couldn't hate that he felt the need to keep her safe. That need, one mirrored in her for him, had been the driving force behind her rolling pin-wielding charge into the fray.

Yes, she needed to be cautious where her heart was concerned. She couldn't take another blow like the one that caused their breakup, but she was feeling cautiously optimistic in relation to him. Like perhaps this time they'd get it right.

And when he gazed at her with such heat, her ever-present ice began to thaw and drip away. Their kiss came back to her with total recall, and her body reacted as if they were in the midst of the action. Butterflies fluttered low in her belly, and her body warmed, becoming achy with want.

She paused outside her door, fanning herself with the map as she shook her head.

"Calm yourself, woman!" she scolded. "You'll have him believing he's in charge with all your fawning and giggling and blushes. You're not a bloody schoolgirl, now are ya?"

"Oh, I don't know. You'd look hot in one of those short

plaid skirts for a uniform," came a suave, sexy voice from behind her.

She squawked her fright and turned to give Quentin a glare. "You'd think for a man so large, you'd make noise instead of sneaking up on an unsuspecting woman."

"To borrow a line from my father-in-law, where's the fun in that?" His grin was a thing of beauty, like the man himself.

"Jaysus. Put that thing away, why don't ya." She twiddled her fingers in the direction of his mouth. "It's dangerous to be casting it about like you do."

His laughter boomed loud, and the wicked sound curled her toes. For a hot minute, all she could do was stare. The twinkle in his eyes said he didn't mind.

"Sure, and Holly will kill me," Bridget muttered with a shake of her head. "Stow the charm so I can get on with me day."

A dimple flashed, enhancing his already disarming grin. Plucking the map from her fingers, he asked, "What do you have here?"

She tried to grab it, but he held it above her head as he unfolded it. At times like these, Quentin Buchanan was as childish as her brothers.

"Do you need a swift kick in the bollocks, man?" she snapped. "Yeah, and that's what you're likely to get if ya don't hand that back over."

"Bloodthirsty. I love it." He had the nerve to wink. "Holly just put Frankie down for a nap. Let's explore your treasure map."

She'd planned to spend the time doing that with Ruairí, and her disappointment at having her time with him intruded upon was keen. And apparently not easily hidden.

"Ah, you don't want me to help with whatever *this* is." He narrowed his eyes and brought a hand up to his chin as if to concentrate. His laughing eyes gave him away. "Why, I wonder?

Could it be that you want to spend time with your ruggedly handsome employee? What's his name... Rocco, Ronald..."

"Ruairí!" she ground out between clenched teeth as she managed to snag the map from Quentin's hand. "As you bleeding well know!"

"You're beautiful when you're angry, Bridget. And I was just helping put color in your cheeks for your little assignation."

"Assignation indicates sneaking around, and I'm doing nothing of the kind."

His teasing gaze traveled over her face and locked on something beyond her shoulder. "She says she's not meeting you for a lovers' tryst. Sorry, guy."

She whirled to see Ruairí leaned back against the wall, his arms crossed over his chest and a grin fading from his face. A look of hurt flashed.

"You've abandoned me yet again, *mo ghrá*? Sure, and I'm crushed." He placed his fingertips over his heart and pretended to brush away tears with the knuckles on his other hand.

"I'll crush something," she said in disgust. "The bollocks on both of you!"

They shared a commiserating look to which she stalked off.

Men! No smarter than oxen, the lot of them!

CHAPTER 8

*R*uairí found Bridget in the study with a pad of paper at the ready and a pen in hand. The O'Malley grimoire rested on the wide round table in front of her, and her concentration was total.

"It took you a lifetime to get here," she said, never looking up from jotting down her notes.

"Quentin and I were licking our wounds and commiserating over the abuse heaped upon us. Seems we both have women who like to inflict pain."

She laughed. "Poor Ruairí. Should I be throwing you a pity party and inviting all your friends from the pub, then?"

He grinned as he sat next to her. "That would be sporting of ya. Are drinks on the house?"

"Pfft. The lot of you would drink me dry." Bridget turned the parchment so it was facing him and tapped the fake notation in the corner. "Look, what do you make of this? I've written down a few things that came to mind, and I'll need to consult the book, but I believe these three additions are clues for retrieving the Sword of Goibhniu." She practically danced on the edge of her chair.

Ruairí had written *"Hidden in the hearth inside the heart, now fallen to ruin."*

Pulse racing, he pretended to consider it along with what she'd scribbled. "The old castle ruins? We played within those crumbling walls too many times to count as children. Do you think it's as simple as all that?"

He'd chosen the site to remind her of their first kiss. It was where they snuck away to meet and where they'd once written their names encircled within a heart, in permanent marker on the stone inside the room-size chimney. They huddled together, laughing with glee as they did it, certain no one would ever find their scrawled promise to each other. But the two of them would always know it was there. Ruairí hoped, if they spent time wandering around, the old memories might further soften her toward him.

"You don't believe it is?" She gave the map a skeptical look. "I thought the clue referred to our ancient family home. That's the only one I've ever known about, but I could ask Cian when he returns if you—"

"No!"

She looked up in surprise.

"I mean…" He searched for an excuse to explain away his panic. "Well, with Moira's attack, it seems we should act sooner rather than later. Cian might get back and not know of another O'Malley family estate, all the same."

With curious eyes, she studied him, and he felt hot under the scrutiny. Bridget was the only person able to see through him when she cared to, and her thoughtful gaze was an indication she might care to now.

A smile curled her full lips, and her eyes—normally a murky green from the trials of life—brightened. "I've a mind to get started tomorrow. I'll have Carrick and Roisin take over so we can leave at first light. It's a drive."

"Did you forget I can teleport us?"

She paused, then laughed. "I did, yeah. How is it I've forgotten? You transported us everywhere."

"I'm thinkin' it was too painful for either of us to recall those early years. To have such love and lose it… It makes one shy away from the memories or die of a broken heart." His voice was gruff as the emotions overwhelmed him, and he found it difficult to meet her eyes. With a small shrug to rid himself of his embarrassment, he absently reached for the O'Malley grimoire—and got the shock of his life!

He went arse over teakettle and landed flat on his back with the room spinning above him and his heart pounding like he'd sprinted uphill.

"Ruairí!" Bridget's worried cry cleared the circling birdies and had him delicately turning his head to look at her. Her horror was genuine. Dropping to her knees beside him, she ran her hands over his face and neck, then cradled his head to her breast. "Jaysus! I thought that feckin' thing killed ya dead."

"It's nice to know you'd miss me, *mo ghrá*." He snuggled closer, content to lie in her arms until doomsday. As he saw it, that fecking spellbook did him a favor.

Her arms tightened a fraction, then she dropped him like a hot rock. The woman lacked compassion and didn't even react when his head banged the boards. Yes, there was a plush rug to cushion the blow, but she could've at least *looked* contrite.

"I'm wise to your ways, Ruairí O'Connor," she said with a wry tone. "I half believe you used your own magic to play at falling down so I'd hold you close."

"I would've if I'd have thought of it first," he admitted with a wicked grin. Rising up on one elbow, he rubbed the back of his head and winced. "I can't say it didn't hurt this hard noggin of mine, though."

"Here, and let me look. Sit up." She positioned herself behind him, and with tender fingers, probed the area at the back of his head.

He hissed in a breath when she hit a particularly sore spot.

"Should I call round to the doctor for you?" she asked with a light caress of his neck. "Or I can call GiGi Gillespie to see if she can examine what's left of your brain."

Twisting to face her, he gave her a look of exasperation. "Sure, and I might have a brain bleed, but you'll bust my bollocks. If I die in my sleep it will serve you right, you shrew."

She laughed and bussed a kiss on his lips. "Poor Ruairí, I'll be bookin' that party for you after all but in the form of a wake."

He joined her in laughter, and as the last of it died away, they stared into one another's eyes, their frayed connection somehow beginning to weave back together into a stronger bond.

One of friendship.

He had lied when he said he didn't want to be friends. He absolutely did, but he also wanted so much more.

Her gaze dropped to his lips, and a becoming blush colored her cheeks. If asked, he'd have said Bridget had seen more than most and didn't possess a shy bone in her body, but her reaction made him curious how much of herself she held back from others. She'd always seemed like a free spirit, but perhaps she didn't allow herself to let go as she once had.

Turning more fully and lifting a leg to rest his forearm, he created a more intimate position for them. When he reached for her, cradling her nape in his palm as he drew her forward, she showed no reluctance, and instead shifted to her knees to meet his mouth halfway.

The second their lips touched, he was transported. Back to when it was the two of them against the world, and they lived for the time they could sneak away to meet at the old ruins to talk and makeout for hours. Each brush of her tongue fired his desire, made him eager to get her beneath him once more. His heart sighed its contentment as she moved within the circle of his arms and straddled his lap. Her clever fingers explored whatever skin they could find and tangled in the hair above his ears. Even in the throes of passion, she was mindful to avoid his injury, and the care she showed made his love for her swell. His Bridget possessed a hard outer shell, encasing a soft center, and the little ways she showed her caring and concern made them all the more momentous.

When they drew apart to suck in air, they simply stared at one another. Her irises were now a deep forest green, and the sight sent a shiver of awareness through him. Those were the eyes of Wanton Bridget. The woman who intuitively knew how to rock his world and make him beg for her special charms. Oh, how he'd dreamed of her, of this, of the way she would tease and toy with him before they joined in a perfect mating dance only the two of them knew the steps to.

Cupping her beautiful face, he caught her full attention. "I love you, Bridget. More than any other person or thing on Anu's green earth, I love you. And I've paid a terrible price for the eejit boy I was. But here, now, as a man who knows what he wants, who'll promise you he'll never so much as look at another, I'm humbly beggin' you for another chance to prove my worth."

When she remained silent, his heart dropped to his stomach, hitting as hard as a pebble crashing upon the jagged rocks of Moher.

"You said no, yesterday. You might say no today, tomorrow, and all the days after that, but I'll not stop askin'. I'll not stop trying to win you back," he declared hoarsely.

Her expression softened into a faint smile. "And I'll enjoy every minute of it, I will. But you have to swear there will be more snogging with the tryin'."

He closed his eyes in relief. Bridget had given him leave to woo her, and woo her he would.

. . .

SEEING RUAIRÍ'S RELIEVED REACTION TO HER TEASING CLARIFIED Bridget's decision to give him a second chance. Yes, she'd make him work for it. Prove he was as worthy as he claimed this time around. But she intended to enjoy herself in the process.

He was right about one thing; he'd been an inexperienced boy who didn't know the first thing about women. She was his first as he'd been hers, and they'd not had the knowledge between them to deal with the situation properly at the time. But life was for learning and using those lessons to make better choices in the future. Until now, Bridget had let his kiss with Molly Mae define her actions toward him and other men. Never trusting. Never giving one hundred percent of herself to another. She wasn't positive she wanted to give that much of herself even now, but she was open to the possibility of change. Of love.

"I said I forgive you, Ruairí, and I do. Just give me time to remember how to trust again, yeah?"

The hope in his eyes was humbling—and flattering to boot. All the years he'd tried to make the mistake right made her feel like a fool for rejecting his overtures. He wasn't the one who had wasted seventeen years of their lives; *she* was.

"I'm sorry I didn't forgive you sooner," she whispered past her tight throat. "You deserved better."

"Oh, Bridg," he whispered back, as if he, too, was fighting not to cry. "I deserved everything I got, and if you decided to never give me another chance, well, sure, and I deserved that, didn't I?"

Cupping his face, she blinked away the moisture blurring her vision. "No, Ruairí, ya didn't. But I was too hurt to see any other way. I loved you that much."

His arms tightened around her, crushing her to his chest in a fierce hug. "I'll earn your trust again. And if you should find it in your heart to love me like ya once did, I'll never give ya another reason to cry, *mo ghrá.*"

Clapping hands ruined their tender moment, and Bridget looked over her shoulder.

Cian was leaning against the doorway, suntanned and arrogant in the way only he could. "It's about bleedin' time the two of you got out of your own way. The rest of us were taking bets on when you'd finally shag."

Embarrassment at being caught on Ruairí's lap burned Bridget's cheeks, but she lifted her chin as if the teasing meant nothing to her. "And shame on you for interrupting a private moment. It's like you were never taught manners, which I happen to know you were."

"Should I leave and come back later, then?"

"Why are you home so soon?"

Cian's expression and tone turned serious when he said, "Aeden."

Bridget scrambled up, careful not to knee Ruairí in the process, and lent him a helping hand to stand. "What's going on, and why has no one told me there's a problem with Aeden?"

"That I don't know. It's why Piper and I teleported home the instant Carrick's text came through. Did he not text you to meet him here?"

"My mobile's in the other room," she said irritably. Scarcely ever did she leave it behind for reasons just like the one they were dealing with. That she'd gotten so caught up in finding the sword and failed to remember the phone was disturbing.

Ruairí gave her shoulders a quick rub. "Tell me where, *mo ghrá*, and I'll fetch it for you."

After he left, Carrick and Roisin walked in, followed by Holly and Quentin.

"Where's Piper, and what's the emergency?" Bridget demanded.

"She's agreed to watch the little ones," Carrick said and gestured for the others to sit down. "Aeden's had a message from Anu. He—" With a wary look for Ruairí as he returned to the room, Carrick paused his dialogue.

Oddly, Bridget felt offended on Ruairí's behalf. He'd only been a friend to her brothers and had come charging over a time or two when things had gone tits-up, during his cousins' attack. He'd also manned the bar if the rest of her family were too busy.

When he would've left, she clasped his hand and led him to the sofa. "He'll hear what you have to say unless Anu has indicated otherwise," she said stiffly.

A wide, satisfied smile curled Quentin's lips, and he gave her a nod of approval. She wasn't certain why it mattered that he found favor with her gesture, but it somehow did. Perhaps it was because he displayed a calm collectedness and, as a Traveler able to alter time and space, was privy to future events because he'd lived them already. Maybe he already knew how her relationship with Ruairí would turn out. It was food for thought and one she'd explore later as time allowed.

"As I was sayin', Aeden's had a message from Anu. The time is now to complete the final leg of the prophecy." Carrick gave her a pointed look. "She said you needed to have faith, Bridg. Your ability to trust is about to be tested."

Cold washed through her, and she instinctively dropped Ruairí's hand. Wasn't she just talking about trust? And why did the message come through Aeden at that precise moment? Was Anu trying to tell her Ruairí had a hidden agenda?

"Is that all?" she croaked.

"No." Her brother shook his head. "The threat is on our doorstep, and we're to gather together to defeat it by using the resources at our disposal."

"What the devil does that mean?" she snapped.

Ruairí's phone buzzed, and he removed it from his pocket to read a message. "We'll find out soon enough," he said grimly. "Ronan is on his way."

CHAPTER 9

"*W*e're supposed to welcome him into our home and have a grand ol' time of it?" Bridget's outrage and worry showed in the tight lines around her eyes and the glance she darted toward the door.

Ruairí shifted to comfort her, but she backed away, avoiding meeting his inquiring gaze. Aeden's prediction now hung between them, creating a distance Ruairí might not be able to bridge. But he had to try. If it meant doing whatever it took to retain her trust, he intended to do it.

"I'll meet him outside. You can keep the wards against him in place."

"No." Roisin's fierce denial was unexpected, and they all stared at her in varying shades of disbelief. But it was her husband who was the recipient of her severe look. "He saved Aeden. For that, we'll hear what he has to say."

Ruairí knew the story from Ronan himself. How Moira and Seamus planned and executed an attack on Aeden and Sabrina, the beloved daughter of Damian Dethridge, the Aether and the most powerful magical being on earth. The children had been clever enough to glamour, changing appearances to reflect

Aeden as Sabrina, thereby saving the girl from certain death. The boy's actions had fulfilled the second part of the prophecy —*the golden Son sacrifices for the One*—thereby securing the gift of Carrick's magic.

And Ronan had been on hand to help stop his cousins and heal Aeden at great risk to himself. He'd effectively painted a target on his broad back since he refused to allow women or children to be pawns in the game for power that the O'Connor clan was fond of playing.

Carrick was quick to acquiesce to his wife's demand. "Aye. We'll hear what he has to say, Ro."

"Do you think he's here to bring us the sword?" Bridget asked in an odd voice.

Ruairí choked down a disbelieving bark of laughter. "Doubtful."

"And why would you say that?"

Thinking fast on his feet didn't come as easy to him as it had when he was younger and needed to be at the top of his game to survive, but he could still weave a diversion when he needed. "A feeling. Do you believe he's your Enemy at the Gate? Seems to me he's more of a reluctant ally, if anything."

A frown formed between Bridget's brows, and she sported a disappointed expression. The return of her magic meant a lot to her, and Ruairí would make it happen. Whatever it took, whatever hoop he needed to jump through, whatever she needed for him to provide, he'd do that too. Basically, he lived to make Bridget happy.

"Tell him to use the back door," Holly said with a speaking glance at her husband. "We'll cloak ourselves and be prepared should anything go sideways."

"You remind me more of your father every day, love." Quentin rose and gave her a quick kiss on the mouth. "You stay here, and I'll stand guard until our visitor arrives." When she objected, he patiently waited her out as if he had all the time in the world. Eventually, he said, "Frankie needs her mom, Hol. I'd prefer you not take chances when I can easily handle this."

Although her mouth opened and closed as if she wanted to argue further, she eventually squeezed his hand and sat back down. "Do what you have to."

The love in the man's eyes as he looked down at her was awe-inspiring. Never had Ruairí seen such emotion shining so fiercely. He glanced at Bridget to find her watching him, and he couldn't look away. If he could find a way to tell her what was in his heart, actually get her to listen and understand it beat only for her, perhaps she'd trust him enough to give him a second chance—or rather *them* a second chance—at happiness.

Quentin clapped him on the back. "Send the text."

Two minutes later, with Quentin cloaked in the garden behind the house, Ruairí went to meet his cousin Ronan.

STANDING OUT IN THE OPEN GAVE RONAN THE WILLIES. He couldn't shake the sensation of being watched, and he spun in a slow circle twice to search out the source. If his bleedin' cousin would've just sent an image of the O'Malley drawing room, he could've teleported right in and all this cloak-and-dagger nonsense could be avoided. Yeah, and he wasn't visiting this fecking inn for his own health, was he? If he was a smart man— and here his brilliance was questionable, as was his sanity— he'd have stayed on the other side of the pond, away from his heinous father.

Surprisingly, Ronan liked New York. The size of the city had given him a sense of comfort. The ability to get lost in a crowd, even at his towering height. His accent had been telling, though, and it wouldn't do to stay in one place longer than necessary.

Just as the feeling of being observed became too much and

Ronan was ready to bolt, the back door opened.

"Jaysus, man! I've been out here a lifetime, and I've developed a case of paranoia." He shot a glance to his left where the sensation of magic was strongest. "Let me in the feckin' door, so I'm not a sitting duck, yeah?"

Ruairí smiled and shook his head. "Only you and I knew you'd be here, Cousin. You've got to learn to relax, ya do."

"With *my* father runnin' around? You've got a screw missing now, don't ya?"

The two men shook hands, and with one last look around, Ronan followed him inside. But the second the door began to shut, someone or something unseen shoved in behind them. Acting on instinct, Ronan blocked Ruairí's body with his, prepared to take the brunt of the attack.

One that didn't happen.

The entryway door was closed with a soft click, and the air crackled an instant before a dark-haired, god-like creature revealed himself. The man sported shoulder-length hair, muscles for days, and a shite-eating grin that said he believed cloaking himself and scaring the bejeezus out of others was some craic.

"Who the feck are you?" Ronan growled, advancing a few steps with balled fists. "Did Loman send ya?"

"Loman?"

"My father."

The man tilted his handsome head slightly as if considering, his smile never wavering. "Never met the man. I'm Quentin Buchanan, a guest of the O'Malleys." He paused a heartbeat and narrowed his eyes before adding, "And son-in-law to Alastair Thorne."

There wasn't a magical person on the planet who hadn't heard the name or who didn't know the story behind the legendary man. Alastair Thorne was favored by the Goddess Isis and was as wily as the day was long. Few went up against him and lived to tell the story. If the man in front of him was married to Thorne's daughter, then he was a worthy opponent —or ally, depending on what side of the war one happened to be on. But Alastair also happened to be cousin to Hoyt Thorne, the guy Ronan had wronged a lifetime ago.

"Sure, and I've heard of the man. Who hasn't?" Ronan said with a casual ease he didn't feel. "Were you the peeper in the garden, then? Making sure I didn't stage a strike against my own cousin?"

"Blood is an accident of birth. It doesn't make you trustworthy, friend."

"Yeah, I know that's the truth of it. Can we have a pint and quit the pecker-measuring contest? I'll gladly concede to you, and I've things to impart that might save a wee bit of heartache for the O'Malleys."

Quentin laughed, and the booming sound was so contagious Ronan found himself fighting back a grin. Since all his concentration had been for Quentin, he'd forgotten Ruairí, and when his cousin slapped him on the back, he jumped and whirled, ready to strike.

"I'm getting too feckin' old for this shite," he muttered.

"Alastair continually says the same thing." There was genuine humor in Quentin's tone, as if he enjoyed irking his father-in-law, and perhaps he did. A devil danced on the man's shoulder, and he had an ever-present twinkle in his eye to go along with his engaging grin.

"Yeah, well the man has my sympathies with you as an in-law. I've no doubt ya bedevil him daily," Ronan retorted with a dismissive snort.

"I live to please, man."

Life in the O'Connor household had required snap judgments and decisions. Ronan was quick to sum up the potential threat, but he found he liked Quentin. It was impossible not to. Yes, the resplendent glow radiating off the guy was mesmerizing, and he didn't imagine there was anyone on the planet, witch or non-witch alike, who wasn't charmed by the man or warmed by his magical aura. It made Quentin dangerous. The deceptively easygoing vibe was a ruse. Yet, Ronan couldn't fault him for the gifts he'd been born with, though he was highly envious.

His own power had disappeared when he healed Aeden then had been infected by Moira's blood curse. The Aether had saved him, but at the cost of Ronan losing whatever magic he possessed. Gradually, small abilities had returned. Things like conjuring necessary food, the art of glamouring to disguise himself, and teleporting. Nothing more meaningful.

All disheartening, yet much deserved for his part in trying to retain the O'Malley magic to begin with. Sure, he'd only wanted it to keep Loman and the remaining O'Connor clan in check, but he'd done some shady and questionable actions to manage it.

Once, he might've been as powerful as Quentin, able to go toe-to-toe if the need arose. But now, Ronan didn't possess the necessary abilities to keep the other man from wiping the floor with his face.

"Like I said, I've news for the O'Malleys, I—"

"*Ronan!*"

He turned just as a small body barreled into him and hugged him about the waist. Recognizing the child as Aeden, he patted him on the head, detangled himself, and squatted eye level. "Well, sure, and you've grown since I saw you last."

"I've been building me muscles so I can be like you when I'm grown."

Ronan's heart hiccuped in his chest. Somehow, this boy had managed to melt the colder side of him and had captured a softer part of his heart Ronan hadn't known existed. Dutifully, he squeezed the presented bicep. "Aye. I've no doubt you'll grow to be bigger. More like this beast of a man here." He gestured to Quentin with a thumb over his shoulder and grinned at the boy. "Is that your aim, then? To be as big as a mountain?"

Aeden laughed as only a small child could, clear and without restraint. His voice still had a raspy quality, but it didn't seem to pain him to talk as it once had. "You're bigger than him, you are!"

Leaning in as if to impart a secret, Ronan said with a stage whisper, "Well, yeah, but he's got more fat around the middle, don't ya think? Perhaps a little more mutton for brains if we're to be honest."

The child's bright green eyes danced with his merriment as he snuck a look at Quentin. "I think he's all right."

"Well, I suppose if you like him, I'll be givin' him a chance, I will." He rested a hand on Aeden's shoulder and squeezed. "I'm happy to see ya healed, boyo. But you'll be promising me here and now you'll not be going up against anyone in my family again, yeah?"

Some of the happiness left Aeden, and his eyes turned solemn. "I promise, Ronan. Anu said to leave it to you, and I will, but I don't want you to be hurt either."

Nerves ate Ronan's insides. The only reason the child would say something of that nature was because the outcome of Ronan's battle with his relations was questionable at best. He drew Aeden in for a quick, tight hug. "You'll not worry about me, yeah? I'm resilient and inclined to save my own skin when the need arises." Standing, he ruffled Aeden's golden hair. "You'd make a man proud to call you son, boyo."

Beaming, Aeden darted off as quickly as he arrived. The moment he was out of sight, Ronan's forced smile fell from his face, and he addressed the others as he stared at the empty space where Aeden had been, tone as tough as steel. "Loman and Moira must be stopped at all costs. I'll not let Aeden suffer again."

CHAPTER 10

*B*ridget swallowed her tea wrong the second she spotted Ronan walk into the room. She hadn't been prepared for such a beautiful man. In her mind, she'd build him up to be a monster, but the person in front of her possessed kind eyes. Eerie with the flash of silver, but kind, all the same. A memory tried to make itself known, like a pesky fly buzzing about her, but she couldn't recall where she might've met him.

His gaze flitted around the room as if he were marking all the exits for later use. A single glance allowed him to sum up all the occupants and weigh the threat.

What must his life be like that he always needed to be on guard?

After rising and placing her tea cup on the table, she approached him. It was disconcerting to realize she only came up to his armpit. With grim determination and a whole lot of trepidation, she held out her hand.

"Welcome to the Black Cat." His large hand swallowed hers, and she felt the small zing that told her despite what the others had said about him losing his magic, he still had enough to cause trouble. "It's thanks I owe you for helping Roisin and my nephew," she said. Fairness dictated she offer that much.

"You owe me nothing, Bridget O'Malley, and believe me, you'll prefer it that way." His warm smile could be felt to her toes, and she released a girly sigh. She hadn't realized she still held his hand until Ruairí separated them with great purpose, keeping his arm around her, lest she be unable to control herself in the presence of their company.

Ronan's wicked laugh nearly took her out at the knees, and she understood where his true power lay. His charm. Just like Quentin, he possessed a lethal side disguised by a tantalizing smile. Two such men in one place was enough to make a woman lightheaded.

Roisin and Holly sent her understanding looks, and Bridget poured them more tea in an attempt to compose herself.

"I've a mind for something stronger if you have it," Ronan said with a grimace. "I've a lot to impart, and it isn't all pleasant. None of it is in fact."

"Sure, and stronger you'll have," Carrick said, walking to the sideboard to grab the whiskey and enough glasses for everyone present. After everyone was served, he sank down on the arm of his wife's chair, absently caressing her neck. "You should just come out with it, man. Makes it easier all around."

With a silent toast of his whiskey tumbler, Ronan downed the contents and closed his eyes to savor the burn. Bridget noted the fine lines around his eyes and mouth, as if he had once laughed frequently but now wore a grim expression much of the time. For a man like him, on the run from the only family he'd known, his existence was grim indeed.

He lifted his lids and pinned her with a stare, as if he knew exactly what she was thinking. A shiver ran through her, and she inched closer to Ruairí for added warmth. The gesture wasn't lost on Ronan, and he looked between the two of them with a faint smile, one that seemed to mock her, although she didn't understand why.

Focusing on Carrick, Ronan said, "I don't know how much

Ruairí has told ya, but my father has escaped from the Witches' Council prison and is in the wind. He's the worst of our lot, and lethal to boot."

Her brother glared at Ruairí. "He's told us nothing."

"That's not true." Bridget placed a hand on Ruairí's knee in a show of support. "He told me about Loman O'Connor when he arrived, but we've not had a chance to talk to the rest of you about it with the exception of Dubheasa."

"Why the delay, Bridg?" Roisin asked quietly. "Seems that's something we should've known right away, yeah?"

How did Bridget tell the others she'd been so tangled up in Ruairí's presence, she forgot all about the threat? It was an eejit move to leave them all in the dark as she had.

"Aye, and I've no good excuse, but I suppose I'd hoped to find the Sword of Goibhniu first. Maybe solve the last part of the puzzle so we could have our rightful abilities fully restored."

"Jaysus!" Carrick jumped to his feet in an explosion of anger and movement. "Why in the Goddess's name would you go off on your own to find that feckin' thing? You've no magic, Bridg. You could've gotten yourself killed. It's a fool move, is what it is!"

Anger coursed through her. She'd been cleaning up his boneheaded messes her entire life, and he had the nerve to take her to task for trying to resolve the prophecy?

"Sure, and exactly why would you think I'd go off on my own? I intended to take Ruairí all along. He has more magic than *you* to protect me, and he's had it longer."

She felt him stiffen under her hand, and she wasn't sure if it was because she'd used him to insult her brother or because, in her anger, she'd squeezed too tight. Taking her hand in his, he entwined their fingers then placed a kiss on her knuckles. "I'll always protect you, *mo ghrá*," he assured her.

A small frown drew Ronan's brows together as he watched

the two of them... or rather as he met Ruairí's uneasy look. What Ruairí had to be nervous about was a mystery, one Bridget intended to get to the bottom of when they were alone. As it was, she didn't want to bring suspicion on him since she'd just defended him to her family.

"I hate to interrupt this little family spat, but perhaps one of you can fill me in on who this Loman character is, other than Ronan's undesirable sperm donor," Quentin said.

"Loman O'Connor is the meanest bastard you'll ever meet," Ruairí said, with another wary glance at his cousin. "He relishes pain, both for himself and what he can inflict on others."

"He's mad and bent on mayhem," Ronan added grimly. "The abuse he heaped on my cousins is what twisted their minds."

"What about your mind?" Holly asked softly.

Ronan seemed to turn inward as he thought about his answer. "I don't know," he finally said. "I have a warped sense of right and wrong it seems, and I've no problem crossing a line when it comes down to it. But I've a fierce problem with women and children being used as pawns."

"With the exception of Moira," Roisin added with a hard look.

"Aye." He met her look with a weary smile. "With the exception of Moira. If it comes down to her life or one of yours, I'll see it's hers that's ended."

"You trust him?" Bridget asked Ruairí in a whispered aside.

"I do. He's as tired of the feud as I am, *mo ghrá*. He's a good one to have on your team when it comes down to it."

"But what if he's playing you, too?"

Ruairí took time to think about it as they watched his cousin in deep conversation with Roisin and Carrick. As Bridget waited for him to reply, she noted Quentin's watchfulness. For all his easygoing ways, he wasn't as trusting of Ronan as he appeared. And with Quentin on guard, she felt marginally better. They'd have the magical backup when they needed it. But she also worried about the children. If Loman wasn't opposed to using them in his war, then they needed to be protected, as did Piper, who was pregnant with hers and Cian's first child.

"I don't think Ronan's playing us," Ruairí eventually said. "He's been a victim in all of this as much as your family, and I'm of the mind he wants to do the right thing."

"If you vouch for him, it's good enough for me, it is."

He gave her a startled look, followed by a delighted grin. "You're taking my word? Sure, and have I died and gone to the Otherworld? Because I never thought I'd see the day."

"Go on with ya!" She nudged him with her shoulder, trying and failing to maintain a stern expression. She laughed when he tackled her down on the sofa and rained kisses on her face. "Stop, you fool!"

"Sure, and I don't care if they all know of me undyin' love for you, Bridget O'Malley."

His playfulness caused her to giggle and had everyone around them gaping in surprise. Rarely did anyone see this side of her. The Bridget they knew was the forceful big sister, the sharp businesswoman, the protector of their small family. Not the giddy girl who adored the silly boy next door.

Clasping his beloved face between her palms, she stared up at him. "You're an eejit, Ruairí O'Connor." And there was fondness in her tone for all to hear. It was as far as she'd go to declare her feelings for him, because she wasn't sure she was ready for what any stronger sentiment would commit her to. "Now get off me before I send your bollocks into up into your stomach, yeah?"

He scrambled to his feet and pulled her up with him. "You've only to ask me nicely, *mo ghrá.*"

. . .

R<small>ONAN WAS JEALOUS OF HIS COUSIN HIS CAREFREE EXISTENCE.</small>
Always the rebel, always the one to reject the ongoing feud,
always the one on the side of the O'Malleys, Ruairí had
brought down hell upon himself. Yet, never was he swayed
from his deep abiding love for Bridget. 'Twas as if they were
one soul in two bodies. Even as a child, Ronan had envied their
bond. He'd watch as they snuck away to be together, giggling
all the while in their belief no one knew of their trysts.

But Ronan never told another.

Part of him believed any O'Connor with a soft side was
destined for disappointment and pain, but he also believed if
they had the grit and determination to try, then more power to
them. Who was he to destroy what those two had built?

Ruairí had done that all his own by kissing Molly Mae in
his effort to provoke Bridget's jealousy and her desire to fight
for him. His gross miscalculation had subjected him to endless
years of heartache. But his cousin hadn't been wrong about
Bridget's reaction, or what it should've been. He'd just failed to
consider any outside influences.

Ronan had the ability to alter Bridget's mind at the time,
and he'd chosen to do so. It had been before he himself had
experienced love and the crushing hurt that it could leave in its
wake. Before he knew what it was like to lose the woman you
adored above all others. If he'd have known, he'd never have
interfered.

"I'm sorry."

Ruairí and Bridget shared a confused look before turning
their gazes to him.

"Sure, and what do you have to be sorry about, Ronan?"

Admitting what he'd done would find him no favor with his
cousin, nor the O'Malleys, but Ronan needed to do it anyway.
"For turning Bridget away from you on the day you kissed
Molly Mae."

"But I've never met you before today," Bridget protested. "And I think I'd know my own mind on such matters, I would."

"But you *did* meet me, Bridget O'Malley. The moment you decided to return to give Ruairí and the girl a piece of your mind, I intercepted you and used my magical persuasion ability to alter your decision."

The moment his words sunk in, Ruairí was on his feet, an unbecoming shade of scarlet, with fists balled. "Yeah, and this had better be malarky, Ronan, or I'll be after rearranging the bones of your face."

Roisin gasped and covered her mouth as she reached for Carrick with her other hand. *She* knew the influence he'd been capable of—once. Before he'd lost the gift of hypnotism that went by way of his magic. He'd made her forget their meeting on the night Seamus had abducted her, after which Ronan had teleported her back to her cottage. Eventually, her memories had sorted themselves out. But she knew he spoke true now.

"Why?" Ruairí's anguished cry stabbed Ronan right in the heart. "Why would you do that to me? You were like my own brother. And didn't we have a pact to look out for each other in the midst of all those fucking jackals?"

"Because I didn't want you to leave me," Ronan confessed roughly. Admitting his need was difficult. "If you and Bridget went away, what did I have? I'd have never held out against my father. I'd have become just like him." Emotion clogged his throat as he witnessed Ruairí process the betrayal. "I'm sorry. You were my brother in every way."

"You broke my heart. You broke Bridget's. It's not something I can ever forgive," Ruairí said harshly. "Say what you need to, then I never want to see you again."

Inside his chest, Ronan's heart shriveled to the size of a raisin. He'd known if his cousin ever discovered the truth, hatred would be his burden to bear, but he'd never thought seeing the two of them together would have the confession pouring from his own lips, bringing on that hatred he so richly deserved.

CHAPTER 11

*T*he buzzing in Ruairí's ears drowned out half of what Ronan said after his confession. All he could do was stare out the window toward the glen where he used to meet Bridget. To the scene of that disastrous day.

To know he hadn't been wrong about Bridget's reaction, to know she might've come back and they'd have resolved things, to know they'd lost seventeen years to Ronan's scheming... was to have a thousand pound weight around his neck. The man he'd loved as a brother had betrayed him in the most horrendous of ways.

Was that why Ronan had given him the sword? Had it been his misguided attempt to get Ruairí and Bridget to reconcile?

Ruairí wanted nothing more than to ask, but he couldn't reveal he was in possession of the weapon. Bridget still needed to trust him fully, and he could sense she wasn't close yet.

Lost in thought, he jumped when she touched his back. Turning to face the sitting area, he was startled to realize the two of them were alone. "Where's Ronan?"

"In one of the upstairs bedrooms."

"I don't want him here, Bridg. He's a fucking backstabber, he is!"

"He had his reasons. And when your temper cools, you'll be seeing it, too."

"Reason? He swayed your mind from me. He stole years of our lives!"

"No, Ruairí. Your actions swayed me from you," she corrected with her hands on her hips. "You were the one to kiss another. You were the one who'd set about to trick me first. Had you not done that, Ronan's trick wouldn't have changed anything between us, now would it?"

"You would've come back that day," he said hoarsely.

"Aye. Probably to punch you in the bleedin' face and drown the skank. But not to get back with you. That wouldn't have changed. So if I'm able to forgive you your mistake, you'll need to be forgivin' Ronan his."

"Bridg—"

She held up a hand and shook her head. "What's done is done, and he's about apologizing for it. You can be man enough to accept it as I accepted your apology."

They glared at one another for a long moment. Ruairí conceded the point first, knowing he'd never hold out against her. He groaned and drew her close. "Are you sure you wouldn't have dragged me away by me ear to marry ya?"

Her laugh was muffled against his chest. "Positive."

"Then I'll forgive the sneaky scut, but only because you're forcing my hand." He drew back to look down into her flushed face. "How is it that you haven't murdered him for his part in this?"

He felt her light shudder and hugged her tighter.

"I can't say I'm not sporting a fine temper over his trickery, but I can also see how it wouldn't have made a real difference either way. Seems you were his lifeline in that horrid family of yours, yeah? How else was he supposed to react when he found out you wanted to run away with another?"

"When did you grow to be so wise, *mo ghrá?*"

"It's taken a few years," she said with a light laugh. "What do you think of the rest of it?"

"The rest of what?"

She gave him a dubious look. "What Ronan had to say."

Scrubbing his hands over his face, weary to the bone, Ruairí admitted he hadn't been listening.

"Your crafty cousin has been tracking Loman through his finances and putting the squeeze on dear old da by hacking into his investment accounts." She grinned, and Ruairí experienced a twinge of jealousy toward Ronan that she admired him so. "With his magic not one hundred percent, Loman has no way of correcting the hack."

"Which makes my uncle even more dangerous!" Ruairí was angry at his cousin's lack of insight. "Loman will strike sooner rather than later, to be sure, and we all need to be prepared. Without the finances to keep him afloat and hidden from the Council, he'll make a play for your power. And I'd be surprised if Moira hasn't already told him of our connection."

All traces of amusement died from Bridget's face to be replaced by worry. "Then we need to get Piper, Aeden, and the twins to safety."

"Where will they be safe from the very devil?"

With a wary look around, she lifted his arm and pushed back the sleeve of his jumper. With the tip of one nail, she traced letters onto his arm: T H O R N E S. He nodded his understanding, drawing his sleeve back down and grabbing her hand, pulling her in close enough to whisper.

"If I'm not mistaken, there was jewelry created for all of you to communicate without words, yeah? Let's put them back into play, so we have the advantage should anyone be listenin' in."

Looking up at him, she nodded and mouthed, *thank you.*

I love you, he mouthed in return.

Some of her tension drained away, and the smile she graced him with was soft and affectionate. The smile of older, wiser Bridget, and one more valuable in his opinion because those were harder to come by.

RONAN WAS EXPECTING THE VISIT, SO WHEN QUENTIN SHOWED up, he wasn't surprised. "You could've knocked."

The other man shrugged and proceeded to meander about the room with its ample space, touching things as if he'd never seen everyday trinkets before.

Ronan toed off his shoes and folded his arms behind his head as he leaned back against the headboard. "Will you be gettin' to the reason for this little meetin' sometime today?"

With Quentin in profile, it was easy to see the flash of his grin before it disappeared. Just as Ronan suspected, the man was toying with him.

"What do you know about your ancestry, O'Connor?"

"It's a long one, filled with gobshites."

Again, the other man grinned. "Fair enough. Anything else?"

"Why don't you save us both the time, friend, and tell me what you want me to know, yeah?"

"Can't do that. I'm waiting on someone else to kick off this *little meetin'* of yours."

"Sure, and you do a passable accent. It'll amuse those ignorant of the real thing."

Quentin laughed off the insult. "I find myself liking you in an odd way. I suppose that will be a good thing if what I suspect is true."

Dropping his arms and all pretense of casualness, Ronan leaned forward and drew on all those vicious years of training he'd received. Tone as frigid as an arctic evening, he said, "Get to the point, man. I'll not be toyed with."

As he approached the foot of the bed, Quentin did away with all the games. "I noticed your resemblance to someone close to me right away. I wanted to see what you both have to say about it."

Right when Ronan opened his mouth to reply, the air around him became heavy and sparked with magic. The sharp crackle sounded like professional fireworks on an American holiday weekend. He wasted no time standing and preparing for battle. Only his father had magic enough to cause that type of entrance.

Quentin, on the other hand, didn't appear fazed in the least. In fact, he looked as if he found the entire thing hilarious.

A ripple in the fabric of the space around them opened, and a blinding light poured into the room, forcing Ronan to shield his eyes or go blind. When the brilliant glow faded, Loman was standing next to Quentin, and Ronan's stomach dropped below his bollocks.

"You told me you didn't know my father, you fucking maggot!"

"And I don't." Quentin gestured to the man next to him. "This is mine."

Knees weak, Ronan closed the distance to stare into the face that was almost a mirror image of Loman. The eyes were different, less cold, perhaps a little bluer, but still arrogant. His build was a little leaner, too. Loman had spent many years honing his fighting skills, all in an attempt to frighten and manage the others around him with that fear.

The white-blond hair was the same thickness. The hairline, too. But that's where the similarity ended. This man wore his longer, almost identical to Quentin's, and not short like Loman.

"Are you related to him? My father, Loman O'Connor?"

The stranger's eyes turned frightening as the blue leeched away, replaced by an icy silver gray. Anger radiated off him and could be felt with each breath the man expelled.

Ronan quickly put distance between them. "What's this, then? Who are you?"

"You're Loman's son?" The tone was the same as his father's, the accent was not.

"Aye, not by choice. And if the fucker fell into a volcano tomorrow, I'd not be sheddin' a single tear as the lava swallowed him."

The frost left the other man's eyes, and after summing up Ronan one last time, he held out his hand. "Alexander Castor."

Confused, Ronan looked between father and son. "Not Buchanan?"

"I was adopted." Quentin took up a spot on the bed, copying Ronan's earlier pose. "By people who wanted me."

Castor shot him an exasperated look, but otherwise ignored the barb.

"How is it you look the spittin' image of my father?" Ronan demanded.

"Twins are quite frequent in the magical world." Castor shrugged as if it were nothing. "The cells are ofttimes too powerful for one embryo, so they split."

"You're Loman O'Connor's twin? You're tellin' me there are two of you bastards in the world?"

Behind him, Quentin snorted. "Disturbing, isn't it?" he said dryly.

"Immensely." That single word was probably the shortest dialogue in Ronan's history, and yet, it said it all.

"I think this calls for a longer conversation," Castor said. "And plenty of alcohol."

"Fuck me, you're tellin' it true." Ronan ran a shaky hand through his white-blond hair, belatedly realizing he probably looked more like the man in front of him than his own father with the way he wore it. "Are you an O'Connor?"

"*No.* I'll never acknowledge the name. If you were smart, you'd change yours, too."

"Don't think I didn't consider it, man."

"No hug for your Uncle Alex, Cousin?" Quentin asked with a cackle.

"Sure, and I'd appreciate if ya didn't call me that. With the exception of Ruairí, the only ones using that address are wankers and mad cows." He paused and shot Quentin a curious look. "Which one are you?"

After casually flipping him off, Quentin stood and stretched with a faux yawn. "I'm going to take Frankie, Piper, and Aeden somewhere safe while you two become acquainted. Maybe if you use what little brains the two of you possess, you can find a way to defeat dear old Uncle Loman."

"Don't call him that," Castor snapped. "Never call him that. He's not your dear anything. If I can this time around, I'll bury him six feet under and save us all the headache."

A small part of Ronan relaxed upon hearing Castor's curt reply. Until that very second, he wasn't convinced the two brothers were at odds. But it wasn't as if Loman inspired loyalty. Ronan was also thrown by how casual and dismissive Quentin was of his father. He'd have liked to be that way with Loman, but the man would've killed him before he allowed that type of *disrespectful* banter, as he'd see it.

"Are the two of you not close?"

"He's just the sperm donor my mother used to conceive," Quentin said in a hard tone on his way out the door.

"It's more complicated than that," Castor assured Ronan with a weary sigh. "He hates me for what he perceived as abandonment. The truth is I left him so he stood a chance at survival."

"I wish Loman had done that for me." Ronan shared a

commiserating look with his new uncle. "Maybe in time, Quentin will see it through wiser eyes."

"Perhaps. Shall we find where they keep the booze in this place and go have a much-needed drink?"

"That would be the Lucky O'Malley's pub on the other side of the alley. They've a pint o' plain that will make a man of ya."

"As if I wasn't already one before," Castor said dryly.

"Sure, and you aren't until you've gotten pissed in an Irish pub." He slipped on his shoes and nodded toward the door. "Let's go plot the demise of me bastard da."

"I think I'm going to like you, boy."

Ronan snorted. "That fills me with joy, it does."

"Now why does everything you say sound so sarcastic?"

"Because I'm Irish, man. Because I'm Irish."

CHAPTER 12

"Jaysus!" When Ronan entered the hall with a man looking just like his father, Ruairí about had heart failure. His first thought was to shout a warning to the O'Malleys then try to neutralize the threat. But before that thought took firm hold, the small differences between Loman and this stranger with Ronan became apparent. For one, the genuine laughter wasn't liberally laced with cruelty. For the second, the eyes were different. Just marginally softer, bluer in color.

"Who's this, then?" he asked warily.

"This is our Uncle Alexander." Ronan gave a hard laugh, and his tight expression said he was as suspicious of all this as Ruairí.

"The fuck you say!"

"*Our* uncle?" The Loman clone asked with a raised brow. "How many of my brother's offspring reside in this place?"

"Sure, and you make us sound like those flyin' cockroaches from Florida." Ruairí eyed the man with distaste.

"Palmetto bugs, and if the wings fit…"

The American accent threw him coming from someone

who looked so eerily like his hated uncle. "Are you about insulting every person you meet, man? If so, you can take yourself away from the O'Malleys' inn."

As Alexander opened his mouth to reply, he caught sight of someone behind Ruairí's shoulder, and the haughty expression vanished from his face.

Ruairí already knew who was there. He'd felt the prickle of her nearness, and any man who saw Bridget tended to go all soft around the edges. He shifted to block Alexander's view. "She's not for the likes of you," he growled.

A cocky grin flashed as wicked amusement lit the other man's icy eyes. "You don't know who or what I am, boy, but I can promise, you don't want to try your teeth on me."

"She's spoken for, and I'll not have you stirrin' up trouble with your cauldron of tricks, yeah?"

Alexander eyed him and gave a nod of grudging respect. "You're nothing like your father."

"Loman's not my father, and thank Christ for that. My own was rotten enough, he was."

"I suppose introductions are in order."

The arrogance of the fecker! Opening his mouth to tell the man where he could go, Ruairí was forestalled by Ronan.

"Alexander Castor, this is my cousin Ruairí O'Connor."

"You must be Shane's son."

"Aye," Ruairí bit off. "Though I've not called him father in thirty years. Not since he allowed his brother to knock me out cold."

Some of the swagger left Castor, and real regret shone in his eyes. "I'm sorry. Had I been there—"

"You'd like to do nothing, just like my da. Seems no one cared to challenge Loman in his own castle." He shrugged it off as Bridget joined them, not caring to dirty her with the truth of his miserable childhood. "We've things to discuss, us three. Do you mind if we use the drawing room, *mo ghrá*, or do you have something planned for the space?"

She studied him with curious eyes before leaning into his side and turning her attention to the newcomer. Bridget smiled her greeting, the coolly casual one she reserved for anyone not in her immediate circle, and Ruairí was pleased to see her maintain a professional barrier in the face of such a jaw-droppingly fit man. "The drawing room is free for your use. I've got to head to Lucky's to prepare for the night shift, but I'll let the others know to leave you be."

A feeling of unease settled between his shoulders, and he suddenly didn't want her out of his sight. "Will you stay close tonight, Bridg? Let one of the others man the bar."

In typical Bridget fashion, she took umbrage. "I'll not be shunning my chores, Ruairí O'Connor, and scarlet is your mam that you'd think I would."

"Christ, she's stunning," Castor exclaimed as she stalked away.

"And a right pain in my arse most days," Ruairí muttered. "Looks like I'll be pourin' drinks at the pub tonight if you'll be needing me."

The other men laughed as he hurried after Bridget.

He caught up with her at the bottom of the staircase, and she gave him an arch look.

"I thought you had a meeting with the man upstairs and Ronan."

"Someone's squatting on my grave, and the chill has reached my bones. 'Tis a feeling from boyhood, a warning of sorts. I'll not be letting you out of my sight tonight."

Her expression softened. "Ruairí, go do what you must. I've been taking care of my family and myself for more years than I care to count. I'll be grand."

"No."

Brows almost to her hairline and mouth opened in a shocked O, she stared at him like she was seeing a stranger. And perhaps she was. Ruairí wasn't the type to be insistent and was mellow most days, but when it came to her safety, he wasn't having it.

She surprised him when she didn't argue. Again, her eyes warmed to a lighter green and a tender smile curled her full lips. "All right. You'll be my bodyguard for the night."

The tension drained out of him, and he drew her into a grateful hug. "Thank you, *mo ghrá*. The wee hairs on the back of my neck have been tinglin' since Moira showed her hand in the alley. I can't seem to shake this feeling of doom plaguing me."

"I've had those feelings. I like to think they are warnings from the Goddess. She looks out for her own."

"Aye."

ALEX WATCHED FROM THE RAILING ABOVE. SEEMED THE O'Connors had produced one decent fruit from the batch of rotten apples. He liked the young man's pluck and determination. Spirit like his deserved reward.

Perhaps that was why his son had called him. Having recognized the remarkable resemblance between Ronan and him, Quentin needed the puzzle solved. Of course, the boy would cut off his left arm rather than admit to needing him, but Quentin was smart enough to know when he required backup. With a family to protect, he wouldn't embroil himself in someone else's war without assurances he could win.

That's where Alex came in. He was known to wage wars single-handedly with no care for his own safety. When you had nothing to lose, it was easy to put your life on the line. For his son, he'd do it, too.

"He doesn't deserve the life he's been handed," Ronan said quietly from beside him. "He's the best of us."

"I was thinking along similar lines." Alex faced him. "But I suspect you sell yourself short, Ronan."

"No. I'm little better than the others, and I'll save my own arse first. Never forget it, yeah?"

Ronan reminded him of a small child trying out his bravado. He wasn't boastful or arrogant in a way that mattered, but he didn't want anyone to expect better of him. Quentin had gone through a similar stage before meeting Holly. Perhaps a woman would eventually be the making of the man in front of him.

"I won't forget. I think it's time we had a drink and you told me about your father. Last I heard, he was in a Council cell and they were preparing him for execution."

Ronan cut a sharp look his way. "The execution is news to me. It's a crying shame they didn't carry through with it, all the same."

"Isn't it, though."

Halting Ronan before he would've descended the stairs, Alex shook his head. "We no longer go anywhere without altering our appearance. Also, we stick to crowded areas. If we go to the pub, we pretend to be the hired help, enter through the back door, and blend with the locals."

Comprehension dawned in his nephew's intelligent eyes. "To make it harder to track us with his blood. By blending, we'll be more difficult to pick out of the crowd."

"Exactly. He'll get a general location but not be able to scry and spy on us. Especially if we put Granny Thorne's cloaking spell to good use." He grinned. "I stole that one from Alastair, but if you tell him, I'll deny it and blame it on Quentin."

"*Now* I see more of the resemblance to my da," Ronan said dryly.

Alex's shudder wasn't faked. "Perish the thought."

After they glamoured and were firmly ensconced in the pub, and after the cloaking spell was modified to muffle their conversation, Alex got to the point. "Let me take a stab at the problem. O'Connors and O'Malleys have been fighting for the better part of two and a half centuries. You and your boyscout cousin Ruairí have decided you don't want to play on Team Evil anymore, and without anything more than determination and grit, you've decided to take on one of the craziest sonofabitches alive. That about sum it up?"

"Aye."

"Which means this is going to come down to the blasted prophecy. How many of the three conditions have come to pass? Are the O'Malleys close to getting their magic back?"

"Two of the three. Cian's frozen heart was pricked by a mighty Thorne, Aeden was the golden Son who sacrificed for the Aether's daughter, also known as the One. All that's left is for the Enemy at the Gate to be welcomed by the Keeper of the Sword."

Alex didn't let his surprise show regarding the involvement of Damian and Sabrina Dethridge. As a close friend of the Aether, he'd have thought Damian would've told him what had happened, but it wasn't the first time the guy had kept disturbing news and events to himself. The man was an island and welcomed few to moor anywhere close to shore.

Giving thought to what Ronan said, Alex looked at the couple flirting behind the bar as they served the patrons. "You believe it's those two?"

"Damian Dethridge gave me food for thought, but Ruairí has a plan. He's convinced himself Bridget would view him as the Enemy at the Gate, and she's the rightful Keeper of the Sword."

"Interesting." Alex sipped his beer as he ran various scenarios through his head. He fully intended to have a conversation with Damian, but first, he'd like to discover who really possessed the Sword of Goibhniu after all this time.

"You know, it's disturbing to see the wheels turning in your head. It's too similar to Loman when he's thinking about his next move." Ronan rubbed his hands together as if to ward off a chill. "Gives me the willies, it does."

"I can imagine so. There's only one difference between Loman and myself, and it's important you remember it. His heart is black. Mine, well, it's more of a murky gray with shades of pink for those I care about."

"Would you say you're the more powerful of you both?"

Alex had to give due consideration to the question. As children, Loman seemed like the stronger of the two of them. He knew no fear because he cared for nothing or no one but himself. Alex, on the other hand, was taunted for being "soft" until the day he learned to pretend. He'd grown into a consummate actor. His faux disdain of all things O'Malley would've earned him a Tony Award had he taken his act to the stage. When Loman hurt others, Alex sneered and turned his back as if his stomach wasn't roiling from his need to vomit. He had silently vowed to himself that one day he'd stop Loman and make up for the pain his brother had caused.

At twelve, he'd run away, only looking back to make sure no one was on his tail. It was the day he'd met Damian Dethridge and a young Alastair Thorne. Those two upstanding men had saved his life by creating a new identity for him, and teaching him right from wrong. They'd helped him hone his skills to become the formidable warlock he was today.

Loman had gone from bad to worse. The psychopath inside had developed a thirst for power, and he eventually became the right hand of Victor Salinger, Alastair's nemesis and the second in command of an organization known as Désorcelers, a group of non-witches determined to erase anyone with magic. The irony was that those fuckers had needed people with Loman's abilities to take on their enemy. When Victor was cast into the Netherworld and his band of merry men disbanded, the

Witches' Council saw to it that Loman was incarcerated with his powers bound.

"We both have different talents," Alex finally said. "I'd like to think I'm more powerful, but if my brother has escaped his jailers, then he's found a way to kill those who bound his magic in the first place and get back what he lost."

A sickly look spread over Ronan's countenance, and his hand shook as he lifted his pint. "When Cian and Carrick solved their respective parts of the puzzle, their magic was restored and all of us felt the drain. Did you?"

Alex frowned. "When did this take place?"

"Over the last few months."

"No drain, but then I severed ties with my kin long ago. Damian gave me a magical boost to defend myself should I need it at the time. Perhaps it counters the lost O'Malley magic."

"Sure, and that's something, then."

Reaching out, Alex gripped Ronan's wrist. "I'm here now, son. We're on the same team, you and me. And I'll do what I can to divert Loman's wrath and leave you a clear field to see the ball reaches the goal."

His analogy made Ronan chuckle. "Were you a coach in your last life?"

"No, but I've been watching a lot of Ted Lasso lately. It's inspiring."

The two of them shared a laugh and clinked glasses.

A resounding bang confused them for the split second before the world exploded around them.

CHAPTER 13

*S*ure, and this chapter has been omitted by request of Bridget O'Malley for the obvious witchy reasons. But prepare yourself because shite is about to go down!

CHAPTER 14

A deafening explosion rocked the pub, sending the alcohol bottles and pint glasses along the back wall crashing to the floor and upending tables, chairs, and patrons in the common area. Bridget barely had time to register the threat when Ruairí dove for her, covering her body fully with his. He pressed her face against his chest and cradled the back of her head with his large hand as he lay overtop of her and protected her from glass and timbers raining down.

A broad wooden beam crashed to the ground beside them, and she barely heard his muffled grunt over the sounds of screaming patrons.

"Jaysus! Ruairí, love, are you all right?"

"Shhh, I'm grand," he whispered into her ear. "I need you to stay hidden, Bridg. Can you do that for me, *mo ghrá*? Can you stay quiet long enough for me to get ya out of here?"

She nodded, suddenly terrified at seeing him so grave. Ruairí was seldom serious, and everything was cause for amusement to him.

The fear in his blue eyes was strictly for her as he helped her rise but only enough to huddle behind the bar. "Fire," he mouthed with a glance overhead. She kept her back pressed to the cooler and tried to catch a glimpse in the cracked mirror of the mass exodus out of Lucky's door. Two men, warlocks she'd never seen before, stood in the center of the sea of tables. The dark-haired man with the ice-blue eyes met her gaze and winked. *Winked!* As if the destruction of her pub didn't just happen. Bridget almost stood up to give him a healthy piece of her mind, but all hint of humor left him as he shifted to confront the beefy blond man who walked over the debris as if it were of no concern to him.

"You can drop the glamour, Ronan. You're the only one with the bollocks enough to stand up to me," the newcomer said. The coldness in his tone nearly froze Bridget's blood into ice chips. "Where's the sword, boy? Tell me now, and I won't kill you."

But the man who revealed himself wasn't Ronan. He was the one who had been with Ruairí and his cousin an hour earlier. The resemblance between the two men, standing face to face, was uncanny, leaving no doubt they were twins.

"Antoin?" Disbelief was in every line of the newcomer's face, and his tone was heavy with surprise. "'Tis you returned from the dead, then?"

"I've gone by Alexander for years, Loman. Do keep up with the times."

His reveal caused Bridget to suck in a breath, and she met Ruairí's worried gaze with a matching one. Sweat was beaded on his brow as he kept shooting looks upward to monitor the crawling progress of the fire. It occurred to her he'd somehow slowed the flames, controlling the blaze yet not making it obvious to non-magical patrons who might have stayed hidden. The smoke clung to the ceiling and inched its way toward the door opening.

Confident in Ruairí's ability to contain the fire, she peeked over the bar in time to see Alexander/Antoin casually brush the dust from the debris off his shoulder.

"Alexander *Castor*," he emphasized with a smirk.

Never would Bridget have thought another person could make the fearsome Loman O'Connor pale, but pale he did. In seconds, though, his bravado was back along with what appeared to be a permanent sneer.

"Castor? Are ya cuddin' me, Antoin? Alexander Castor is a legend, not a wee scut afraid of his own shadow. If you think to have a laugh at my expense, brother, you'll have to try harder than that."

But Castor never blinked. Instead, his brows shot up as a mocking smile curled his lips. His confidence seemed to chip away at Loman's shield by the way the other man flushed and shifted his stance as if preparing for a fight.

Ruairí touched her wrist and nodded toward the back room. "Time to go, *mo ghrá*. There's about to be a feckin' battle of the Titans, and we don't want to be caught in the crossfire," he said in a hushed voice.

"He'll see us if we move now," she said just as quietly.

Not losing his challenging look, Castor shifted to the right and sauntered forward as if he didn't have a care in the world. Loman, not fool enough to let his adversarial brother out of his sight, turned in a half circle, causing Ruairí and Bridget to scoot sideways so he wouldn't catch them from his periphery.

Although Castor never looked their way, Bridget mentally blew him a kiss in hopes he somehow understood how much she appreciated his sacrifice on their behalf. He'd seen her in the mirror, so he was absolutely challenging his brother for her benefit.

Ruairí scowled and shooed her forward when she hesitated to leave.

Two feet into their frantic, crawling escape, she came up against a hard object—an *invisible* hard object that very much felt like a man's jean-clad leg. She fell back into Ruairí, unsure what to do now that their way had been blocked.

Before they could react, the cloak fell away and revealed Quentin, deadly intent on the conversation across the room. He didn't spare them a glance as he dropped one arm and used his index finger to gesture to the exit.

Heart close to beating out of her chest, Bridget scrambled for freedom, uncaring if she made noise at that point. Only when she'd reached the alley did she realize she was alone and that Ruairí had stayed behind to help the others should they need him. She ran back for him, but her brother Cian stepped into her path from beneath a cloaking spell of his own.

She really needed to learn that trick.

"I'll go for Ruairí, Bridg. You get to safety, yeah?"

"The fool stayed behind. Why, for the love of the Goddess, would he do that? The ceiling is on fire!" She didn't care that her voice was close to screeching, she was terrified on Ruairí's behalf. He was the softest of the O'Connors, concerned with the welfare of others over his own. The man didn't have it in him to purposely hurt another, and Bridget feared it would get him killed.

"I'll not let anything happen to him. I swear on me life. And I'll be damned if our pub will burn down."

Bridget was torn. As much as she wanted Ruairí safe, she didn't want Cian rushing into danger to save him. But of the two, Cian was better prepared for intrigue and the perils that came with it. As a previous spy for the Witches' Council, he'd been in sticky situations before. "Be careful. I'd not be happy with you if you were hurt because you're too thick to stay out of the fray."

With a kiss on his cheek, she ran for the inn.

———

RUAIRÍ WANTED NOTHING MORE THAN TO SEE BRIDGET SECURE IN her home behind a wall of wards that even Loman, with his disturbingly powerful abilities couldn't breach. But he stayed behind in case he needed to buy her time to escape.

"Where's my son?" Loman growled the question at Castor. "I know he's here because I scryed using my own blood."

"And you're too stupid to realize a spell utilizing your blood might bring you to me?" Alexander taunted.

How Loman kept his cool in the face of his brother's taunt would be a riddle Ruairí wasn't likely to solve. The man had never been one to keep his temper in check, as anyone on the receiving end of his fists knew.

"I've his hair."

With a careless shrug, Castor leaned back against the wall and crossed his arms. "Hmm, okay, so maybe you aren't as dumb as I thought."

Appearing to recognize the tactic to expose his back, Loman shifted and glanced behind him, immediately zeroing in on Ruairí standing next to Quentin. The wide grin of delight was belied by the hatred in his eyes. "Hello, boyo. No hug for your Uncle Loman, then?"

"I'm saving them all for me new Uncle Alex," he said with a devil-may-care attitude and a buff of his nails on his dust-covered apron. "I like him best, I do."

Castor laughed in genuine amusement as a scarlet flush climbed his twin's neck. "Poor Loman. You always were a terrible sport about your toys."

"I will kill you for real this time, Antoin—"

"You can call me Alex."

Loman's skin was the color of crushed mulberries, and he looked like he'd have apoplexy at any moment. Ruairí prayed it would be what took the fucker out. Perhaps ol' Uncle Alex knew what he was about.

"Ronan!" Loman roared. "Yeah, and you'd better show yourself, son. I'll not have you siding with traitors and pantywaists."

"I'd rather side with them than you, all the same," Ronan said coolly as he sauntered around the corner from the hallway to the main room.

"You'll give me the Sword of Goibhniu, or I'll kill ya. Simple as that."

"I don't have it to give you," Ronan said with a shrug. "You've taken back that miserable pile of rocks, yeah? Have a search for it and see if you can't find it there."

Within the span of a blink, Loman had thrown a ball of fire straight at Ronan's handsome face. With no time to duck, Ronan would've been fried to a crisp had time not stopped.

The only ones frozen were Ronan and Loman.

"How... what.... Did you just freeze the two of them?" Ruairí asked in a choked voice. Never had he seen time stand still, manipulated by one's whim.

"Yes," Castor said with a wide grin. "Be a sport and move your cousin out of the line of fire, won't you?"

Unsure how much time he had, Ruairí practically tackled Ronan at Castor's request, knocking his cousin out of the way to avoid the fireball.

"I owe you this one, you fucker," Alexander said savagely as he punched his twin square in the nose.

Time snapped back with a pop, and the fire exploded against the wall as Loman hit the floor from the force of his brother's blow. Before Ruairí could scramble up to extinguish the blaze, Quentin had snuffed out all the flames, both the one from Loman, and the one crawling along the ceiling, searching for material unprotected by Ruairí's earlier charm.

He sagged back against a stool, happy he didn't have to tell Bridget her beloved business had burned to the ground.

"So, this is the infamous Loman O'Connor, then?"

The surprise of another behind him threatened Ruairí's bladder control. He was becoming too jumpy by far.

Cian strolled in, hands fisted and shoved into the pockets of his jeans and a deceptively curious expression on his face. The casualness was all a ruse, and he was actually in his *I'm about to throw your arse out of me pub* state.

Stopping five feet away, Cian's gaze swept up and down Loman as the other man climbed to his feet and spat blood on the floor. With an arctic glare for Castor, Loman worked his jaw.

"I swear on our dear departed mother's soul, I'll kill you, *Alex*," he promised as he swiped the back of his wrist across his bleeding mouth. "You can take that to the bank, ya can."

"I'm quaking in my boots," Alexander deadpanned. "Don't come back here, Loman. You've done enough to those present."

A reptilian smile twisted Loman's mouth, and he looked from one man to the next, stopping on Ruairí. "Moira told me you're the third part of the prophecy, boyo. I'll be paying you a visit soon, don't ya know."

"Say when and where, and I'll be there."

"Not without your magical backup, yeah? Foolish gobshite. You'll learn not to cross me soon."

"You're sounding like a broken record." Castor swept his arm toward the door in a grand gesture. "Do you want to walk out the way you came, or should I send you to hell?"

Loman was gone before another word could be spoken, and four of the five of them shared a relieved look.

"Sure, and I think you'll be handy to have around, Uncle Alex," Ronan said with a shaky chuckle. "Remind me to put you on me Christmas list."

Castor didn't laugh as Ruairí suspected, but gave Ronan a stern look, including the others in his sharp, sweeping glance. "As you probably already know, he's as lethal as a pigmy rattlesnake and a thousand times meaner. All of you had better be on guard. His first order of business will be to take me out because he thinks to make the rest of you weaker. You're not. Together, you can take him."

Ruairí wasn't so certain, but he didn't intend to speak up and be the Negative Nelly of their group. "Let's restore this place, or Bridget will do his job for him and murder us all. As it is, she's likely to be salty about losing the night's profits."

CHAPTER 15

*B*ridget pretended to survey the repairs with a discerning eye, hiding a pleased smile at how well Ruairí and his motley crew of warlocks restored Lucky O'Malley's to its former glory after last night's excitement.

"Well? Don't be standing there like you've nothing to say, *mo ghrá*. You and I both know you're itching to give me hell for something I've missed. Just show me what it is, and I'll fix it to your likin'."

Laughing, she stretched to kiss his cheek. "It's grand, Ruairí. Simply grand." Cupping his jaw, she smiled up into his surprised face. "Thank you."

His brows snapped together, and he gave her a suspicious look. "Don't be coddin' me, Bridg. Tell me what needs done."

"You're too paranoid, ya are. There's not a thing I can see wrong." Her smile dropped and she gripped his hand and led him to a table. Once seated, she said, "You saved me. You saved the pub. And you put yourself in Loman's path without a care for your own safety. Please, don't do it again, yeah? You've no need to prove anything to me."

"I'm not trying to prove a thing to you, *mo ghrá*, other than that I love you. I couldn't walk away and let your business burn. Please don't ask me to ignore anything that might make you happy. If I can make your life easier, I will." He leaned forward and tipped up her chin. "I'll do whatever it takes to make you smile and the light come back to your eyes, Bridget," he said softly.

It gave her an idea. "Anything?"

"And don't I recognize that look." Shaking his head, he said, "Go on, then. Lay it on me."

"I want to find the Sword of Goibhniu." When he opened his mouth, she suspected it was to argue, and she placed her fingers over his lips. "Hear me out. Yeah, and I've given this a lot of thought. If I can discover where that scrap o' metal is hidden, I can end this thing once and for all. All I've to do is welcome the Enemy at the Gate, and I've an idea what that's about."

"Bridg—"

She winced at the warning tone and rose to her feet to pace. "Don't. Just don't. I'm not a green girl. I know it will be challenging, but I have to find it. I won't only be restorin' magic to myself, but to Eoin and Dubheasa, too." She whirled back to look at him. His frustration was a palpable thing. "Will you help me, Ruairí? Please?"

"I've something to tell ya first."

"If it will alter how I feel about you or impact my decision to restore the O'Malley magic, don't," she warned. "I don't want to know if you've kissed a hundred Molly Maes in the last month."

His lips twitched, and humor lit his handsome face. "A hundred? That's ambitious, it is."

She grabbed a pulpboard coaster off a nearby table and whipped it at his head. He caught it with a hearty laugh and rose to his feet to stalk her.

"Bridget O'Malley, you have a temper, you do." The twinkle

in his eye told her it didn't disturb him in the least. "And I've a hankerin' to tame the shrew."

With a snort, she shoved a chair into his path and darted to her right. Anticipating her dodge, he went to his left, effectively cutting off her escape. He laughed as she grabbed a handful of coasters from the center of the closest table and flung them all in his direction as she made a break for it.

"Where do you intend to go now, *mo ghrá?*" His well-muscled arm slipped around her waist, stopping her flight and pressing her back to his front. Burying his nose against the sensitive part of her neck directly below her ear, he chuckled. "I've captured a wee faerie, and I intend to claim my prize."

In their youth, he always likened her to one of the fae. Always teasing her about sneaking away from the faerie realm to tempt him. With a breathless laugh, she wiggled in an attempt to escape his embrace, and unable to break his firm hold, she asked, "And what prize will you be demanding of me, Ruairí O'Connor?"

Turning her to face him, he brushed her nose with his. "I'd request a kiss, but I fear you're Niamh sent to tempt and trick me away. Maybe whisk me away to *Tír na nÓg* on your white horse."

"Hmm, and if I were? Would ya be comin' willingly, then?" she asked with a husky whisper and a butterfly-light brush of her mouth across his. "Or would I have to find a way to tempt you further?"

"No need to do anything but be yourself, *mo ghrá.* I'd follow you to hell and back for one taste of your lips, I would."

Chest heaving with exertion and laughter, Bridget once again tried to break free of his hold, albeit not hard. "I've said it before; you're a silver-tongued devil out to seduce a woman to the dark side."

Laughing, he wrapped both arms around her waist and

lifted her until they were eye level. "It's not a bad plan if the woman I want desires to be seduced by me. Do you?"

Yes.

Yes, she did, but she couldn't tell him.

Not yet.

She had a job to do and a family curse to break first. But then... Oh, he wouldn't leave her room for a good week or more if she had her way.

He must've recognized the deep regret in her eyes, because the teasing left him, and he loosened his grip to slowly lower her to the ground. As each of her soft body parts came in contact with the hard planes of his, her desire to tell Practical Bridget to feck off increased. When was the last time she'd been spontaneous? Just now, when she'd started a game of chase by throwing coasters at Ruairí?

"It's not that I don't want you," she said past her suddenly dry throat. "Because I do, and I'd be a liar to say otherwise, but I need more time."

"I've waited seventeen years for you, Bridget. I can wait until you're ready to give us another try."

Unexpected tears stung her eyes at his tenderness. Cupping his cheek, she nodded. She, Bridget Abigail O'Malley, was for once at a loss for words.

He turned his head and placed a gentle, lingering kiss against her palm then used his hand to press hers into the side of his face, leaning his head into her. Their gazes locked, and in his eyes was all the love she could ever wish for. All the promise. All she had to do was be brave and trust him this time.

But she wasn't brave. Not truly.

"Maybe I would've given you a second chance that day if I'd have been stronger," she said achingly. "Or at least, I should've heard you out."

His sad smile caused her heart to ping. "Magical trickery and a ginger's temper were working against us." Ruairí shifted to press his forehead to hers as he held her lightly within his embrace. "Let the two of us make a pact, here and now, Bridg. Let us promise, no matter how angry, no matter how betrayed we feel at the time, we'll always hear the other out."

Call it premonition, call it the Goddess giving her a warning, but all the hair on the back of Bridget's neck rose on end as a chill caused a slight shudder. "And why would we be betraying one another?"

He drew back with a black frown. "That's not what I said. You've a suspicious mind, is all."

"You said—"

"I know what I said, and you don't need to be parroting it back," he snapped.

With narrowed eyes, she watched as a flush climbed his neck. He wouldn't look directly at her, which was Ruairí's standard tell when he was being dishonest or didn't want to tell her the entire truth.

Disappointed in his behavior and with another potential lie, she pulled away. "I've things to see to before tonight."

"What about the quest for the sword?" he asked, almost frantically.

"It'll have to wait another day. I need—"

"*It can't!*"

Hands on hips, she glared, irritated with this whole line of conversation. "What aren't you telling me? You'd better give me the truth of it, right here, right now."

RUAIRÍ COULDN'T. IF HE DID, HE FACED CATASTROPHIC consequences. She wasn't softened up enough to forgive him his little scavenger hunt ruse. "I want to spend time with you," he finally blurted. It was as close to the truth as he could come. "If we hunt for your sword together, we could find it. I'm sure of it."

He felt like a science experiment as she studied him through narrowed eyes, and he fought not to squirm. Bridget would come to a decision all on her own without help from him.

"Okay, I'll do it."

Elation ran a close second to his first reaction of relief. He needed her to spend time with him to see how he'd changed. How he could be the man she needed him to be.

"When do we leave?"

"Give me one hour. I want to make sure my shift is covered."

After she left, Ruairí looked down at the map she had been consulting. Yes, he felt guilt for his trick, but it would be assuaged by the final outcome. Bridget and him together again —forever this time.

"What have you set that girl up for?"

For a second, Ruairí mistook the chilly voice for Loman until he registered the American accent. He pivoted to face Alexander. "What makes you think this is a setup?"

"You're an O'Connor. None of you do anything without an agenda."

"It could be argued you're an O'Connor, too, couldn't it?" Ruairí taunted with no real heat behind his words.

The coldness dropped from Alexander's expression, and he laughed. "I suppose you have a point. Tell me, son, why are you plotting against the lovely Bridget?"

"Not against, to be sure. I've a mind to make her remember that she loves me. I was a right eejit many years ago, and it's taken me this long to work my way back into her good graces."

Understanding dawned in his uncle's intelligent eyes, and he nodded. "Ah. If you can convince her to spend time with you, she'll be reminded how devilishly charming you are."

With an unrepentant grin and a shrug, Ruairí said, "Something like that, yeah."

"And when this backfires?"

"Sure, and why should it backfire? I've got a foolproof plan, I do!"

Alexander shook his head like Ruairí was the dumbest gobshite on the planet.

"What? What am I missin'?"

"Women don't care to be lied to, son. I suggest you find another way."

"But this has to be the way," he replied with a touch of desperation, then proceeded to explain his plan in detail.

"You actually believe that if you take her to all your old haunts, all those old feelings will come back to her?"

The heavy skepticism in Alexander's voice set Ruairí's teeth on edge. He sounded like a proper fool when his uncle phrased it like that. His stubbornness kicked in, and he decided he had nothing to lose if it didn't work and everything to win if it did.

"She'll find it the craic, she will," he insisted.

Alexander's brows rose, but he remained silent.

"Oh, feck all the way off!"

A moment later, Bridget appeared in the doorway, a sunny expression on her face. "Ready?"

Bridget O'Malley was never bright and sunny.

For a terrifying second, Ruairí thought maybe she had heard their conversation. He thought back to her words the other day in the garden.

"Oh, no. I haven't begun to pay you back. But I will."

"You can't forgive and still take revenge, Bridget O'Malley. Sure, and that's not the way it works."

"Oh, but it does Ruairí O'Connor. It most certainly does."

Looking at her closer, he could see the same wicked smile she'd worn when she said it.

He was fucked.

CHAPTER 16

"*I*'ll have to hold ya to teleport," Ruairí told her.

Alexander coughed into his hand, "Bullshit."

Bridget fought back a laugh. Another lie. But one she could easily forgive. Ruairí, the prince of little white lies, was at it again, but she didn't mind because *she* knew that *he* knew that she wasn't an eejit and would eventually figure out he was codding her. Those small fibs only proved how much he cared and that he wanted to go the extra mile to hold her or remind her what they'd meant to each other.

It was why, when Alexander called Ruairí on his ridiculous game of remember-when, Bridget didn't get upset. Yes, she'd overheard his confession. Yes, it was sneaky as feck. But in the end, he wanted to take her on a trip down memory lane, and she'd let him. Perhaps she needed those memories to recall exactly how good it had been between them. They couldn't go back, but maybe they could have something a little more solid moving forward.

She was also curious what he had planned. Whatever it was, it would be clever. Ruairí had a brilliant mind. It was a rare occasion when he used it to benefit himself, as prone as he was to help others out, so this time, she'd let him get away with it—as long as it benefited her, too. And when she returned home after, she'd look for the sword without him being any the wiser.

As Bridget snuggled into Ruairí's embrace, she grinned at Alexander and gave him a wink. She didn't want him to believe she was so easily hoodwinked.

Her insides warmed to almost burning but cooled just as rapidly. Opening her eyes, she saw they were standing in the drive outside the fully restored grand house.

"What the fuckin' hell happened here, then?" Ruairí looked surly and out of sorts, and all Bridget could do was laugh.

"Ah, so you didn't know Piper restored the old place for Cian and her to settle into?" She shouldn't have taken so much pleasure in his reaction, but she was only human. If he could try to pull one over on her, she had no problem reciprocating.

His look of frustration made her laugh, and she linked her arm through his. "They've given us permission to explore."

"But this was ours. Our place. We had dreams and…"

When his words became choked, the reason for his reaction became clear.

Bridget turned to him and sandwiched his face between her palms. "We did. Once. But Piper fell in love with the place when Cian showed it to her, and you and I were over. For me, there was no looking back, and I signed the papers over to Cian a month after Piper used her magic to restore the place."

"So there's no hope?" His voice was raw and hoarse, as if she'd destroyed all his dreams.

She stretched and brushed his lips with hers. "If we determine we're meant to be, we'll make new memories, yeah?"

For the longest moment, he stared at her, indecision on his face. Her stomach plummeted to her toes and she dropped her arms to her sides when he said, "We should go."

"Then we're not here to find the sword," she asked in a carefully neutral tone.

"It's not here if they already took away the evidence of... well, whatever clues there might've been," he replied flatly.

"Ruairí, look at me." When he reluctantly did as she requested, she said, "If you truly believe there is a clue here, then we'll look. Piper told me she'd restored some of the original features. Perhaps what we seek is still here."

"No. I'm a fool, and what I seek is likely gone. I'm after needing a minute."

As he walked away, Bridget felt a crushing disappointment. Maybe it was for what they'd lost; maybe it was for his reaction. And maybe it was directed inward for her own trick. Had she understood how important this quest truly was to him, she'd have been kinder and told him the whole of it before they left Lucky's.

Left with no choice but to make herself comfortable until he returned, she ascended the steps and knocked on the door. Piper answered with a wide smile and a tight hug.

"Bridget! How did you get here? I didn't hear a car approach."

"I teleported."

Eyes wide with excitement, Piper squealed.

"No!" Bridget grimaced. "Not like that, I didn't. Ruairí brought me."

"Ah." Although she appeared disappointed, her new sister-in-law quickly recovered and clasped Bridget's hand. "Come, have a cup of tea with me. We can call GiGi and make it a party," she said with a laugh.

"A cuppa would be lovely, but I'm awaiting Ruairí's return. When he cools off, he'll be back."

As she led the way down the beautifully refurbished hallway, Piper glanced back over her shoulder. "What's he salty about?"

"I'm afraid I let him believe this—" Bridget waved an arm to gesture to their surroundings "—was still in its sorry state."

"I'm totally confused. Why?"

No plausible explanation came to mind, and she shrugged, hoping Piper wouldn't press the issue. She couldn't understand her own actions. How could she explain them to another?

"Men. Got it." Piper gave her a commiserating smile.

Bridget crossed to the old hearth, now newly restored. No flame burned, and she had the desire to peek inside to see if maybe the words she and Ruairí wrote on the stone still existed. "Did you repair the inside as well, then?"

"Only the chimney. I wanted as much of the original house left alone as possible."

Heart thudding in her chest, she asked, "Do you have a torch or something to light the inside?"

"I could conjure a flashlight if you think the light from your cellphone won't be bright enough."

With a tap of the heel of her palm on her forehead, Bridget reached into her back pocket and removed her phone. Turning on the torch feature, she bent slightly, prepared to enter, but the thought that Ruairí should be there, too, plagued her.

She typed out a quick text to him but held off sending it. "Can Ruairí pass through your wards without a problem, or do you need a quick charm to allow him entry?"

Piper crinkled her nose and squinted an eye. "I'd need to add a charm specific to him."

"I think there's something he needs to see."

"Then I'll get right on that." Piper's look and voice were full of understanding, and with a quick explanation to say she needed to get the items to make her spell work, she was gone.

Turning back to the fireplace, Bridget ran her hand lovingly along the weathered, foot-thick weathered mantle. Many an hour she and Ruairí had hidden out here, away from their families, from the feud. They would wrap in a blanket and discuss their future as they watched the flames whittle down to ash. Never once did either of them believe they wouldn't be together. Though at the time, Bridget did wonder how she'd ever move away from her beloved siblings. Yet she'd never told Ruairí of the misgivings that the thought of leaving them brought.

Had she been foolish to believe two young lovers from warring clans could ever have a happy life together? Especially with an uncle like his and a mother like hers?

With a regretful sigh for all they'd lost, Bridget sent the text. They were older and wiser this time around. They may never find common ground and get past their differences, but she was willing to try if he was.

A tingling started in her fingertips, and she held them up in wonder. Either she was about to suffer a stroke, or that small surge was her magic waking up. Excitement turned her belly into a mosh pit of dancing butterflies, and she wished Ruairí was with her to experience the moment. As quickly as the sensation in her fingertips started, it receded.

Disappointment keen, she gave her hands a dark look. Sure, and hers had to be the power that flickered out like the bloody electricity during the worst of a storm.

Anticipating Ruairí's quick return, she headed for the foyer.

FEELING LIKE TEN KINDS THE FOOL FOR HIS CHILDLIKE NEED TO run away, Ruairí rushed back to where he'd left Bridget, angry at himself for leaving her unprotected at such a volatile time. Moira or Loman could've taken advantage of his momentary lapse in judgment and hurt her... or worse.

He was almost to the driveway when her text came through. *"All is not lost. Get your arse back here."*

He laughed. Trust her to be abrupt and to the point.

As he neared the front terrace, the door opened, and there

she stood, proud and queenly with color high in her cheeks. The vision of her, so achingly beautiful, stopped him in his tracks, and all he could do was stare up at her from the bottom of the stone staircase.

"The sight of you steals the breath from me lungs, *mo ghrá*," he said huskily. "If I live to be a hundred and eighty, I'll never forget how your face causes me heart to dance a jig in me chest."

She gave him a one-sided grin, as if she believed his statement to be malarky but enjoyed it anyway.

"'Tis true enough, Bridg. I'd not be lying about something as real as this."

"Get up here, ya eejit, and kiss me while I'm feelin' charitable."

Needing no further encouragement, he bound up the steps and swept her into a tight embrace, dipping her enough to cause her breathy laughter. Her arms wound around his neck, and in a gesture as familiar as his own face, she tangled her fingers in the hair at his nape and urged his head down to hers with a wicked, anticipatory grin.

He paused an inch away. "Don't think you'll always be bossing me about, woman. I've me pride."

"Shut up and kiss me."

"Fine, but only because I want to, yeah?"

He lowered his lips to hers, and the first taste of her mouth was ambrosia. Sweet. Addictive. Better than he ever remembered even in his wildest dreams. His heart took flight, circling above, never wanting to touch down again. And his desire for her, never far from the surface, made itself known in the throbbing of his cock. He groaned as she pressed fully against him, her hips reaching for his and sending his eyes rolling back to greet his brain matter in ecstasy.

No one had ever had the ability to make him burn like her. To send his pulse racing to such a degree he feared a heart attack. To drive him to abandon all sense of time, space, and location and give into the need to take her on the spot.

Only Bridget.

His one true love.

She trailed one hand down his chest to his stomach, and farther still, cupping him through his suddenly uncomfortably tight jeans. Ruairí groaned into her mouth as she rubbed him.

Just as he would've teleported them to the nearby woods, the door beside them opened.

"Oh!" Piper's light laugh turned naughty. "Should I offer you two a room?"

"I'd be grateful—"

Bridget laughed as she slapped a hand over his mouth. "We aren't there yet, and he bleedin' well knows it. Thank you, all the same."

"Offer stands if you change your mind. You've seen the size of this place. I wouldn't hear a thing." Piper gave them an impish smile then handed Ruairí a ring. "Consider this your free pass beyond the wards. Come on in. We were about to have tea."

As they followed her down the hall to the grand salon, he leaned in to whisper to Bridget, "With the way your hand was caressing me, it *felt* like we were there, to be sure."

She snorted a laugh, and his day became brighter.

As they rounded the corner into the room, he sucked in a deep breath, relieved to see the hearth was just as it had been but with a newer surround. "It's still here."

"It's why I messaged you." She looked up at him with soft eyes that seemed lighter in color. "All is not lost."

Piper left them alone on the pretext of making tea, and Ruairí took full advantage of the fact by drawing Bridget in for another bone-melting kiss. When they separated, her cheeks were as rosy as her lips, and her eyes had a welcoming sparkle.

"Show me," he said.

And because she knew what he wanted, she led him to the fireplace, pulled out her cellphone and hit the torch button, then ducked inside. Sandwiched together, they found the original inscription.

"This encapsulates all we were, all we can still be, *mo ghrá*." He settled an arm around her shoulders and rested his cheek on the crown of her silky soft hair. "Can you not feel the magic here, in this place?"

"I thought I did. Earlier."

The little bit of light was enough to illuminate her face, and seeing her awe was enough to set his heart to hammering. If she felt the blossoming of magic, did it mean Loman experienced a draining? How desperate would his uncle become?

"Tell me about it," he ordered softly.

"Isn't much to tell." She shrugged and looked up at him. "I had just sent you the text, and my fingers began to tingle. Thought I was having a stroke, I did."

He laughed. "Sure, and ya didn't!"

She joined him in his amusement. "Well, maybe not truly. But the spark was there, Ruairí."

"What were you doing at the time?"

Frowning, she looked as if she were trying to recall. Her expression cleared and became one of stunned amazement, and she reached out to touch their hand-written names. "Thinking about us. About starting over."

"Maybe that's the key, then. Maybe you just need to let love back into your heart, Bridg. Let me back in."

She bit her lip and nodded slowly, as if perhaps she had come to the same conclusion.

"I'll be here when you're ready," he promised. "As long as it takes."

And he meant it. He'd been ready to cut ties and run if this didn't work, but spending these last days with Bridget had changed his mind. He intended to stick, and if it took him until he was ninety to convince her to try again, then ninety it would be. They would experience whatever happiness they could in whatever time they had left before they crossed to the Otherworld.

"And if Loman stops us before we start?" she asked, concern heavy in her voice.

"The plan is to stop him first."

$\mathcal{A}$ ll through their tea with Piper, Bridget thought about what he'd said. But more importantly, she thought about what he made her *feel* again.

Loved.

Cherished.

Valued.

Wanted.

And having thought all of that, she needed a break from his company to process the excess emotions overwhelming her.

"Do you mind coming back for me, Ruairí? Give me a while to catch up with Piper about her trip?"

His knowing eyes and lopsided grin told her he knew she needed time away from him to put her mind to rights.

"Aye. Message me when you're done, and I'll be back for you."

"I can bring her home," Piper offered as she inspected and selected another sandwich from the batch on the plate.

If Bridget allowed Piper to teleport her, she'd miss the wonderful warmth of Ruairí's embrace on the return trip. Her indecision apparently gave her way.

"Or not," Piper said with a laugh. "I guess it's up to you to retrieve her, Ruairí."

He rose to his feet and drew Bridget up beside him. With a tender, lingering kiss, he said, "I'll come the instant you call, *mo ghrá.*"

In a blink, he was gone.

"He's a romantic fucker. I'll give him that." Piper's wide-eyed wonder sent Bridget into peals of laughter. "What? He *is* romantic! The man never takes those puppy-dog eyes from you, and he hangs on your every word. I'm positive he'd lay down his life for you if you asked."

A shiver chased along Bridget's spine, and her nerve endings went haywire. "Never say it. It's like inviting trouble, it is."

"Sorry. My bad." With the offer of the plate, Piper gave her a beseeching look. "Forgive me?"

"There's nothing to forgive, is there? But have a care about temptin' the Fates in the future, all the same."

"Consider it done."

"Grand. Now, tell me about your holiday and leave out the part about shagging my brother. No sister needs to be forced to sanitize her mind over her brother's bedroom adventures, but I will after hearing such things."

For the next two hours, Piper regaled her with stories of her honeymoon in the islands with Cian. She did reveal they seldom left their room, but also described in great detail the times they did. The food, the day jaunts, the warm sandy beaches, snorkeling with dolphins. It sounded like heaven to Bridget.

"You look wistful. Should I shut up now?" Piper asked with a rueful smile.

"Not at all. I love hearing about your trip."

"But?"

"No buts. I do." When her new friend raised her brows,

Bridget crinkled her nose. "I might be a wee bit jealous, if I'm tellin' it true. The last time I left home was for the Witches' Council hearing against Ryker Gillespie. After watching that right mess, I was back to work within hours." She sighed. "A real holiday sounds wonderful, it does."

"So it's not the fact that everyone around you seems to be coupling up?"

"Could be, in part," Bridget admitted with a short laugh. "I don't know what to do about Ruairí. He holds a key place in my heart, but I've little faith he won't hurt me again." Honesty was important to her, and if Ruairí betrayed her again, it wasn't going to end well. She might take her rolling pin to him like she'd planned to do to Moira.

"And you're afraid to take him at his word?"

"Aye."

"What if he does something you view as a betrayal but isn't really? How do you plan to reconcile the two?"

"You don't need to be posing the hard questions. I've enough shite running through my mind as it is." Bridget smiled to soften the sting of her words.

"If it helps, I see a man in love. It's not to say men in love don't betray the women they commit to, because I've been there, and they absolutely do. But I can say I'd be gobsmacked if Ruairí was one of those."

"He kissed another once," she said, just to see Piper's reaction. The indignation was gratifying, but she felt the need to clarify, so she explained the trick Ruairí had played when they were barely out of nappies.

"He did it to provoke your jealousy? What an *eejit*!"

There was something about Piper using the Irish version of the word that tickled Bridget's funny bone, and she couldn't prevent a giggle. When they made eye contact, they both laughed until they cried, wiped the tears of mirth away, then laughed some more.

"Sure, and I don't know why we're laughin', do you?"

"No idea, but it's funny, regardless." Piper rose and stretched her back, which caused her protruding stomach to jut out farther. She groaned and rubbed her belly. "Nature calls. This one likes to sleep directly on my bladder."

Bridget stood and began gathering the dishes. "After I pop home, I'll send my brother to you."

"No need. Take a night off and let him take care of the business for a while. You deserve a day to yourself, my friend." Piper grinned and flared her eyes wide. "Besides, I'm going to soak in a hot bath and read smutty romance novels as I eat chocolate covered bonbons."

"Go start your water. I'll clean this up and fix you a bite for dinner."

She removed the dishes from Bridget's hands and placed them back on the coffee table. "What part of take a night off don't you get, woman? Call that smoking hot admirer of yours, go out to dinner, or order in, and bump some nasties. Trust me, you'll be glad you did." She laughed when Bridget rolled her eyes. "From what I saw on the front porch, the man knows his way around a female body. Not to mention you looked mighty invested in his expertise."

"Go on with ya!" Bridget scolded with a laugh. "I need to message my ride home."

With a kiss on the cheek, Piper narrowed her eyes and poked a finger in her direction. "Don't even *think* about cleaning this up! I mean it."

"Pfft. What is it you always say to Cian? 'You're not the boss of me.'"

The two shared a grin, and Bridget was left to her own devices. After shooting a quick text to Ruairí, she began gathering the cups and plates to put on the serving tray. Within a minute, he'd arrived and took the tray from her hands.

"Do you know the way to the kitchen?"

A woman could easily become spoiled by this man. From the day he began helping at Lucky's, he wouldn't let her lift anything heavy, and he was quick to jump in and assist with any chores that needed doing. And until this very moment, she'd been unappreciative of his attentiveness.

"Thank you, Ruairí. For everything. The pub, the protection, this." She shrugged off his surprise, embarrassed by her previous lack of manners. "You deserve my gratitude and not my surly attitude."

"Your surly attitude is part of your charm, *mo ghrá*. I'd not have you any other way."

When she raised her brows in disbelief, he grinned.

"I'm tellin' ya true, Bridg. When you give others shite for whatever they do to deserve your wrath, it heats my blood. You've a fire in you that calls to the one in me."

"You're a few pints short of a full keg," she said with affection. "But I'd not have you any other way either."

"It's settled then. You don't be throwing around gratitude all somber-like, and I won't fall dead at your feet in shock, yeah?"

She laughed and led him to the kitchen.

As Bridget prepared the evening meal, she ruminated over the day's events. Adult Ruairí was impossible to resist when he turned on the charm. He'd been a fun-loving and flirty boy, but the man he'd become was someone she definitely wanted to know more about. He seemed to be someone who had used his life experiences to mold him into a trustworthy, caring man who looked out for his own. Who could be depended on when the chips were down and things got dicey.

Turning off the stove, she shifted to open a cabinet and gasped to see Ruairí resting against the doorjamb and watching her with heavy somberness.

She paused in what she was doing, certain something was about to go terribly wrong. "What?"

"Nothing. I was thinking about the past. And about how much I love just watching you go about your chores, whistling and smiling to yourself. I've missed so much."

The ice encasing her heart melted a little more.

"Aw, Ruairí. We were both eejits."

"But we're grown now. We should be able to find our way back to each other. Should've been able to long before now, if I'm to be honest."

She wanted to agree, but she remained silent. There was still a part of her, the cynical part, that taunted her with the possibility he was using her for his own agenda. She'd overheard him talking with Alex and was flattered he cared enough to recreate a few of their finer moments together. Yet she'd been tricked by him before. If she gave her heart to him and he did it again, she'd never recover. Regardless of his intent.

"Dinner's almost ready. Have a seat." Bridget nodded toward the table and turned her back to him, afraid her face showed her good sense warring with the desire to fling herself into his arms like the senseless females in the old-school romance novels she couldn't get enough of. What would it be like to hand over the decision-making to someone else for a change? To have a husband take charge of the day-to-day running of the pub so she could have free time for long hot baths, bonbons, and a glass of wine?

Instead of sitting, Ruairí walked up behind her and rested his chin on her shoulder, not touching her in any other way. "Where did you go, Bridg? One minute, you were present, and the next, you had a faraway look."

"I've work to do," she said stiffly. "I—"

Taking her hands in his, he guided her toward the table. "I'll make dinner. You put your feet up, yeah?"

"But you don't—"

"I've magic, *mo ghrá*. I can conjure anything you've a mind to eat."

His willingness to ease her plight made her smile. "Porter cake?"

"Consider it done."

"And the wafer bars we ate when we would sneak away."

"Most especially those." Before she could blink, the new bars were on the counter beside her.

She laughed. "I'd settle for you finishing the potato soup for tonight's dinner. There's bread in the oven that needs to come out in five minutes."

"And where would you be going?"

"I've rooms to see to for tomorrow's guests."

"Tell me which rooms, and I'll—" he twiddled his fingers in the air "—take care of those, too."

"I could get used to having you around, to be sure."

"That's the plan, *mo ghrá*. Sure, and that's the plan."

"While I appreciate your grand abilities, I've a need to see to some things myself." She rose on her tiptoes and brushed her mouth across his in a light, teasing kiss. "You finish here. I'll be down soon enough." She stopped when she got to the doorway. "Four minutes on the bread. Don't burn it."

"Aye, now go. The sooner you're gone, the sooner you'll return. I've a mind to see your beautiful face again. I already miss ya."

Again, she laughed. His charm always brought a smile to her lips and a song to her heart. It was impossible not to love him.

"Go on with ya!" she mock scolded, ruining it with a wink. His wide, engaging grin was her reward.

As Bridget headed upstairs, she couldn't seem to wipe the smile from her face. Perhaps, if they could make it work this time, this easygoing camaraderie underlined with the spark of sexual tension would always be theirs. The thought made her feel years younger.

The tingling started in her hands again, and she paused at the top landing to stare at them in awe. *Was it really as simple as allowing him back into her life?*

A flash of yellow distracted her, and she looked up sharply to see who might be in the hall.

No one.

She smelled the fresh, bracing scent of the ocean as a breeze swept across her neck and shoulders. With a small shiver from the chill, she turned to make sure the hall windows were closed, giving another little shudder when she saw they were.

Unsure what caused the fluttering wind, she tentatively made her way down the hallway. From the corner of her eye, she again saw a flickering yellow light. It was either wee wicked faeries out to cause mischief, or she was losing her feckin' mind. Still, she decided to follow.

When the dancing light became a solid, pulsing glow at Ruairí's door, Bridget had a moment's hesitation before entering. Perhaps it wasn't the fae after all, but Anu come to tell her not to be so quick to weave fantasies where he was concerned.

Hand on the knob, Bridget inhaled deeply, prepared to go in and face whatever might be on the other side. The door to the next room opened, and Ronan filled the entry. His surprised expression turned to a wicked grin, and she felt the heat warm her from head to toe.

"Is there a woman you don't get with that feckin' look?" she asked irritably. She gasped when she realized she'd spoken the question aloud.

He laughed and lounged against the wall, arms crossed and decided amusement on his ungodly handsome face. "Oh, there would be a few. Like the one in front of me, mad for my cousin, Ruairí."

"I'm not mad for him!" Her denial was too swift and an obvious falsehood, which they both knew. "Oh, feck off," she grumbled, dropping her hand from the door handle as if she'd been burned.

"Don't let me stop you from your..." He nodded toward Ruairí's room. "I'm all for helping this little romance along this time around."

"That's not the impression I get from that knicker-melting smile." She frowned when he laughed. "Sure, and now I see the resemblance to Ruairí. That bleedin' O'Connor charm."

She had to give him credit for trying to suppress his grin, but the dimple in his left cheek gave him away. With one last frustrated glance at the door, she turned on her heel to head the opposite way.

Ruairí was standing about ten feet away, his eyes wary.

What did he have to be worried about? Was there something in his room he didn't want her to see? Another false clue for his fake treasure hunt?

"I'd decided to check if you need help," he said by way of an explanation.

She had none for her suspicious behavior other than the truth. "I saw a flickering yellow light by your door."

His surprised gaze shot to the door in question. "Anu."

Bridget spun back, expecting to see the Goddess herself, but no one was there.

All amusement left Ronan's face as he straightened from his lounging position and backed away from the wall. "Ya sure?"

"As I can be," Ruairí replied grimly.

"And why would she be flitting around my inn?" Bridget asked, the slight tremble to her voice giving away her concern.

"I guess we need to find out," Ronan said as he approached the door.

"No!"

But it was too late.

CHAPTER 18

$\mathcal{R}$uairí's heart plummeted to his stomach as his cousin whipped open the door. The wardrobe on the far side of the room was lit like a topper on a Christmas tree, casting a warm glow over the rest of the room.

Bridget hung back by the opposite wall. "Why would Anu be hidin' in the wardrobe?"

"Goddesses don't hide in closets," an amused voice said from behind the three of them, causing Ruairí to shout and spin, fist raised, and Ronan to lift his hands and prepare for battle.

When they saw it was Alexander, they calmed and relaxed their stances.

"Those are some quick reflexes you fellas have. I'm sorry it ever came to that," he said with real regret in his eyes.

"Sure, and we're not fond of people sneakin' up on us," Ronan countered, shaking his hands out and dispersing his magic.

As if the threat the two of them presented didn't concern him, Alexander strolled in the room, as pretty as you please, not stopping until he was in front of the wardrobe. "What's in there?"

"Exactly what I'm wondering," Bridget said. "You can do the honors, if you've a mind."

"No!" The word was ripped from Ruairí's soul and came out high pitched. If Bridget discovered the sword in the closet, he was completely fucked.

They all turned to look at him, Ronan and Bridget with varying stages of disbelief and Alexander with wry amusement.

"What are you hiding, my dear nephew? For sure, it's not going to be a happy reveal if it's got your undies choking your balls that tight."

After giving Alexander a shut-the-feck-up glare, Ruairí faced Bridget, ignoring Ronan altogether. "It's nothing, *mo ghrá.* I'm asking you to trust me."

Wrong thing to say. Wariness settled on her visage, and she cast another look at the glowing doors of the cabinet. "What's in there?" There was no denying the demand in her voice.

"Bridg, please." He was begging for his life. *Their* life.

She gestured to Ronan. "Open it."

Locking eyes with his cousin, Ruairí slowly shook his head.

The disbelief intensified on Ronan's face. "You brought it *here?*"

With a defeated sigh, Ruairí closed his eyes. Shite was about to hit the fan and splatter all over him.

"What? What did he bring?" Bridget's forbidding tone caused the sick dread building in his chest to settle into a leaden ball in the pit of his stomach.

The instant Ronan caved to Bridget's unwavering stare, Ruairí knew he was a dead man walking. She'd not forgive him again. He'd only meant to make a game of the hunt so they could spend time together and she could remember what it was like to love him, but he'd grossly miscalculated by not telling her the complete truth.

Ronan opened the doors, and the golden light flared so brightly, they all shielded their eyes, right before it died out. And lying on the bottom shelf was the Sword of Goibhniu, pretty as you please and betraying Ruairí in every way.

Like a marionette with frayed strings being forced to perform, Bridget turned to face him with slow, jerky movements. Her eyes—so bright and lively only an hour before—were dull and lifeless, as if her body no longer contained its soul.

"You tricked me? Again?"

Her hoarse question was lacking in the expectant rage. Lacking any emotion at all. And that lack caused terror in his heart. "Bridg—"

"*Again*, Ruairí?"

He was wrong about her anger. "I—"

"You were willing to let me run all over hell and back, lookin' for that fuckin' thing, and you had it the entire time?"

He winced at the screech in her voice.

"'Twasn't meant as anything to hurt you. It was meant for the two of us to spend time together. To help you remember what we shared."

"Oh, it helped me remember, it did. It helped me remember what a lyin' gobshite you are!"

"No, *mo ghrá*. I—"

"You'll save your pathetic excuses, Ruairí O'Connor. You can pack them up in that bag of yours and leave my inn."

Her fury was palpable, and as the victim of her wrath, he was helpless to do anything but comply. Alexander and Ronan were silent and sober as judges as he crossed to the wardrobe and removed his bag from the top shelf to begin stuffing his clothes inside.

Color crept up his neck, and he wanted to defend his actions, but he didn't have the right. He'd taken a gamble, and he'd lost the roll of the dice. Lifting the sword, he stared down at the metal weapon that had caused all his woes. From birth, this thing had cursed him. It was only proper he give it back to the rightful owner.

Silently, he held it out to Bridget.

For a long moment, she stared at the sword in his hands, seemingly unwilling to take it. Finally, she did, immediately looking disappointed as if she were expecting something to happen when she took it from him.

"If I may be the voice of reason..." Alexander stepped forward and removed the weapon from her hands to toss it on the bed. The blatant disregard he showed for the object that started a two-hundred-and-fifty-plus-year feud was laughable —*if* Ruairí had felt like laughing, which he didn't. Not even a little. "It isn't safe for my nephew out there, Ms. O'Malley."

"And I should care, why?" she snapped.

Alexander's gaze bored into her, waiting for her to understand the significance. When she remained defiantly mute, he sighed. "You love him," he said simply. "You might be angry with him at the moment, but think of the regret you'd feel if he were to go back to his house, alone and lacking the necessary abilities to fight Loman, and get hurt or worse."

She cast Ruairí a sullen look. "You can stay, but don't think I love you, because I don't. I've no desire to have your death on my conscience." Stopping by the bed, she touched the hilt of the sword. "Is this really the one?"

"Aye," Ruairí said quietly.

Her cool gaze met his, and he was disheartened to see they were once more a murky green, not a hint of the emerald to be seen. "If you stay here, I don't want to see you again. You can conjure your own food here in your room."

"Bridg—"

She held up a hand. "I knew you were playin' a game because I'd overheard you tell your uncle. But to keep this from me, from my family, when it could've restored our magic and protected us from Loman? That's beyond low, Ruairí."

"I always intended to give it back to you. You have to believe me, Bridg." His voice cracked from the strong emotion he was experiencing. Helplessness combined with hopelessness.

"I don't care for excuses or for your fool reasons. You put my family in more danger with this little stunt of yours, ya did. That I can't forgive." When her voice broke over her last words, she compressed her mouth and lifted the sword from the bed.

"I won't ask you, then." Ruairí was sure he could hear his heart crack in two. "I'll be gone in the morning."

She nodded once and exited the room.

"She'll forgive you, son." Alexander gripped his shoulder and gave him a light squeeze. "She loves you."

"But she doesn't want to. And she's always looked for an excuse to reject me. I've provided it time and again."

"Do you ever ask yourself why?" Ronan's question was softly spoken, designed to make Ruairí think hard about the cause of his fuck-ups.

"I'm sure you'll tell me, now won't ya?"

"You don't think you deserve happiness, Cousin. You're into self-sabotage."

"Oh, and you're one to be lecturing me about me choices when you're shaggin' married women," Ruairí snapped.

"One. One married woman, a lifetime ago, and I loved her," Ronan snapped back.

Because he'd known the why of it, Ruairí felt like shite for picking the scab covering his cousin's lacerated heart. "I know. I'm sorry."

Alexander watched them silently for a time before he finally said, "My brother doesn't stand a chance when the two of you fellas are united. Remember that, won't you?"

BRIDGET SAT ON THE EDGE OF HER BED, STARING AT THE SWORD of Goibhniu on the dresser across the room. That scrap of metal had caused so much strife over the years, it deserved to be melted down and buried at the center of the earth. If she was an earth witch with any power, she'd likely do it, too.

How could Ruairí have lied to her about something so important? Made it another of his games? He'd said he intended to give the sword to her eventually, but had he?

Oh, how he must've gotten a good chuckle at the fact the bleedin' thing was under her very roof while she was ready to search the globe so she could be the one to restore her family's magic. How laughable!

The irony was now that it was back in O'Malley hands, the last line of the prophecy was wrong. Their magic hadn't been restored. She'd not felt a single spark when she touched that feckin' thing. Not even a tingle.

Her disappointment had been keen, and it galled her that Ruairí had witnessed it and recognized her emotions for what they were. She'd seen it in his watchful expression.

When the Enemy at the Gate is welcomed by the Keeper of the Sword, all that is lost shall be restored.

She'd welcomed him into her home, but perhaps he wasn't the true Enemy at the Gate. Or perhaps she wasn't the true Keeper of the Sword. Maybe that fell to another. She'd have to put the sword with the O'Malley grimoire and see if it triggered any reaction from the temperamental spellbook.

Maybe there was more to this than the simple act of receiving the weapon back.

A knock on the door startled her out of her musings.

She was almost afraid to answer. If it was Ruairí come to beg forgiveness, she didn't know what she'd do. Tell him to feck off, most likely. But she didn't want to be angry anymore. Oh, she couldn't help but be furious; however, there was nothing productive in that type of rage. She'd prefer he stay out of her sight until she had a better handle on the riot of emotions all vying for dominance inside her.

She was no coward, though, and she took a deep breath to call out to whoever was on the other side of the door. Of all the people she *didn't* expect to see, Ronan was the one. His gaze darted to the sword but just as quickly locked on her.

"What do you want, Ronan?" she asked wearily.

"He's a broken man, Bridget."

There was no need to define who "he" was. They both knew perfectly well Ronan was talking about Ruairí.

"And how is that my problem?"

"He'd intended to give you the sword all along. He only wanted to take you on a stroll down memory lane so you could recall the better times together. I've never known a man to love a woman more than he loves you. You're more important to him than anyone in his entire world."

"Then he shouldn't have lied!" she snapped. She felt the sting of tears she refused to shed. Forced to blink away the moisture, she looked away from him in an effort to compose herself. "'Tis all he does."

"No. He's the most honest person I know."

Lifting her chin in challenge, she said, "Then you should keep better company, shouldn't ya?"

His mouth tightened and disappointment shone in the depths of his silvery gaze. "He always speaks so highly of you, and yet you don't have a kind word for him. He's better off without ya, he is!"

The shock of his angry retort washed her in cold awareness. She had little doubt of the truth of *that* comment. Ruairí did love her, he just had questionable people skills. And wasn't that the crux of the matter? Should she overlook his little white lies in favor of fun and laughter, or should she call him on his behavior and try to curtail any future problems?

Future problems.

Was she set on forgiveness then?

She stared hard at Ronan, wondering if he was somehow influencing her mind again. "Are you using your magic on me?"

"I don't have enough left to penetrate that thick skull of yours," he said sourly.

Just as she would've given him the tongue lashing he deserved, Ruairí filled the doorway behind him. "Ronan, I'd like to talk to Bridget if you've a mind to leave us alone for a while."

His voice was solemn, subdued, but it still held a hint of command, and Ronan was quick to depart.

Bridget opened her mouth to tell him to go to the devil, but he forestalled her with a simple gesture of his hand.

"I've things that need saying, then I'll go." When she gave a short nod, he continued. "I've never lied about the fact I love you, Bridg. Never once. You are my one true heart, and I want no other."

Biting the inside of her cheek to hold back the venom she was tempted to spew, she glared instead.

"I can see what I'm saying doesn't mean anything to you anymore, but I'll finish what I came to say." After a deep inhale, he said, "I've lied to you exactly twice. Once over the trick with Molly Mae, and once over the whereabouts of that feckin' sword. Both were in an effort to have you do my bidding as I wanted you so badly. The first time to run away with me, and the second to spend time with me. To get to know me again."

"You succeeded. I've gotten to know you can't be trusted," she said coldly.

"Aye, you would see it that way. But it's not true, Bridg. When it mattered, I've always been there for you."

There was no honest retort in reply to his comment. The truth was he *had* been there for her. "Why did you have to lie?" she asked tearfully. "Why? Why couldn't ya have just given me the bleedin' thing and be done with it? I'd have respected you more for it."

"I didn't think you'd grant me the time to take you to all the places that would remind you of what we were to each other," he said simply.

"I don't want to be reminded."

His face lost all expression, and he gave a single nod then turned to go.

"Ruairí."

He paused but didn't turn.

"I don't want to be reminded because the past doesn't matter, yeah? It's the future that's important because we can't change what was, what happened. No matter how much we want to."

"Sure, and I'll leave you alone, Bridget. I understand what you're sayin'."

"No, I don't think you do."

She rose to her feet and crossed to where he stood. As much as she wanted to hug him, to convince the lonely boy inside him he was worthy, she resisted. Her desire to help and heal always overruled her good sense. Not this time. "I need you to promise, no more lies. Not a one. Not as a trick, not to make me view you in a better light, not for my own good, as the case may be. Not a one."

He faced her, wariness and hope plainly displayed. "I can do that."

"I'm not ready to begin anew, but I don't want to be angry anymore. Can you understand that?"

"I can." His light of hope went out. He gave her a sad half smile. "Then I suppose friendship is all we'll have moving forward, yeah?"

She opened her mouth to reply that she would like for it to be more, but a shout from downstairs caught their attention.

CHAPTER 19

"Stay here!" Ruairí commanded as he ran for the door. Of course Bridget wasn't one to listen to a man's dictate when it was unreasonable. If one of her family was in trouble, she'd do what she needed. Grabbing the sword from the dresser, she charged after Ruairí.

When they got to the bottom of the steps, the laughter stopped them short. They shared a confused look and cautiously peered into the sitting room. Alexander was center stage, mid-story with Sabrina Dethridge and Aeden staring in rapt attention, huge grins on their adorable faces. Leaning against the far wall, Damian Dethridge was in a deep discussion with Alastair Thorne, Cian, and Carrick.

The Aether had to be the most fit man on earth. His nose was straight and perfect—not too long, not too short, and without a bump on the bridge to speak of. Every feature on his face was symmetrical, from his almond-shaped eyes to his full lips to his chiseled cheekbones and jaw. He stood with a casual elegance, but deep down, Bridget assumed he always had to be at the ready. There was undeniable power there, and his radiance eclipsed everyone's in the the room.

Alastair was the opposite in coloring, blond to Damian's dark, but he too was a throwback to the Old Hollywood heroes. Bridget had only ever seen him wearing a suit and tie. His gracefulness belied his lethal abilities.

"What the devil?" Ronan muttered from behind them. He jumped back as Bridget swung the sword. "Watch where you're aimin', woman! You almost cut off me prized possession."

She snorted and rolled her eyes, struggling not to laugh at his indignation. "Then don't be sneaking up on me, ya eejit."

"You're getting as bad as Ruairí, with his *strike first and ask questions later* attitude, you are."

Bridget did laugh then. "Don't be such a *ween*. It's a wonder anyone fears you at all."

"Now you're just out to wound me pride, you are."

"Stop flirting with her," Ruairí growled. "She's not for you."

"She's not for any O'Connor," Ronan countered. "She has no sense of the absurd."

"How about you both stop determining who I am or who I'm not for, and let me decide that for myself, yeah?"

"If you children are done squabbling, there are things to discuss," a droll voice said from the entrance to the sitting room.

As one, they turned to see Alastair Thorne tug at his cuffs.

Bridget smiled at the telling sign he was readying for battle. "It's grand to see you again, Alastair."

"And you, too, Bridget. You're more lovely every time we meet, child." His gaze traveled over Ruairí and stopped on Ronan. Displeasure caused him to grimace. "Although the company you keep is questionable."

"They grow on you," she deadpanned.

An amused smile curled Alastair's lips, and a twinkle lit his sapphire-blue eyes. "I suppose it's the influence of the pub? Do these two look like savory characters compared to most of your patrons?"

His teasing made her grin. "I have a soft spot for ne'er-do-wells."

"Must be why you like me."

She laughed and opened her arms for a hug, which he obliged with an added kiss to her temple.

"GiGi will be sorry she missed this, but our cousin Leonie and her new husband, Matt, are having their first child, and she was determined to be there for the birth."

"Another baby to spoil. She's in her element, she is."

"Truer words were never spoken. Now come. We need to discuss Loman O'Connor and how to stop him for good this time." He spared Ronan a glance. "That is, unless you don't care to stand up to your father, but Castor assures me you will."

"I hate the man, and the sooner his reign of terror is done, the better it'll be for all involved." The edge of steel in Ronan's voice left no one in doubt of his commitment to ending that reign.

"There may be hope for you yet, boy."

"I've spent forty-two years on this earth, man. I think I've outgrown the title of boy."

Alastair's engaging smile started slowly and spread across his handsome visage. "I can understand what Rebecca saw in you." The smile dropped as his eyes turned frosty. "But don't mistake me, Mr. O'Connor. You're not in charge here. You'll follow any plan Castor comes up with, and you'll do it without question. Do I make myself clear?"

Ronan's defiance was in every line of his body and as obvious as the perfect nose on his face. Submission wasn't in his vocabulary.

Alastair raised a brow.

Bridget locked eyes with Ruairí, silently giving him the do-something cue.

He clapped a hand on his cousin's back and gave an abrupt

laugh. "He'll do what's necessary. We *all* will," he added when Alastair and Ronan continued their staring contest.

"See to it." Without a by-your-leave, Alastair Thorne turned his back on them and held out his arm to Bridget. "Come, my dear. We've much planning to do."

With a worried glance over her shoulder, she allowed herself to be led away.

"Do you think you were a bit harsh, Al?"

"No."

She snorted. "Sure, and would you admit if you were?"

"Probably not." He leaned closer and lowered his voice. "The truth is, I get a conflicted energy from him. It could be fear, it could be he plans to betray us all, but he needs to be pushed hard to make a decision. Either he's one hundred percent with us, or he isn't." He shrugged. "He can't sit both sides of the fence."

"We have Ruairí and Alexander. Ronan seems to care for them, so I believe he'll fall in with your plans when it's necessary."

"Good. We won't get a second chance to stop Loman, and he's lethal." He glanced down and gestured to the weapon in her opposite hand. "It looks as if you're preparing for a battle all your own. Is that what I think it is?"

"I believe so." She frowned as she lifted it for him to inspect. "But I don't think it holds the magic I assumed it would."

"Ah, the final part of your family's prophecy." He nodded sagely. "Perhaps you haven't welcomed the proper Enemy at the Gate."

"That's exactly what I was wonderin' a short time ago."

"We'll work it out. I've no doubt your magic will be fully restored soon."

Ronan was quite certain Alastair Thorne was determined to test him at every turn. He'd started with the initial verbal challenge and hadn't let up since. But Ronan was an old hand at confrontation and pecking orders. It had taken every magic trick in his arsenal to keep his cousins in line. Theirs was a large family, and there were more O'Connors, Doyles, and McLearys than he could shake a stick at. Their family rivaled the Thornes in size, but while the Thornes were made up of stellar individuals who all supported one another, Ronan's family was the polar opposite. They were likely to slit each other's throats rather than band together for the good of the whole.

Ruairí was the exception. He was the best of them. Which was why Ronan was willing to go face down the formidable Bridget while she was in high dudgeon over the perceived betrayal. Had she truly understood Ruairí and saw what was in his heart, she'd never believe he'd intended any harm.

Alexander Castor caught Ronan's eye and gave him a small, understanding smile as if he knew what was running through his mind. Perhaps there were *two* good souls in the lot. The last one remained to be seen. It was hard to believe Alexander and Loman were twins. Not in looks—that was quite eerie—but their personalities differed so greatly, it was disconcerting.

"Okay, to recap, Loman O'Connor is on the loose, he's somehow restored the bulk of his abilities, and he's determined to steal back the Sword of Goibhniu. Do I have this straight?" Damian Dethridge held out his hand to Bridget, who promptly handed over the weapon in question. His long, slender fingers caressed the blade as he examined it in the light. "And this is it? What everyone is squabbling over?"

"Aye." Ronan needed to express exactly how relentless Loman truly was. "If I know my father, and of everyone here, I'd say I'm the expert, he won't stop until he has it."

"Remind me, what is the last line of the prophecy?"

Ruairí answered first. *"When the Enemy at the Gate is welcomed by the Keeper of the Sword, all that is lost shall be restored."* He gave Bridget a wry smile tinged with sadness. "I assumed I was the Enemy at the Gate and Bridget was the true Keeper of the Sword. I've tried a number of ways to be welcomed, all to no avail."

Blushing furiously, she elbowed him but remained silent.

Damian's lips twitched as if he were fighting back a smile, but he otherwise ignored the exchange. "No sudden influx of magic, Bridget?"

"No. A slight tingling in my hands a time or two, but nothing like my brothers experienced."

"Tingling?" Ronan dropped his arms and stood straighter. This was the first he'd heard of it, and if her powers were trying to manifest, his father's would be diminishing. The result would be deadly. Loman wouldn't tolerate a drain of his magic, as the dead guards at the Witches' Council prison could attest. "When did you feel that? What exactly were you doing?"

She appeared horrified to be put on the spot and gave Ruairí a helpless look. "I... that's to say... well... I..." Closing her eyes, she touched her fingertips to the place between her brows and rubbed. "I was thinking about Ruairí. About second chances."

"I see." Damian returned the sword to her and touched her on the shoulder. "We've all been where you are, Bridget. There's no need to be embarrassed." Crossing the room, he paused and stared out the window, becoming completely silent.

They all shared a look behind his back, unsure what to say next.

Sabrina walked to where Bridget and Ruairí sat side by side, not looking or touching or acting as if the other existed. The girl cocked her head to the side and studied one, then the other.

Here it comes. The girl would throw a prediction out there and immediately be curtailed by the Aether for revealing everything she knew. Of course, Ronan shouldn't take such pleasure in Damian's trials, but it was great fun to witness so powerful a man flounder in the face of his young daughter.

"Papa?"

"Yes, Beastie. You can tell them, but not too much, mind."

With a joyful laugh, she clasped first Ruairí's hand then Bridget's, joining them together and keeping them sandwiched between her smaller ones. "Your magic will come, Ms. Bridget, but only when you see the truth in Mr. Ruairí's heart. Yours will have to thaw all the way." Her earnest gaze bored into Bridget. "Do you know what I mean?"

"Aye. I think I do," Bridget replied softly.

Sabrina nodded and addressed Ruairí. "You will need to help her make the new sword to fight your uncle. You will hold the true one for her and be the arm that strikes the evil man down."

"I would die for her." Ruairí looked right at Bridget when he said it, and Ronan's heart stuttered in his chest. That type of sincerity, the unwavering commitment to another, would get his cousin killed in the end.

"This is feck—uh, this is pointless. I'll not let him go up against Loman," Ronan said angrily. "He's not equipped, sword or no."

"Don't worry, Mr. Ronan." Sabrina gave him a knowing smile. "You'll be there to help them, too."

"You can't just give us a location and be done with it, ya wee wild beastie?" Ronan said with a resigned sigh.

She ran and leaped for him, and he caught her midair. "You're a true hero, you know."

"I'm no one's bleedin' hero," he growled, touching his nose to hers. "Don't be spreadin' vicious rumors."

With a giggle, she wrapped her arms around his neck and

hugged him tight enough to choke him. Her adoration warmed his cold, dead heart, causing it to beat again with purpose. This child had a magic all her own, and it had nothing to do with her abilities. She was genuine and loved everyone, crusty old villains like himself included.

"You're too generous with your praise, wee wild beastie," he whispered against her temple.

"You're a nice man," she whispered back.

Giving her a final squeeze, he set her on the ground and ran a hand over her black curls. When she gazed up at him, those obsidian eyes full of trust and hero-worship, his heart swelled.

"You've too much faith in me. What if I disappoint ya?"

She grinned. "You won't." In a blink, she turned serious. "You'll be careful, won't you? You'll come back?"

"Sure, and where would I be going?"

She looked to her father who shook his head. With a sad expression and an exaggerated shrug, she looked down at her feet, scrapping her black patent leather shoe back and forth across the rug.

"I'll return, wee wild beastie. If only to stop my father and Moira, yeah?"

She nodded up at him, tears shimmering and making the dark depths of her eyes seem fathomless. "I want you to be safe," she said in an achingly sweet voice.

"I'll try me best, darlin'." He squatted down and tapped her nose. "But if I don't return from this mysterious destination, you take care of young Aeden for me. He needs a good friend."

"Aeden is my forever friend," she said simply.

Ronan took it to mean she'd always use what magic she had to look out for him. If it came down to Sabrina and Damian Dethridge versus Loman O'Connor, he'd put his money on the child before him. "Good. That's good."

"Run upstairs and play with Aeden, Beastie," her father urged. "We have adult things to discuss."

CHAPTER 20

*A*fter the children left, hand in hand and whispering all the way, the adults got down to business. Alexander listened, weighing the pros and cons of every suggestion tossed around that might get Loman to confront them on their turf. He couldn't see it happening.

"My brother is too clever by far to fall for any of these ideas," he finally said. "Loman will smell a trap coming from a mile away. The best you can do is be prepared for his strike when it happens."

"And don't forget, he's not alone. At the very least, he has Moira. But if he's been in touch with any of his old cronies, he's likely to have a small army at his back," Alastair inserted.

"Moira and I will have a reckoning one day soon," Damian promised.

Alex had heard the story firsthand from the Aether himself of how Moira, along with Seamus, went after Sabrina and Aeden when the kids crossed the border of Damian's property to a memory garden. Once the kids had left the protection of the Dethridges' warded land, they were fair game. Moira had then tried to shoot Damian in the back when he visited Roisin and Carrick to bring Aeden home after a sleepover. And for the second time, that rotten bitch's plans had been foiled by Roisin.

"The worst thing you can do is leave her alive without her magic." Ronan gave Damian an evil little smirk. "She'll die a thousand deaths when she can't conjure what she wants at a second's notice."

"No. I have a score to settle."

Never in all the time Alex had known Damian had he heard him so cold. The anger rippling off him was barely contained, and had the Aether been any more furious, they'd all have felt the backlash of his fury like acid in the air, burning their skin. If the man ever lost control, there would be no stopping the explosion of power able to decimate a city block... or worse.

"Try to remember to keep your rage in check, Dethridge. The rest of us will pay the price if you don't," Alastair warned.

With a droll look in his friend's direction, Damian said, "You're one to talk, Al. If I remember correctly, when your anger surfaces and you forget yourself enough to swear, you bring on a plague of loc—"

"Enough of that," Alastair said with a narrow-eyed glare. "Let's get back to the subject at hand. Castor's evil twin."

"Sure, and I never thought I'd ever hear that in a real world settin'," Cian said with a short laugh.

"Nevertheless, my brother is the vilest creature you're likely to come across in this lifetime." Alex shot a look at his two nephews. They didn't argue. "His favorite pastime is picking on those weaker than himself. Make no mistake, half the people in this room don't hold a fraction of the power he has. He's likely to try to divide and conquer then use your lack of abilities to his advantage."

"Who does hold it?" When all eyes turned to Bridget, she clarified. "The amount of power he has? Who does hold it? You, Alastair, and Damian, I'm assuming, but what about any others?"

"My son, Quentin, yes, but he has a young daughter, and I'd prefer to keep him out of the fray if possible. These two—" he nodded to Ruairí and Ronan "—should be strong enough together. And if we find a way to restore Ronan's abilities completely, he might be able to go toe-to-toe with his father."

"Sabrina seems to have limitless faith in me. So how do I get this magical restoration of abilities?" Ronan asked with a less-than-enthused expression.

Alex couldn't blame him. Even after all this time and all the power he'd accumulated, he found it difficult to confront his brother. Loman's mind games could erode another's confidence in themself.

"I can restore it with a blessing from the Goddess," Damian said. "I'll need a specific talisman that only she possesses so we don't risk Moira's black-magic blood spell reactivating in your cells."

"What did I miss?" Alex asked.

"When Ronan was in the process of healing Aeden, Moira sliced his back with a poisoned blade. The infection spread too quickly, and the only way to save him was to remove his power. She'd designed the spell that would attach to the magical side of his DNA."

"Clever."

"Extremely." Damian gave Ronan a commiserating look before he addressed Alex again. "Unfortunately for our friend here, he was forced to endure the removal of any abilities he possessed. I had to separate the magic from his DNA to save his life."

"But his magic is returnin', so how do you explain that?" Ruairí asked.

The Aether shrugged. "I can't. He should be one hundred percent mortal at this point. I've never heard of anyone's power returning once I extracted it. It shouldn't be possible."

"Uh, fellas…" Bridget pointed to the golden glow starting in the far corner of the room. "I believe you'll be gettin' your answers soon enough."

A rift split the fabric of their earthly plane, widening to reveal two women on the other side. Alex recognized the black-haired beauty with kohl-lined eyes in the flowing white dress as Isis. But he'd never seen the woman with the fiery red hair the color of the sunset and eyes the shade of Ireland's greenest fields.

As one, with the exception of the Aether, their group dropped to their knees and bowed their heads in respect.

"Rise, beloved children," Isis said in her soft, seductive voice. "We've come to bestow a gift."

Alex smiled. The tide was about to turn in their favor.

As Loman lounged against the wall across the street from The Black Cat Inn, he shook his head in disgust. Their naiveté was astounding. There they all gathered within sight of the sitting room windows, no doubt discussing a plan about how to trap him. He'd have thought the Aether, Alastair Thorne, and Antoine would've known better than to make themselves sitting ducks. All it took was one bomb, not even a magical one at that, to take down the entire group.

The key to setting up the explosives would be in getting close. That feat was a little more difficult. The Aether had the gift of sight, and Alastair Thorne was an empath. Both would sense his arrival before he set foot on the property.

Rumor had it Alexander Castor—and here he found it hard to believe his twin was such a formidable warlock—was a Traveler, the type who could manipulate time and space. The rarest of the rare. Like hen's teeth. Oh, if he could only channel his brother's magic for his own!

He straightened.

Why couldn't he?

Loman had the knowledge, and what he might lack, Moira certainly knew, skilled in the black arts as she was. What couldn't he do if he had the power to manipulate time?

"If I had your ability, I could go back to when you were a *ween* and finish you for good, Brother," he muttered.

"I'm afraid that's not how it works."

Loman spun, prepared to strike, when he saw his nephew Reginald. "Who told you I was here, lad?"

"It didn't take a rocket scientist, Uncle." His nephew's look was pure cold amusement, his jade-green eyes reptilian in nature. Of all those spawned from the O'Connor line, Reginald was the most like him, and he was the only one Loman held a remote fondness for. That's not to say he wouldn't kill the young man should he have to, but he might regret it —eventually.

"Why wouldn't it do me to go back in time to kill Antoine?"

"The time-space continuum doesn't work that way. Should you go back and alter things, the present would change. Uncle Antoine would never transform himself and become Alexander Castor, and he might never gain his Traveler abilities." Reginald shrugged as if it made no difference to him either way. "It also means you'd never get his powers. If you decide to try for Castor's powers, you shouldn't go back to do him in, or you'll forfeit what you worked so hard to gain."

"You're a bleedin' know-it-all, you are," Loman grumbled, irritated he hadn't thought that far ahead. He'd have eventually figured it out. Likely after killing Antoine and getting stuck in the past, but still. "And you're Irish, boyo. Stop jabberin' like you're a feckin' Brit. It's sacrilege."

One of Reginald's perfectly groomed blond brows shot up, but he remained quiet, not daring to contradict Loman, proving he was, indeed, one of the smartest of their lot.

He nodded toward the inn. "What do you think we should do?"

A golden light filled the room, shining out through the panes of glass and casting rays on the ground like sunlight through the clouds. The glow could mean only one thing; a deity had entered the fray.

"Fuck!"

"Retreat would be my suggestion," Reginald said with a hard laugh. "Come back to fight another day."

CHAPTER 21

"We've decided it's time to restore magic to you, Ronan O'Connor," Isis said with a gracious smile. "With the caveat that you use it to protect those present." She gave a significant look at the ceiling, including everyone in the house. "I believe you've learned your lesson."

Ruairí shot his cousin a concerned glance. Ronan hated the responsibility of looking out for others. He'd only ever cared and sacrificed for Ruairí and received beating after beating for his efforts. Loman had tried to remove Ronan's innate kindness in the only way he knew how. Abject cruelty.

"Sure, and it appears the wee wild beastie was right. I'm to be a feckin' hero, whether I want to be or not," Ronan said with deep disgust.

Bridget bit her lip to conceal a smile, but Castor didn't bother to hide his amusement, and his laughter boomed out as he clapped Ronan on the shoulder and gave him a little shake. They all treated it as if it were a cause for grand entertainment, but Ruairí knew well Ronan's internal struggle to do the proper thing.

He'd been programmed at a young age to do dastardly

deeds, and as an adult, he had to fight the influence of years of conditioning. It wasn't to say he wasn't naturally kind, but perhaps that was why he'd sought oblivion in the arms of Rebecca Walsh-Thorne, Hoyt Thorne's beloved wife and the mother of Cian's wife, Piper. As a gifted doctor and surgeon, Rebecca had likely recognized Ronan had a deeper wound that needed healing. She would've taken one look at his angelic face and battered soul and decided to be the balm his hurting spirit needed.

"You seem awfully contemplative of a sudden," Bridget said in an aside. "What is it?"

"I'm worried about Ronan." Ruairí nodded to the goddesses in deep conversation with his cousin and Damian.

"You don't think he'll do the right thing, then?"

"Oh, I do, to be sure, but he's conflicted."

"Loman's influence, I'm assumin'."

"Aye."

Bridget's thoughtful stare caused sweat to pool at his lower back.

"What?"

"You've never given in to the pressures of your family, Ruairí, or not that I'm aware of at any rate. Why?"

"I had you, *mo ghrá*. The memory of your smile, your laugh, your faith in me, yeah, those images got me through the worst of the abuse. I clung to every moment we'd spent, and I had hope for the future. Ronan had none."

"Yeah, and that makes his deceit seventeen years ago more understandable, doesn't it?" she said absently as she studied Ronan from across the distance. "He needed you as you needed me."

"Yeah."

She turned tear-bright eyes on him. "I'm sorry either of you ever had to go through what you did. No child should suffer so."

And her caring for two men she should be happy to see the last of was what made Ruairí love her to the extent he did. One moment, she could easily put a man in his place, and in the next, her kindness to a stranger was humbling.

"No, they shouldn't." At the age of three, he'd been locked in a damp, dark closet after it had been discovered Ruairí had made friends with the girl next door. He'd been talking to her through the slats of the gate between their two properties when his da caught him. The memory of that dank hole made him shudder whenever he recalled it. "I still hate pitch-black nights and wake from dreams in a sweat. I can only imagine what Ronan suffered at the hands of his father, who was the worst of men."

The shout of "Guardian!" drew their notice.

"Feck no! Keep your bleedin' magic," Ronan said, complete disgust heavy in his tone. "I'll not guard a tomb."

They all sucked in a collective breath at the blatant disrespect for the Goddesses' gift, letting it out again only when Anu laughed and Isis smirked.

"It looks like I won that bet," Anu said with smug satisfaction.

"Who knew he'd be so difficult?" Isis countered.

Hands went up around the room, and both deities laughed.

Ruairí and Bridget shared a relieved look.

"What's he talkin' about? Do you know?" he asked her. While Bridget didn't have any magic of her own, she knew a lot of talented witches and had been a member of a coven for years until she stopped attending because of her overall sadness that she'd never be able to practice as they did. Ruairí trusted her knowledge.

"Guardians are one step below the Aether on the magical ladder," she explained. "But they're always tasked with the difficult jobs. The last two of their kind were to watch the tomb of Isolde de Thorne and take action should she waken."

Ruairí's brows shot up. "The Enchantress?"

"Yeah, one and the same, and wake she did. The male Guardian was killed in the process, and the other, his wife, followed him not long after." She shrugged. "And as far as I know, there's been none to take their place... until now."

"But if she woke up, what tomb is Ronan to watch?"

Bridget gave him an exasperated glare. "Sure, and how am I to know that? I'm just learnin' he's to be a Guardian, aren't I?"

The sound of silence registered on them both, and they turned to see the entire room of people, goddesses included, watching them in varying stages of disbelief and amusement.

A side glance showed Bridget's cheeks were flushed, and Ruairí couldn't help but chuckle. "Scarlet is your mam for yellin' at me like ya did," he whispered.

His comment earned him a side pinch, and he laughed outright. Goddess, he loved a feisty woman.

Bridget rolled her hand in a gesture for the others to continue their discussion. If Ruairí hadn't been plaguing her with questions, she might know what was going on with the others. But like always, he was the perfect distraction. His mere presence could make her forget herself most times.

"No tomb, Ronan O'Connor," Isis said. "Should you choose to accept our offer, you'll be the Guardian of the next generation of children. The three Fates have warned us there is a potential for war in the years to come, a war the likes to make that of the Désorcelers society seem tame. You and your mate will play a vital role in training those with powerful magic and seeing to it they are on the right side of that war."

"Mate?" Bridget asked, unable to help herself. "He's mateless at the moment, he is."

Anu's lips twitched and dimples appeared in her porcelain-smooth skin, making her even more beautiful than she first appeared. "He will not be long without a mate." Her brilliant green eyes swept the length of Bridget's body and came to rest on her face. "Would you care to fulfill the position?"

Speechless, Bridget stared at Anu. How did she insult a goddess by saying as fit as Ronan was, he didn't appeal to her half as much as the man sitting beside her?

"Fuck no!"

She breathed out a sigh of relief at Ruairí's emphatic response and tightly gripped his hand.

A wink accompanied Anu's knowing smile. "I thought not."

"I'm crushed, to be sure," Ronan said dryly.

"Hush, you plonker," Bridget said with a laugh. "You're not disappointed in the least, and you know it. You'd live in fear of me every day of your worthless life."

He grinned. "You don't speak for me, Bridget O'Malley. But you'd have made a formidable Guardian."

The second it registered on her that she'd have been granted powerful magic, she dropped Ruairí's hand and stood. "Wait! Does this mean I'll not have abilities at all, then?"

With a sexy swish of her hips, Isis was at her side and tucking a stray strand of Bridget's hair behind her ear. "It doesn't mean that at all, Beloved. No need to sacrifice yourself to gain your rightful power."

"Sacrifice?" Ronan said indignantly, apparently still smarting over the decree he was to be called into service. "I'll have ya know—"

Isis waved a hand, and the rest of his words were choked off. Alastair's muffled laughter gained him an arch look in reprimand, but he was completely unrepentant. She continued as if she were never interrupted. "That will come when you fulfill the rest of the prophecy."

With a lingering look at the sword resting against the sofa's side, Bridget muttered, "I thought I had." Despite her personal feelings for Ruairí in the past, she'd allowed small concessions like entry to her pub, giving him a job—although that benefited her more than anyone else—and access to her inn.

"No, dearest, you haven't. You will need to open your heart for that to happen," Isis told her in a low voice. "There lies your true magic, and once found, it will never go away."

But I can't trust him with my heart, she thought silently.

"You can," Isis said aloud, startling Bridget with her ability to read minds. "You've only to trust yourself and what you feel."

With a helplessness she couldn't shake, she stared at Isis, wishing she knew how to get beyond the overwhelming sense of dread and the terror of another betrayal. Maybe it was because she loved *too* much that she feared opening the gate.

Isis gave her a tender smile.

That's when it occurred to Bridget the prophecy had nothing to do with the physical "gate" to their garden and everything to do with the one guarding the secret place where her soul resided. She closed her eyes in resignation. Either she had to trust Ruairí, or she had to let him go and any chance of magic with him. She almost laughed, and bitter the sound would be if she did. Loman O'Connor was closer to winning than he knew, and he didn't need to do a feckin' thing to make it happen.

She felt the heat of Ruairí at her back when he rose and placed a comforting hand on her shoulder. Close enough to have heard everything, he offered her the support she didn't know she needed.

"I believe you will come to the right decision and be happier for it, Bridget O'Malley," Isis said kindly. "But should you choose a different path, your life will be as fulfilling. This is my promise to you."

"Thank you, Exalted One." Bridget bowed her head, overwhelmed and grateful for the choice. Beside her, she felt Ruairí stiffen, but he remained silent. They'd yet to finish the discussion they'd started in her room, and things were left unresolved. The atmosphere was heavy with his disappointment.

Isis smiled at him, and her expression was filled with gentle understanding. "All will be well, Ruairí O'Connor. Trust the process."

His steady regard brought Bridget's head up, and they locked gazes. "There's only one way this will be well, but I'll not stay where I'm not wanted."

She felt a desperate need to tell him he was wanted, and yet, she wasn't quite ready to confess or commit. When the time was right, she would know.

"Now." Anu's sharp clap caused Bridget and Ruairí to flinch. "It's time to secure Ronan's commitment. What will it be, Beloved?"

Sabrina and Aeden entered the room as Ronan paused in his answer. The Aether's daughter gave him a confident nod, and he shook his head in resignation. "Aye. I'll be their Guardian."

"Excellent. This next part might sting a little."

"Sting?" His expression was wary. "Sting in what way?"

Alastair snorted. "That's goddess speak for it's going to burn like the very devil. It will feel as if they're searing your cells, similar to a steak on a grill."

"Fuckin' grand."

CHAPTER 22

*T*he restoration of magic was just as Alastair Thorne said. The heat building inside Ronan's cells felt as if a nuclear reactor explosion was eminent and he was the Chernobyl plant. There was no twisting away or escaping from the pain. For a brief second, he thought perhaps he was held in a dreamlike state under his father's watchful eye while Loman devised torturous ways to make him suffer. The only consolation was his father had never had the ability to alter minds or reality as Ronan once had.

His scream rang out from where he lay on the stone altar, echoing off the cavernous space surrounding him. A small hand found his, and he felt an instantaneous relief. Shifting his head sideways, he met the worried gaze of Sabrina Dethridge, who had tearfully insisted she be present. No amount of protesting by either her father or the Goddess had made a difference. She was one determined little girl and refused to be dissuaded.

"It's okay, wee wicked beastie. I'm all right," he lied hoarsely. In reality, he felt like he was dying again. As if Moira's black-magic poison was coursing through his veins and eating him from the inside out. He thought about inspecting his chest for the black vine-like marks that had spread across his skin prior to the Aether removing the poison, but he was afraid they might truly be there. And then what was he to do? Live without his magic for the remainder of his days?

"It will be over soon, Mr. Ronan." The earnestness in her face stabbed him right in the heart. No child should possess the knowledge this one did. As a future Oracle, she could see alternate realities and endless possibilities. How she kept from losing her mind was beyond his capability to understand.

"You should go home now, love. I'm grand."

She shook her head. "Papa always tells me not to tell tall tales. You shouldn't either."

His laugh quickly morphed into a scream as another wave of fire washed through his bloodstream. Once again, a pulse of magic from Sabrina took away the worst of it.

"You'll drain yourself if you keep this up," he warned on a pant, fighting the desire to vomit.

"Nah. Mack says I'm the Baby Aether, and that makes me better than Supergirl," she said with a cheeky grin.

He didn't know who Mack was, but he assumed the person held a special place in Sabrina's heart based on the adoration in her young voice.

She became serious in an instant. "Thank you, Mr. Ronan. For taking Grandpa Nate's place and staying to protect me."

"You have your da for that, don't ya? I'm just the backup—or I will be if I live through this." He gave her the best smile he could muster, which probably looked as sickly as he felt.

"You and Dovie."

Dubheasa.

He hadn't thought about her since he left New York. Didn't deserve to. He'd blatantly lied to her to steal the information he needed to locate his father through his banking accounts. Then he'd disappeared without a by-your-leave and probably left her in a heap of trouble from the financial mess he created. It couldn't be helped. If he couldn't attack Loman magically, he intended to make his life a misery by cutting off his funds.

What Sabrina said finally registered on his knackered brain, and he almost shot off the altar. "Dovie? Dubheasa O'Malley? What did you see for us, then?"

After casting a cautious glance over her shoulder to see where the others were, Sabrina leaned in to whisper, "She will be the other Guardian."

Ronan shuddered and grew chilled. He didn't want to see Dubheasa in battle should it come to that. But he also couldn't dismiss the implication that she'd be his mate. She'd been the first woman he'd felt a connection to since Rebecca. The only one who had made him forget he was a despicable person who had hurt people in the past and likely would in the future.

Another influx of magic burned him, erasing any thoughts of her from his mind. He concentrated on not wetting himself in front of a child. And as his body began to cool, he braced for another surge. It never came.

"You're done, Mr. Ronan." Sabrina sweet little voice trembled in her excitement. "You're my Guardian!"

"*A* Guardian, Beastie. Not *yours* specifically," Damian said with an indulgent chuckle.

"But strong enough to beat that right bastard Loman!"

Her triumph was short lived.

Damian picked her up and touched his nose to hers, and in a tone as stern as Ronan had ever heard him use with her, he said, "No swearing, Sabrina Dethridge, or you'll face punishment. Little girls don't say words like bastard. Do you understand?"

"But that's what *you* call him, Papa," she retorted with a pout.

There was no argument against the truth, and Damian gave

her an exasperated look and set her down with a light pat on her bottom. "No swearing until you're at least eighteen."

"Sixteen," she said with an elfin-like grin.

"Perhaps seventeen, but no younger."

"Deal." Her mischievous face gave away her obvious lie, but it appeared her da was in no mood to scold her further.

Ronan rested his head back against the foam pillow, the one item provided to offer comfort on the stone altar he rested upon, and closed his eyes. "Sure, and I don't envy you the merry chase she'll be leading you on, man."

"Leading *me* on?" Damian laughed. "You heard her. *You're* her Guardian. You're the one tasked with keeping her alive to adulthood. You'll be little better than a nanny to children, my friend."

"The feck you say!" Ronan shot up like a vampire coming out of a coffin, his horror lending him strength.

"Relax. You're going to need your strength for what's to come." Damian whistled a jaunty little tune as he strolled away, his daughter's tiny hand tucked in his.

RUAIRÍ FOUND BRIDGET ALONE IN HER UPSTAIRS SITTING ROOM. She was standing at the window, gazing out over the backyard.

"I plan to move back into my home tonight," he said without preamble. "I thought you should know. The room has been cleaned, and fresh linens are on the bed, so it will be ready for your next guest whenever they arrive." He grimaced when she turned to face him. "Although, I'd probably find a way to cancel future bookings until Loman is caught. It wouldn't do to have innocents caught in the crossfire."

"It's not safe for you to return home. What if his intent is to harm you?"

"He could've harmed me at any time since his escape, but he hasn't. I imagine it's Ronan he's after if the truth be told."

"I thought you said you wouldn't lie to me again," she said in a tight voice. "Cian's already told me Loman threatened you."

"Yeah, and Cian's got a big mouth, he does." He looked past her out the window, and it occurred to him that it wasn't the yard and tree line she'd been staring at, but the gate. Had she been remembering the first time they'd met? Or was she thinking about the prophecy, and what it truly meant? "I'll be grand, *mo ghrá*. And you'll be, too. The Goddess decreed it, didn't she? Promised you a happy life."

Uncertain what he'd see there, he avoided her gaze and turned on his heel. "I'll text Alexander in the mornin', and he can give me the details on his plan to trap Loman."

"We should shag and be done with it."

The blood rushed to his head, and not the one on his shoulders. Putting a finger to one ear, he wiggled it back and forth. "Sure, and I didn't hear ya properly. What?"

She stomped across the floor until she stood in front of him, hands on her hips and a scowl scrunching her beautiful face. "I *said* we should shag and be done with it."

"Yeah, and that's what I thought ya said. Don't take this the wrong way, but you're mad, Bridg."

"You don't want to shag me?" Her tone rose to a dangerous level, and the red color climbing her neck was a clear indication he needed to tread carefully.

"I didn't say that, now did I?"

"Then why are you still dressed?"

"Because I'll not make love to a woman who is only interested in getting her family's magic back," he snapped. "Admit it, you only want to have a go because you think it will restore what the O'Malleys lost."

If anything, her face turned darker in color, and her eyes

narrowed. "What does it matter why I want to have a go? You're a man, aren't ya?"

He pointed at her face. "That! That right there is why you've earned a terrible reputation for bustin' a man's bollocks! You treat us all like eejits."

"You all *are* eejits!" she scoffed.

"Well, you can find another eejit to fuck, because I'm not it." He strode around her to the door, and just as he touched the knob, he heard her sigh.

"Please."

He glanced over his shoulder, not truly expecting her to be contrite, but she was. "Please, what?"

"Please don't go, Ruairí. Stay with me."

Because he didn't quite understand in what exact way she meant, he remained quiet.

"Here, at the Black Cat. Not here in my bed. You've already rejected me, and I'll not ask again."

"I didn't reject you, *mo ghrá*. I rejected your reason." He spun back and pointed at the rock-hard bulge in his pants. "No sane man is going to tell you no, as beautiful as you are. And before you say a word, I'll be tellin' ya true, I'm not sane. I never have been where you're concerned, now have I?"

"If you want me, and I want you, and it could restore my family magic, then what's the problem?"

Maybe he *was* an eejit, because when she stated it that way, he couldn't come up with a plausible explanation that didn't make him sound like a girl. Why *not* give into his desire?

He wanted her to love him as madly as he loved her.

That was why. Anything less would leave him unfulfilled.

"I love you."

A deep frown marred her lovely brow. "The problem is you love me? You make no sense, Ruairí O'Connor."

"I love you, and I want more than a pity shag."

"Who's pitying you, you dammed fool? Certainly not me. I

said I want you, and I meant it. Sure, maybe not as my husband, but enough that it's not a pity shag."

He'd never been more frustrated with her nor more aroused. Bridget, throwing about the word *shag* and appearing as she was with the flush of desire on her cheeks and an appreciative look in her eye, turned him into a randy goat.

"Fine. You want to shag? We'll shag," he growled, ripping his henley over his head and tossing it to the ground. "Get undressed."

Her triumphant smirk drove him mad.

CHAPTER 23

*B*ridget knew she'd taunted him into the rash decision to have sex, but she didn't care. First, she desired him, and she'd been fantasizing about this moment since he'd set her on the pub cooler and kissed her senseless. Probably longer, if she were honest with herself. And second, if he was the Enemy at the Gate as she suspected and as Isis hinted at, then sex with him would unlock the curse.

Unlocking the curse meant a drain of Loman's power, and should he show up to challenge or hurt any of them, he'd be weaker than when he started. Whatever it took to protect her family and friends, and by extension, Ruairí, from Loman O'Connor's brand of evil, she'd do. Even if it meant shagging the one man she'd never been able to forget after.

"What are you waiting for? Start strippin'," Ruairí demanded, three-quarters of the way to naked.

She couldn't help it; she giggled. A surly Ruairí tickled her fancy. Yeah, and she might be warped in her thinking, but ruffling his feathers and causing this normally unflappable male to lose all sense of reason made her happy. Could be she enjoyed the challenge. Or it could be that, like many a woman, she wanted her man to lose all sense of decorum and go caveman over her.

When she didn't undress fast enough for his peace of mind, he snapped his fingers and had them both stripped bare in the blink of an eye. Such effortless magic always left her breathless, or perhaps she was simply breathless seeing him without a stitch of clothing after all this time. Either way, she had to struggle to inhale a proper lungful of air.

He was magnificent. Perfect in every way that mattered. Looks, a fit body... Her gazed dropped to his rampant erection. And yes, that too.

"You certainly filled out since we were last together," she said.

"I could say the same for you, but then it was harder for you to hide your figure over the years, so I didn't miss much."

For as irritated as he'd been when she suggested sex, Ruairí approached her with great care as if afraid to spook a wild horse. And perhaps the description was fitting because her heart was pounding madly in her chest and, as much as she desired him, she suddenly felt ready to bolt.

"It's all right if you've changed your mind, Bridget," he said softly.

Her eyes snapped to his. Tenderness was what she saw there. A calm acceptance that she might say no. No pressure. No expectations. Nothing but love.

It gave her the courage to step forward and into the arms he raised to hold her. Barefoot as she was, the top of her head only came to his chin, and he lifted her to make their lips align. She needed no encouragement to wrap her legs around his waist or to weave her fingers into his shaggy blond hair.

With a slight tug, she tilted his head back to kiss the line of his strong jaw and nip his chin.

"You've become bitey," he teased. "I like it."

"Good because I intend to bite you in all the proper places."

"Yeah?"

"Yeah." She emphasized the point by lightly biting the column of his neck then tracing the spot with her tongue.

"Mmm, that's a grand place to start, *mo ghrá*."

He walked with her to the bed, and using one arm to brace their weight and one arm to secure her against him, he lowered them on to the mattress. For the longest moment, he stared down at her, his eyes touching on every part of her face as if he intended to memorize every square inch.

Embarrassed by the scrutiny, she sandwiched his face between her palms. "It's time to get to the snoggin' part, love. You definitely excel at that."

His wicked laugh curled her toes. "I excel at all the parts, Bridg. Or so I've been told."

"I swear, if you bring up that minger's name—"

He covered her mouth with his, slipping his tongue inside to steal the vinegar from her words, turning her sweet once more. As their kiss grew heated, she became familiar with this new lover, and he tasted of broken dreams and future promises. Passion and caring. He tasted of pure Ruairí, her first and only love.

His capable hands trailed up her ribcage, careful to apply the right amount of pressure to avoid triggering her giggles. Of course, he'd remember how ticklish she was, of the time when they'd first made out and how their necking session ended abruptly with her full-blown gales of laughter. A woman's hilarity during hot and heavy petting tended to ruin the mood for most men. But he'd taken it in stride, never becoming angry as some men might, but he'd never tickled her again—unless it was intended.

She smiled at the memory.

Ruairí took his time exploring her breasts, tasting, teasing with his mouth and hands. Taking one beaded nipple into his mouth, he moaned in his pleasure, and she reveled in the sound, echoing her agreement. He'd once told her he could spend hours tasting her skin, suckling her breasts. And she always let him until he drove her mad with desire and her passion became too much, as was happening now.

Drawing his head up, she kissed him more fully, impatient for him to be buried deep inside her to wait any longer. And when he gave in to her unrelenting need and stroked her core, she surged upward and rubbed against the palm of his hand. Sitting back on his knees, he spread her legs wide and used the head of his penis to caress her folds, running the tip up and down until her body wept with her hunger for him.

Ruairí bent and touched his tongue to her, sweeping it along her opening and stopping only when he touched her clit. When she arched into him, she could feel his lips curl into a smile as he sucked on the tiny bud.

She cried out in her pleasure, greedy for more.

And he gave it to her. Fingers, tongue, penis, whatever she demanded in every way she demanded until she was mindless. Using her feet to propel her lower half up, she met each of his forceful thrusts with a moan and a plea for more.

She wanted to tell him she loved him, but she held back, afraid to expose that part of herself. And when she looked up into his loving eyes, she couldn't look away.

"Come for me, *mo ghrá*. Come *with* me."

No further coaxing was needed, and she threw her head back as she cried out. He pumped harder for a few more seconds then shouted her name as he crested the wave with her.

As their bodies cooled and their hearts returned to a normal rhythm, she lay beside him holding hands and waited for the magic to sweep through her.

And waited.

And waited some more...

· · ·

"It didn't happen." Disappointment rode her harder than Ruairí had ten minutes before.

His blond head came off the pillow, and he lifted up to rest on one arm, staring down at her in horror. "You didn't come?"

"What?"

"Get off. You didn't get off?"

"*Oh!*" She laughed. "Of course I did. How could you not tell?"

"I... well... I thought... but sometimes a woman fakes it." A blush colored his cheeks, and he'd never looked more boyish and adorable.

"Oh, Ruairí. Yeah, and I doubt any woman has ever faked it with you." She caressed his cheek. "Never change."

A frown marred his brow. "I thought you hated me the way I was."

"When did I say that?" She dropped her hand and scowled.

"Well, not in so many words, ya didn't, but it was implied."

"Never once have I asked you to change who you are. Sure, and I don't like what you consider little white lies, and I'll rip your beating heart out with my bare hands if you lie to me again, but never have I asked you to change who you are here." She patted his chest. "I like you just the way you are."

He laid back on the pillows and grinned. "This feels like a Bridget Jones moment."

With a laugh and a quick peck on his lips, she said, "You're a right tool. And I'm going to ride you mercilessly about the chick flicks you watch."

Taking her hand in his, he kissed her fingertips. "I don't care. For you, I'll take a ribbin'. What didn't happen, then?"

"This." She wiggled her fingers. "The return of my magic."

He rolled on his side and propped his head on one hand. "It's because you refuse to open your heart to me, *mo ghrá.*"

"What?"

"Think about it. What was Isis sayin' to you today? Something about you needin' to open your heart for it to happen?"

Gobsmacked, her mouth fell open at the simplicity of the solution. "That's it, then. I thought it was a simple shagging. Opening the gate, so to speak."

Ruairí began to laugh. Deep, booming guffaws that irritated her to no end.

"Sure, and what are you laughing at?"

"Your face!" he crowed.

"Get out."

"Bridg—" He couldn't quite muffle his continuous chuckle.

"No. This is no laughin' matter. I've need of the magic to defeat Loman."

Her comment sobered him. "Then I hope you never get your magic, because you'll not be goin' up against my uncle. I don't want you within a mile of that fecker."

"You're not the boss of me, Ruairí O'Connor, and the sooner you realize that, the better."

"You've a death wish, woman! If you think for one bleedin' moment that any of us will let you confront him, you've lost your feckin' mind, ya have!"

He'd worked himself up to a full steam, and Bridget decided to let him have his say. She intended to do what she intended to do, and he'd not stop her, but if he felt better venting, she'd let him.

"He's dangerous, and he eats little girls like you for breakfast," Ruairí said. In his frustration, he began jerking on his clothes, glaring at her all the while. "Of all the foolish, most asinine—"

She sat up and let the sheet drop to her waist, resting back on her hands.

He trailed off as his fiery-hot gaze locked on her bare breasts.

Bridget almost laughed at how easy he was to distract, glad

to see nothing had changed in seventeen years and the technique she employed to shut him up still worked.

Trailing one fingertip between the valley of her breasts, she gave him a wide-eyed, innocent look. "Sure, and what was it you were sayin'?"

"You're an evil woman." Reluctant admiration replaced his dark scowl. "And maybe you *are* a match for Loman."

She grinned and patted the spot next to her. "Come back to bed, love. We've an entire night ahead of us."

He dove atop her, and she giggled as he felt up all the right places.

CHAPTER 24

*A*s Ruairí listened to Bridget whisper-quiet snore, he stroked the tangle of curls back from her face with a butterfly-soft touch, never taking his eyes from her, unable not to stare. Never had he thought this moment would come, and his heart was almost full to bursting. Only a declaration of love from her lips would've made it better, but he understood she wasn't ready yet, and might never be. If it came to that, he'd have to find a way to accept her decision to keep her heart locked away.

Never was there a woman as stubborn or determined as Bridget O'Malley. Never one so beautiful and sure of herself. One so honest and true. But he loved her in addition to all those qualities. Her light shone brighter than anyone else's, and it never failed to entrance him. Hers was the beacon that guided him home and would never go out.

"Why are you still awake?" she murmured, her voice husky from sleep.

"I'm treasuring this moment, so don't spoil it." He shifted to drop a kiss on her temple, taking the sting out of his comment.

She tweaked his nipple in response and triggered a deep laugh.

"*Mo ghrá. De shíor.*"

"You always say the sweetest things to me, even when I don't deserve them." Voice and expression dreamy, she gazed up at him with bright emerald eyes.

His heart stuttered at the obvious sign of her happiness. That particular shade of green he'd yet to see in seventeen years. "You deserve all the best things in life. I'd give you the moon and stars if I could."

She snuggled down into him, her head on his chest, and he could feel her smile in response to his words. That smile, along with the contentment in her eyes, gave him hope he probably had no right feeling.

"You should try to sleep, Ruairí. We've a long day when we finally get to it."

The truth of her words intruded on the spell she'd woven here in her bed. By now, Ronan should have the powers of a mighty Guardian and be recovered from the painful influx of magic imprinted on his DNA. With any luck, Loman's ability to scry or track him through their blood would be a thing of the past since Guardians were next-level beings. Maybe then, if Loman couldn't be defeated, Ronan would still disappear off this father's radar and have a chance at a decent life. One without the constant threat of his mad da breathing down his neck and trying to kill him at every turn.

"Who do you think will be Ronan's future mate?" Bridget asked, clearly on one wavelength as Ruairí.

"As long as it's not you, I don't give a feck."

"It will never be me. Your cousin's too pretty for my peace of mind, to be sure." She rolled her head slightly to meet his eyes, giving him a tender smile. "And perhaps I'm satisfied with the man in my bed."

Stroking the silky skin of her shoulder, he thought about

her question. "I don't know if Ronan has cared for anyone but Rebecca Thorne. But I can't see her abandoning Hoyt and Piper to run off with Ronan after all this time."

"No. I met the woman, and she's mad for her husband. I think she cares about Ronan, but not to the degree she loves Hoyt."

"The Goddess must have another picked out for him. It should be interesting to see how this unfolds."

Bridget's expression turned to one of quiet contemplation. "Yeah, *if* we live through the upcoming battle."

"We will, *mo ghrá*. The Fates aren't cruel enough to part us when we are close to finding our way back to each other again."

The arm around his waist tightened, but she didn't reply. They both understood what was at stake should Loman get the upper hand.

"I do love you, Ruairí," she finally said. "I'm still struggling to find my footing, though. Be patient, yeah?"

Since no other words needed to be said, he snuggled her close, resting his cheek against the crown of her head. He would die for this woman if it came to it, and he needed this one perfect moment should he be forced to await her in the otherworld.

"Bridg, if anything should happen to me, if—"

She stretched and covered his mouth. "No. Don't put a thought like that out there. Thoughts are things. They're a living energy, and if you should put it out in the world, it could happen. We'll only believe in a perfect outcome, you and me."

He nodded and kissed her palm. If she wanted him to collect unicorn horns and chase their rainbow farts, then that's what he'd do. Whatever it took to make her happy and whole.

"You have to argue with me on occasion, Ruairí, or this relationship will be boring as feck," she said tartly.

He laughed and rolled on top of her, sighing his pleasure

when she wrapped her legs around his waist and tilted her pelvis toward him. "I'm a lover, not a fighter, *mo ghrá.*" Rubbing his erection against her silky wetness, he kissed the hollow of her throat. "Or have you forgotten?"

"Sure, and why don't you remind me?"

Isis waved her wooden staff, topped by its baseball-size amber gemstone, and the image shimmering in her pond dissolved into ripples, allowing the couple their privacy.

"She still hasn't accepted him completely?" asked a deep, raspy male voice from behind her.

Turning, she pasted on a welcoming smile. "Goibhniu, it's good to see you again."

And it was. As provincial as the lessor god was, he was still quite handsome. Today he appeared in a leather jerkin, left to hang open over his barrel chest. He didn't bother with a shirt underneath, and all his endless muscles rippled with the tiniest movement of his body. It was all Isis could do not to release a girly sigh in the face of all that blatant masculinity.

"Why is the woman being stubborn?"

"I'm sure she has her reasons. Women don't like to be played by men. It makes them... What's the word my beloved Thornes are so fond of? *Salty.*" Isis was clad in a strapless dress of the finest white silk threaded through with gold, and it seemed to fascinate him, based on his unwavering attention. She shrugged one delicate bare shoulder and noted with satisfaction how his hot gaze fell to her breasts. Men were predictable, and she like predictability.

He shook his dark head and managed to tear his attention from her curves. "Yeah, and I don't know what that means, but I can guess."

"You were always happy making your weapons, Goibhniu,"

Anu said as she joined them. "The intricacies of human interactions are beyond your scope. There's something to be said for a basic man such as yourself." She bussed his cheeks then turned and repeated the gesture with Isis. The two women locked gazes, and Isis recognized the twinkle in Anu's intelligent eyes for what it was. Mischief. "Tell me, what's the trick to the sword the O'Malleys hold?"

"'Tis no secret. If the wielder of the sword has a true heart, the blade will always find its target," he explained with a casual disregard to polite social norms as he picked the dirt from beneath his fingers with the fine tip of a dagger.

When they remained quiet, staring at him with raised brows, he whirled the knife and shoved it into a scabbard at his hip. "Pardon me manners. It's only me two brothers and me. I forget women are more refined, I do."

Isis and Anu exchanged another conspiratorial look. They both knew he was more than a simple blacksmith. He'd been embodied with godly powers for his skills. His were the weapons that always struck true, be it sword, arrow, or war hammer. As skilled as he was with metals and magic, he created impenetrable armor and amulets to protect those he'd gifted the items to. But he liked playing a country bumpkin or a hulking brute, and Isis suspected it was so others underestimated him.

"Goibhniu, I'd like to ask you a favor." Anu sauntered over and touched his bulging bicep, fluttering her lashes in a seductive manner.

The man didn't so much as bat an eye as he stared down into her enchanting visage. As attentive as he appeared to be, he didn't strike Isis as a fool, and she couldn't wait to see how this request played out. They were two practiced flirts trying to outdo one another.

"I need an amulet for one of my descendants. Can you do that?"

"Can I? Ya doubt me skills?" A flush started across the exposed V of his barrel chest, worked its way up his thick neck, and settled on his sculpted cheekbones. Goibhniu might be a bit unsophisticated, but he was the perfect eye-candy as far as Isis was concerned, and she could watch the emotions play on his interesting face all day.

"Not at all," Isis inserted smoothly, gracing him with a warm smile she hoped appeared sincere. "Our beloved Anu was merely wondering if you had time and the inclination to help us."

His dark brows snapped together, and he sought confirmation from Anu. Her smile blossomed and widened to encompass them all, and she shrugged daintily. "Truth be told, we have a problem on our hands, and we believe you're the only one who might be able to help. Those wayward humans…" She tsked.

"Are they the ones who lost me sword? I don't hold them in favor, I don't." His growl sounded like thunder in the clearing, and the forest creatures roaming free lifted their heads to sniff the air uncertainly.

Capturing her plump lip between her perfect white teeth, Anu shot Isis a lend-me-a-hand-here look.

"I think what she's trying to say—and this is strictly my interpretation—is that Bridget O'Malley needs protection from the villainous warlock who absconded with your precious weapon to begin with. She's been able to retrieve it, but the curse hasn't been lifted." With a gesture toward the pond, she said, "As you witnessed, she's overly cautious about giving her heart."

Adding an approving nod, Anu touched his bicep again, and Isis assumed she couldn't help herself. The urge was hard for *her* to resist, much less an earthy goddess like Anu. "A nonmagical woman against the descendant of Zeus? She likely doesn't stand a chance without your help."

Lips compressed in a straight line, Goibhniu's suspicious gaze darted back and forth between them. "Yeah, and I think you're trying to trick me, ya are."

"No." Isis's sharp retort and cool, steady stare conveyed her displeasure. "I've laid the problem at your door. Help us or not, Goibhniu, but never believe we have set out to trick you. I don't work that way. If you know nothing else about me, know that."

"Then why help a worthless witch with no magic?"

"She's not worthless. She's honest, hard-working, and innately kind. Go. Disguise yourself as a mortal and judge for yourself. Weigh her worthiness against whatever guidelines you have for bestowing a gift and see if she doesn't measure up." She crossed her arms and arched a brow. "I'll wager she will."

His ocean-blue eyes lit, and the unholy glow told Isis that Goibhniu was about to rise to her challenge. "And what will ya give me if she fails me test?"

"What is it that you want?"

"You. For a *coicís*." His wicked grin made her heart beat faster.

With a slow perusal of his body, she met the dare in his intense eyes. "Deal. But no cheating. You have to be honest in your evaluation. We shall be observing you, and if you don't weigh the scales fairly, you won't have me and you will be required to make the amulet anyway."

He narrowed his eyes as he studied her. "Who's to say what's fair or not? If I deem she's not worthy and say I've been honest but you don't agree, how do we find the middle ground?"

She glided forward, stopping a few inches from touching, and smiled up at him. "I have my ways of judging honesty, my dear Goibhniu. If you lie, I'll know. And on my bad side is not a place you'd care to be."

His bark of laughter thrilled her to her bare toes, but she didn't show it. "Fine." He turned to Anu and grinned at her affronted expression. "It's not that I don't find ya attractive, but me brothers would hold me down and cut off me bollocks if I were to try to seduce ya. They've claimed you for their own, they have."

"You're forgiven. Where are these randy brothers of yours? I'd like to meet them."

He held out his arm, glancing back over his shoulder to wink at Isis before vanishing.

With a laugh, she went to check on Ronan. His training was of the utmost importance according to the Fates.

CHAPTER 25

$\mathcal{M}$orning dawned, and with it came a weighty sense of dread. Needing the comfort, Bridget reached for Ruairí only to discover he wasn't there. She sat up, half worried she'd dreamed the entire night. A quick shower later, she pulled up her damp hair in a ponytail, drew a jumper over her head, and shimmied into her favorite jeans. If she had magic, she'd have accomplished it all in a fraction of the time, but she was still earlier than usual today.

Pausing outside her door, she listened for the sounds of the inn stirring. When she was satisfied she was the only one awake, she crossed to Ruairí's designated room to see if he'd crept back there to avoid anyone learning about their night together.

She knocked lightly. When no one answered, she twisted the knob and eased the door open. The bed was perfectly made, and Ruairí's duffel bag resided in a chair at the far corner of the room. She didn't hear shower sounds, so she assumed he wasn't there.

With a shrug and a huge amount of regret that he'd not hung around for morning sex, she descended the stairs to make breakfast for the guests. As she turned the corner to the kitchen, she stopped short, a gasp escaping her lips.

When Ruairí looked up from his place at the stove and smiled in welcome, her heart thawed completely, leaving her raw and aching with the need to accept everything he was willing to offer. He'd done this to let her sleep in and to please her, and she was undone by the small kindness.

"You don't need to do my chores, love." She approached, rested a hand on his lower back, and leaned in to take an appreciative sniff. "You made *crêpes?*" Stealing one from the plate, she spread the fresh strawberry mixture on top, rolled it, and took a hearty bite. The hint of vanilla mixed with the berries was ambrosia. *"Ohmygoddess!"*

After a second bite, washed down with the coffee he set in front of her, she sighed her pleasure and kissed him. "I'll shag you every night and twice on Sundays if you take over the cookin' and continue to make these for me."

He laughed, and she relished the joyful sound.

With a plate in one hand and her coffee in the other, she raised them up to his line of sight. "Thank you for this."

"My pleasure, *mo ghrá*. Go and have your breakfast. I'll finish here, brew another pot of coffee, and wet the tea."

"Thank you. It'll give me time to tackle the administrative side of things today." Despite Loman and the threat he posed, she couldn't ignore her business. Somehow, Ruairí had understood and provided her with the help she needed. Something her brothers sometimes failed to do, wrapped up as they were in their own lives. "I'm not looking forward to rescheduling our upcoming guests. It'll hurt to do it, but I'll refund their initial deposit and give vouchers for a future stay."

"I'll see you're reimbursed."

"No!" Shaking her head, she sat at the table and spread the strawberry topping on another crêpe. "It's not your fault, and it won't make us paupers to lose a few visitors."

"It's the fault of my family, all the same. And I refuse to let yours suffer for it." His expression was determined, and Bridget let it go for the moment. When this mess was over, she'd settle the debate for good.

He set down the spatula and faced her fully. "You're going to argue the point, aren't ya?"

"Not right now, I'm not. Right now, I'm going to enjoy another crêpe, drink my coffee, and bask in the morning-after glow." She gave him a cheeky grin, realizing for once, all was right with her world. Or at least eighty-five percent right. The rest would be resolved when Loman O'Connor was dead and buried and when she could have an honest conversation with Ruairí about love and trust moving forward.

Mouth open as if he intended to respond, he glanced beyond her, and the transformation of his facial expression indicated an end to that particular conversation. "Ronan. Welcome back, man. How are ya feeling?"

"Surprisingly well for someone who had his insides turned out." The hoarse quality of his voice suggested he'd screamed or shouted a time or two during the process.

Her desire to help him was strong, and she jumped up to mix specific healing ingredients with the tea Ruairí was brewing. "Roisin stocks just the thing for sore throats," she said, measuring out the recipe as her friend had previously instructed. "There's a bit of earth magic grown into the herbs, so it'll take care of what ails you."

"I'm grand, Bridget. No need to fuss."

"You're not grand as we can see and hear. You'll drink the tea I've prepared, with no argument, mind."

"I've the feeling it wouldn't do me any good."

She smirked her triumph. "Not a lick. As soon as you've downed it, you can tell us all about the process and what we're to do next."

Dutifully, he drank what she gave him, admitting to feeling

better almost immediately. For certain, he didn't sound as hoarse.

"Hurry and tell us what we're meant to do," she demanded.

"Nothing."

Half convinced she hadn't heard him properly, she turned to Ruairí for clarification.

With a chuckle, he said, "I heard it, too, *mo ghrá.*"

"Well, you're no help, you aren't." She smiled to indicate she was teasing.

"Isis—"

The backdoor practically flew off its hinges as it slammed open, and both Ruairí and Ronan positioned themselves with hands raised for battle. A flaming ball swirled in each of their palms as they prepared to lob fire at whoever might enter. The entire scene was so instantaneous, Bridget didn't have a chance to react. It bothered her to think what their lives must've been like that they should automatically affect a fighter's stance rather than assume the wind blew the door open.

She pushed through them with a light laugh and abruptly stopped short when a bear of a man stepped through the opening. Her first instinct was to shy away, but she held her ground, knowing Ruairí would always have her back. That realization gave way to the knowledge that she likely trusted him more than she wanted or planned.

Lifting her chin, she offered a welcoming smile to the glowering stranger. "Sure, and that's one way to make your presence known, but if you're wanting a room, you could've come through the front door."

A twinkle appeared in his ocean-blue eyes, but his scowl remained. "Are you the owner of this place, then? Bridget O'Malley?"

Ruairí answered before she could. "Depends who's askin'."

"I'm askin', and it wasn't you who I was addressin'," the stranger growled, narrowing his eyes in challenge.

Ronan shifted in front of her, and she once again darted around him and closer to the posturing newcomer.

"I am... Bridget O'Malley, that is." She held out a hand and was surprised when he took it in a gentle hold to shake.

"Then I'm happy to meet ya, girl." He turned contemplative as he studied her face, not releasing her. "You're meant to be a great witch, ya are," he said softly. "What's holdin' ya back?"

"Fear," she blurted, then nearly choked on her tongue. Never would she have told another living soul her innermost secrets. She wasn't usually forthcoming with her weaknesses. Roisin had only ever received a watered-down version of Bridget's thoughts and feelings when she asked. "How... are you... how...?" she sputtered.

His smile was devilish, and his impossibly blue eyes crinkled at the corners. "I've a few more questions for ya, child. Are you willin' to sit with me a spell and have a pint?"

She thought about it for less than ten seconds before she nodded. "One condition."

"What's that?"

"You don't try to murder me or abduct me from my own pub." She placed her hands on her hips and gave him a saucy smile. "It's too bleedin' early in the morning for drama."

He laughed, and the rumbly sound was oddly soothing. "Aye. I can promise you that."

"Good." She turned toward Ruairí and wasn't surprised to see his anger simmering below the surface. His flushed cheeks and snapping eyes were laser focused on the stranger.

"You'll not be alone with her. Not until we know you don't work for Loman O'Connor."

"I owe you no explanation, boyo, but I'll grant that I don't know the man you speak of if that will make you stand down."

Bridget walked to Ruairí and placed a hand on his crossed arms. "If you would stay and make breakfast for the others, I'd be grateful."

Never breaking his staring contest with the dark-haired stranger, he lifted a hand and snapped his fingers. Three towering stacks of crêpes, paired with three large bowls of various berry toppings and a heaping bowl of whipped cream, now took up half the table. A long platter filled with a variety of meat took up the other half.

"Breakfast is served," he said shortly.

"You forgot the juice, coffee, and tea," Ronan said with a muffled laugh.

Again, Ruairí snapped his fingers. "Is everyone satisfied we've a complete meal prepared, or would you like me to bake some feckin' scones?"

"Ruairí. Look at me, love." She lightly pinched his chin between her finger and thumb, trying to tug his face down to hers. When he dipped his head and met her gaze, he sighed.

"Bridg—"

"Don't ask me how I know, but he's not here to hurt me," she said in a low voice. "I need you to trust me."

"Trust?" He snorted. "Are *you* playing the trust card?"

Her temper sparked. "Aye. I'm playing the trust card because I've given you no reason *not* to trust me, unlike your feckin' games in the past."

His dark-blond brows clashed together, and he opened his mouth to argue, only to be stopped by Ronan.

"I'll go with her, Cousin."

"Sure, and what part of the word *alone* do either of you eejits not understand?"

The stranger laughed and crossed to the table to pick up a plate. As he began piling on food and shoving sausages in his mouth, Damian Dethridge sauntered the room. Both men froze when they saw the other.

"Goibhniu."

"Aether."

"Wait, what?" Bridget charged across the room to confront

the stranger. "Goibhniu? As in the maker of our sword? *That* Goibhniu?"

He picked his teeth with his pinky, looked at the meaty treasure he dug out, then sucked it off his finger. "Aye."

"Jaysus!" Swaying—and not because of the disgusting gesture—she used the table for support as she sat down.

He straddled the bench, facing her. "I'm to judge your worth."

"My worth?"

"Aye. To see if you should remain the Keeper of the Sword and if I should restore your family's magic."

Curious, she forked up another sausage and plopped it on his plate. "Bring that and come with me. We're going to be needin' that pint after all."

He grinned and reached to help her up. She took one look at the grease on his fingers, and ignored his outstretched hand.

CHAPTER 26

*T*wenty minutes and two pints later, Bridget stumbled back into the kitchen. Rauirí had been impatiently awaiting her return with her family, Ronan, the Aether, Castor, and Alastair Thorne. They had all gathered around, either at the table, sitting at the counter, or holding up the wall with their brawny shoulders.

"Sure, and this is an odd sight," she said with a giggle.

"Where's your friend?" Ruairí asked as he abandoned his chair to let her sit down.

As she passed him, she wrapped her arms around his neck and drew him down for a heated kiss. "You're my friend," she murmured with a happy sigh.

He was amused by her unexpected show of affection. "Yeah, and I'd like to know what he used to spike your pint, because I'm going to need whatever it is on days when you're on a roll."

With a laugh and a light slap of his cheek, she plopped down in the chair. "Ah, Ruairí O'Connor, never change." She released a dreamy sigh and propped her chin on her fist, giving them all a happy smile.

"Oh!" She blinked like an owl. "He gave me a present, he

did." She fumbled with the new chain around her neck and withdrew an amulet. It measured roughly seven by five centimeters and had an intricate Celtic knot surrounding a ten-carat, marquise-cut emerald. "Isn't it grand?"

"Does this mean you're going steady?" Alexander asked with a laughing look at Ruairí.

After shooting his uncle the bird, he squatted next to Bridget. "May I?"

She placed the amulet in his hand and began running her fingers through his hair as if she'd never experienced its feel and texture before.

"I love your hair. 'Tis soft and silky, but still thick enough to grip when you—"

To save her future embarrassment, he clamped a hand over her mouth and placed his lips close to her ear. "Save that thought for later, *mo ghrá*, yeah?"

With a giggle, she snuggled against him and dropped a light, lingering kiss against the column of his throat. "I love you, Ruairí."

"And it's glad I am of it," he said. "I've a right powerful love for you, too, Bridg."

Scooping her up and cradling her in his arms, he addressed the others. "I think we should all adjourn to the salon for this discussion. Our Bridget needs a lie down."

Once in the main room, he placed her on the largest sofa and sat to cradle her head in his lap. He stroked her wild main of hair back as she stared up at him, stars in her lovely eyes. The color rivaled the stone in her amulet.

After everyone was seated, Ruairí tried again for answers. "Why did Goibhniu give you the amulet, *mo ghrá*?"

Tilting her head, she tried to view the necklace resting against her breast. "He said he lost a bet with a goddess, and it was to protect me from the Loman O'Connors of the world. I think it's the most beautiful thing I've ever seen," she said on a happy sigh. "Don't ya think so, Ruairí?"

"No. I think you're the most beautiful thing I've ever seen."

She laughed and rolled on her side to face the others in the room. "Goibhniu said he's satisfied his weapon is in the proper hands, and we're to gain our full abilities very soon." She frowned and blinked. "Or I think that's what he said."

Alastair smiled indulgently. "Can you recall his exact words, my dear?"

Her frown deepened, and she blinked sleepily. "No. I..."

"And she's gone," Castor said, tone wry. "I didn't expect it would be long."

"How will we learn what Goibhniu was here to impart?" Cian asked, standing and preparing to lift his sister.

Ruairí waved him away. "I'll see her to bed in a minute. Alone and unmolested," he added under pressure of Carrick's stern look. "In the meantime, you might want to see what he dosed her with. She's—"

"You may want to put down the torches and pitchforks. Goibhniu didn't hurt her. It's the power of the amulet mixed with the alcohol," Alastair said. "Bridget isn't used to such a strong magical influence, and it's made her drunk."

Cian nodded. "Yeah, our Bridget can usually drink many a man under the table, so I suspect you're right."

Damian grew still and his eyes lost focus. "Leave her where she is," he ordered, jumping to his feet and throwing his arms wide. "Prepare yourselves!"

A blinding explosion rocked the house, blowing out windows and raining only small bits of fiery debris on them all thanks to the Aether's quick, protective action. Ruairí's first instinct was to cover Bridget, but as he shifted over her, a viridescent beam of light shot straight up from the emerald of the amulet, spreading out and creating an impenetrable umbrella over their entire group. Wooden beams, glass, insulation, furniture… anything and everything bounced against the barrier and tumbled away. A man-sized hole now existed in the front wall, and across the street, Loman stood, igniter switch in hand and a bone-chilling smile on his face.

Ruairí charged only to be stopped short by Ronan and Alexander. "Let me go," he demanded. "I'll finish the scaldy bastard."

"But you won't, son." Alexander gave him a hard shake. "He's trying to draw us out for a larger scale attack. You need to stay with Bridget and let me handle this."

"He blew up her fucking house!" A second blast rocked the neighborhood, and the sinking feeling in his stomach told him it was her pub. "Bridget's going to be devastated."

"We can rebuild with little effort, but we can't restore a life lost," Alastair reminded him as he rose from where he'd fallen and brushed off the dust from the sleeves of his suit jacket. Once he was somewhat tidy, he straightened his silver silk tie and tugged down his sleeves. "Dethridge? Shall we?"

"He's mine," Ronan said, and his lethal tone was enough to make the hairs on Ruairí's body stand on end.

"Are ya up to it, Cousin? I'll not have you going after him at half power."

"I've never felt better, nor more determined, to kill that vile fucker."

Carrick stepped forward. "We need cooler heads to prevail, but first, we need to put the fire out—"

Alastair lifted his arms wide, closed his eyes, and appeared to draw the moisture from the outside atmosphere. From where Ruairí stood beside Bridget, he could see the rain clouds gather through the hole in the ceiling. The flames, licking up through the opening and billowing black smoke, were immediately snuffed out.

"Sure, and that was a grand trick," Cian said with an approving nod. "Now for the plan to kill Loman O'Connor."

"No plan, just a show of force," Damian said. "Ronan, cloak yourself." He left the protection of the amulet and walked steadily toward the opening in the wall.

"He's so impulsive," Alastair lamented as he followed in the Aether's footsteps.

Alexander ran to catch up. "You two aren't having all the fun without me, Al."

"Do keep up, Castor."

LOMAN COULD BARELY CONTAIN HIS GLEE WHEN THE AETHER, Alastair Thorne, and Antoine stepped through the opening at the side of the inn. His attack, designed to draw them out, worked perfectly.

The C-4 he'd used was able to destroy the house the man-made way. He'd managed to circumvent the wards by paying the mail delivery service to place a package on the stoop, claiming it was a present for his lover. Over the roof of the inn, Reginald had used a drone, and for the other business, Loman had simply lobbed a stick of dynamite. Blowing things up was great fun, as he'd discovered in the years he'd worked for Victor Salinger at the Désorcelers society. As a magical demolitions expert, there were many witches he was able to take down without ever having to get close.

Currently, Loman had another ace up his sleeve, and he was getting ready to play his trump card. Moira was waiting nearby, gun at the ready to take out Alastair, and Reginald had prepared a gas combination of witchbane and moonseeds to poison Damian and Antoine, weakening them in the process. Loman owed them both a violent death. Alastair didn't know it, but he was getting off lucky with a bullet to the brain.

After the major players were off the field, it would be time to finish the O'Malleys. Years ago, he'd wanted Victor to use the Désorcelers resources, but witches without abilities were beneath his notice. But now, they would be extremely vulnerable with no magic of their own, and with Moira and Reginald beside him, his life-long enemies didn't stand a chance.

Loman held up a hand, and his adversaries stopped in the center of the road. "If ya think to capture me and send me back to the Witches' Council, think again, ya feckers," he shouted. "I'll not go back alive."

"We weren't intending to send you back at all," Antoine said with a cold grin. "Your reign of terror ends here, Loman."

The buzz of the drone drew their notice and caused Loman to chuckle. He loved a solid well-thought-out battle, especially when the others had no way of knowing what was coming. "No, Antoine, I don't think I'll let ya kill me today, I don't. But you, on the other hand…"

But just as the drone topped the house, it froze in place.

A second later, he heard Moira scream.

Sweat beaded his brow, and he straightened from where he'd been lounging against the stone wall. "How'd ya do that?"

Damian Dethridge tilted his head and studied him like a bug under a microscope.

"How?" Loman screamed.

"Me."

Ronan appeared beside him, and the glow coming off him was almost blinding. Somehow, some way, his son had amplified his powers to exceed those of Loman's own.

"Ronan, me boy." He hated that his voice sounded wheedling, but he needed to appear weaker so that perhaps he'd appeal to Ronan's softer side. His son's Achilles heel was those who were at a disadvantage, and he refused to attack anyone unable to defend themselves.

"I'm not your anything, ya gobshite," Ronan spat. "Don't look to be paternal now. You were the worst sort of father."

Outraged that anyone would dare insult him, much less a

disappointment like Ronan, Loman struck. But the fireball didn't reach its intended target, instead fizzling out to nothing but a smoke bomb.

"You did that?" he asked in disbelief.

"Aye. It seems you're no longer the strongest O'Connor, yeah?" Shifting forward, Ronan looked him in the eye. A mocking smile curled his lip. "How does it feel to be helpless for a change?"

"Did you forget I always have a backup plan, son?"

For a brief instant, Ronan's self-assurance slipped, but he replaced it tenfold. "Yeah, I'm afraid your backup is out of commission, and you're on your own."

"What did you do to them?" By attempting conversation, it allowed him time to formulate a new escape plan.

"Let's just say Moira is a little tied up right now, and your drone-driving minion has already taken off and left ya high and dry, he has."

"Reginald was always out for himself. He's like his mam that way." Loman grinned like they were sharing a joke. "Do you remember the time—"

"I don't give two shites for your fond memories. Quit your yammerin', and start walking toward the inn. I'm sure you don't want me to drag your old feeble arse across the yard by your ear and embarrass you, now do ya?"

"Too much of a coward to kill me in public, boyo?" he taunted.

Ronan's bolt of electricity struck him without warning, and Loman screamed from the searing pain.

"Get moving," Ronan barked.

CHAPTER 27

"No." Ruairí emerged from the destroyed wall opening and glared at Loman. "If you bring him on the property, it will negate the wards. It's what he wants."

Ronan gave Loman a thoughtful look. "Aye, that may be, but he's helpless against this many people."

Hating to admit it, Ruairí shook his head and said, "We're too vulnerable, Cousin."

"I propose a death match." Castor stepped forward, his eyes so cold and calculating, Ruairí had a moment's unease.

"Between which contestants?" Damian asked. His look was contemplative, as if the idea held merit.

"Loman and myself of course. What could be more entertaining than twin against twin?" The evil grin on his uncle's face worried Ruairí. The man he'd come to know over the last few days wasn't mean-spirited or cruel, and yet his expression rivaled any Loman had ever had. Was it all an act? If so, to what end?

"Sure, and if I win, I get your abilities," Loman stated with glee.

Castor shot a sharp look toward the Aether, who shook his

head. Their gazes remained locked for a long moment before Damian closed his eyes and nodded. An exchange of thoughts had happened, one Ruairí wasn't privy to, and the churning in his gut was telling him this was all about to go terribly wrong.

"Sure, and this is a bad idea. The worst I've ever heard if I'm tellin' it true."

"You always were a pansy, boyo." Loman curled his lip into a disgusted sneer. "I tried to get Shane to be rid of you when you became a turncoat and started hangin' out with the O'Malley girl, but he thought he could reform you. A fat lot of good it did."

"I'd rather be an O'Malley than an O'Connor any day of the feckin' week," Ruairí retorted, well aware of the punishments for not toeing the O'Connor line. He'd suffered every one of them. "They know what true family and loyalty means, they do, and all you know is how to inflict pain and suffering on those you consider weaker than you. You're not my uncle. You're not my anything."

"Yours will be the first death I celebrate after Antoine's," Loman cackled. "Or maybe I should kill your *hor* in front of you. Show you what the penalty is for betrayal. Would you like that, boyo?"

Castor stepped between them. "You betrayed your family a long time ago, Loman. You bought into our father's madness and embraced it for your own. It stops with you. The next generations will not be made to feel worthless or conditioned to hurt others."

"You won't know, now will ya? Because you'll be dead."

Alastair yawned and stretched as if waking from a nap. "Oh, are you still talking incessantly, O'Connor? I thought it was a yappy little dog from the high-pitched, repetitive sound." When Loman opened his mouth to deliver some scathing comment, Alastair held up a hand, boredom on every line of his countenance. "Yes, yes, yes, we've heard it all before. This one will die, that one will die, everyone will die, and you'll be all powerful. Blah, blah, blah. You really need a new line. You're beginning to sound like a broken record."

"Oh, look, Al! I think you've caused him an apoplexy. How fun!" Castor clapped his hands together like a kid in a candy store. "If he strokes out, it would save time but not be nearly as fun as me kicking his ass."

Loman turned positively rabid and lunged for his brother, but Castor had anticipated his move, freezing him in place. He delivered a sidekick to Loman's stomach, then reset time. The effect was immediate, and his brother doubled over, coughing from the pain of the blow.

"You're a cheat," Loman spat.

Castor laughed as if it were the funniest thing he'd ever heard, and perhaps it was, considering Loman used every underhanded trick in the book to get what he wanted.

A prickle started along Ruairí's arms, alerting him to potential danger. "Someone else is here. Watching." He scanned the area, looking up and down the street and in the upstairs windows of the homes closest to the inn.

"I don't see anyone," Ronan said.

"They're there, all the same."

"I feel it, too." Alastair closed his eyes, a frown playing between his brows. When he lifted his lids, he zeroed in on a location to the left of Ruairí. "About twenty yards beyond the shrubbery."

"I'll go," Damian said.

"No, it should be me. You need to find these two a battle ground and secure against Loman's escape."

"Al—"

"Don't go getting all soft on me now, Dethridge. It's unbecoming of an Aether."

"Fuck off."

Alastair chuckled and departed in a blink.

"And then there were four." Loman's lips curled in a satisfied smile.

"There are many more than four of us. You just can't see them, Brother."

Castor's comment confused Ruairí until he remembered the cloaking spell Quentin had used in the bar. Somewhere around them, there were other allies. His relief was profound.

"Who do you think took out Moira and the drone?" Ronan asked Ruairí in an aside.

"You?"

His cousin's lips twitched, but he didn't respond.

"Why are they toying with him?" he asked Ronan in a low voice. "He's likely to escape, he is."

"I don't know, but the three of them have their reasons. You and I will remain on guard."

"Is it possible that he has a full army hidden around here?"

"Yeah, anything's possible, and with him, probable. Go find Bridget and make sure she's all right."

Needing no further urging, Ruairí ducked through the opening and went in search of the O'Malleys.

BRIDGET WOKE TO FIND HERSELF IN THEIR CEREMONY ROOM beneath the inn. Roisin, Carrick, and Cian were all present and in deep discussion over a grimoire.

"Yeah, and what are the three of you plottin'?"

The relief on Roisin's face was plentiful. "When we couldn't wake you, we got worried. You slept through the entire—"

Carrick quieted her with a look.

One that Bridget found disturbing. "As you can see, I'm fully resurrected. So how about one of you tell me what I slept through?"

From the uneasy glances her brothers shared, she assumed

the telling would fall to Roisin, but the trap door above her opened and Ruairí descended the stairs, interrupting any explanation her sister-in-law might've given.

Relief flashed across his face as he saw her up and moving about. "I'm sorry about your inn and pub, *mo ghrá*, but we'll get them restored."

"What the feck happened to them?" She charged for the stairs, determined to see the destruction for herself.

He caught her with an arm around her waist. "It's not safe up there. Structurally, it could all come down around us. This room is the only safe place for you right now."

"Let me go, Ruairí, I need to see the damage."

"Bridg—"

She pulled away and frantically searched the area where she'd been resting. "This is Loman O'Connor's doing, isn't it? Where's my sword? I'll cut that fucking gobshite from gut to gullet!"

"We hid it."

She pinned Cian with a glare. "Unhide it right now!"

"Yeah, and that's not going to be happening, Bridg. You're in no state to face anyone. Ya were out cold for the last hour."

"Cian O'Malley, I swear by all that—"

"Careful! You're in a sacred space, and you're a witch, Bridg." Roisin pointed to the pentagram on the floor, inside which they were all standing with the exception of Ruairí. "You could conjure a spell and not be aware of it. It's dangerous to let emotions come into play in a ceremony room, to be sure."

Frustrated beyond measure, she faced Ruairí. "And I suppose you think I should just hide out, too?"

He took an extraordinarily long time answering. Finally, he shook his head. "No, *mo ghrá*. I think you should be in the middle of the fray. This leg of the prophecy is yours, and you need to finish it like your brothers did before you."

All her rage evaporated, and she rushed to him and threw

her arms around his neck. He caught and held her to him as if he never wanted to let her go.

"Thank you," she gushed. "I needed one person to have faith in me. Just one."

"We all have faith in you, Bridget," Carrick said from behind her. "But you're the one who keeps us together. You're the one we all rely on to make things better, to make us better." He ran an affectionate hand down the back of her head and settled on the middle of her back. "We love you, and if something were to happen to you, well sure, and we'd all fall apart."

"It doesn't mean you can keep me caged for what you believe is my own protection," she said, giving him a half smile. "I've more to contribute than cooking and cleaning our places."

"We know that, Bridg." Cian, not to be outdone by their brother, stepped forward and hugged her. "Sure, and we do. But you've no magic, and Loman O'Connor is a madman."

"But I do have magic." She held up the amulet. "Between this and the Sword of Goibhniu, I'm a right badass."

Thunder boomed overhead, and they all glanced up.

"The clash of the twins, I would expect," Ruairí murmured.

"I'm assuming Loman and Alexander are who you're referring to, but I've no idea what you're talkin' about," Bridget said.

"My uncles are to duel to the death, it seems. It'll make for grand entertainment as long as Castor wins and we don't become casualties of their fight." He mock shuddered. "One is almost an exact copy of the other, and yet they are vastly different, they are."

"A copy…" She tried to recall what the Aether's daughter had said to them. "What was it Sabrina said to you, Ruairí? About the swords."

"You will need to help her make the new sword to fight your uncle. You will hold the true one for her and be the arm that strikes the evil man down."

"That's it then! We need to conjure a matching sword!"

"You think her prediction was meant for you and me to fight Loman together?" The disbelief in his voice was comical.

"Aye."

With a resigned sigh, he nodded. "Sure, and I'm the feckin' eejit you're always calling me, but I'll do it if that's what you want, *mo ghrá.*" He caressed her cheek. "This is foolish, all the same. But I've loved you from the moment I saw you, and I'll love you until the day I take my last breath. Let's pray to the Goddess today is not that day, yeah?"

"And I've loved you, Ruairí O'Connor, from the moment I saw you, and I'll love you until the day I take my last breath."

The sconces on the wall lining both sides of the room, flared to life, and the pentagram at their feet lit as if it were illuminated from beneath. The grimoire on the wooden altar shuffled its pages and stopped somewhere around the first fifth of the book.

The tingling she'd experienced before was nothing like the burning in her veins now. She cried out and looked at her brothers, who both seemed to be hit with a similar infusion of magic. The atmosphere around them crackled and snapped and the torch flames danced on the breeze from some unknown air source. Atop the altar, her black cat, Lucky, watched intently, and she'd have sworn he had a look of smug satisfaction on his furry little face.

"You broke the curse, Bridget!" Carrick shouted over the roar of the wind. He lifted his arms and stared at his hands in wonder. Blue flames snapped and crackled from his fingertips. "Ya did it!"

"Look, and I've never felt anything like it before," Cian hollered with a hearty laugh. "It's incredible, it is!"

Bridget was too enthralled with what was happening to answer. The sheer power flowing through her body was heady, and she could understand why the Loman O'Connors of the world wanted to amass all they could.

When she faced Ruairí, ready to share her excitement, she saw him sitting on the ground, his back to the wall, with Roisin bending over him. Fear took the joy of her family regaining their ancient magic, and she ran to where he sat, crashing to her knees beside him.

"Ruairí!"

He waved her away with a weary smile. "I'm grand. Don't fuss."

"What happened?"

"You gained your power, and I lost mine."

CHAPTER 28

"*What?*" Bridget could scarcely process what he was saying. "Completely?"

"It remains to be seen. But yeah, I had a dizzy spell, and now I've nothing but a hollow feeling inside."

"But that's not what Sabrina predicted. She said you'd conjure the duplicate sword. You've a need of magic to do that."

"Maybe she was wrong."

Roisin shook her head. "No, she's never wrong. If Sabrina told you that you would conjure a sword, you will."

"So this is temporary then." The absolute relief Bridget felt was overwhelming. To think of Ruairí vulnerable to his relatives without his power was terrifying to the extreme. She cupped his face and pressed her forehead to his. "I'm sorry, love. If I'd have known it would take your magic…"

He drew her down onto his lap and wrapped her in a tight embrace then tenderly brushed away the single tear that fell from the corner of her eye. "I'd give up my magic every day and twice on Sundays if it means you get to experience what it's like and if you can protect yourself should the need arise."

"Oh, Ruairí." She laughed that he'd quoted her reaction to the crêpes he'd made earlier that morning.

He grinned, and the love shining from his worshipful blue eyes filled her heart to full.

"We've need of the Aether. He can restore Ruairí's power to him," Carrick said. "I'll go."

Ruairí shook his head. "No, it's important you wait, Carrick. When I left them a bit ago, things were getting heated. I've no doubt if you go up there now, you risk your life."

Bridget, Carrick, and Cian all shared a look. None of them cared to have another fight their battles.

"What page did the book open to?" Roisin asked, and Bridget was almost sure she'd done it as a distraction.

Carrick gave her a long look, and he smiled as if he, too, understood what she was trying to do. He held out his hand to help her up, and they strolled to the grimoire to see what the temperamental tome had displayed.

"Cian, may I have a moment alone with Bridget, please?"

Her brother nodded and joined the others, leaving her alone with Ruairí.

"Bridg—"

"You have that *if I don't make it through this tone* goin' on again, and I'll not listen. You and I are meant to have a future, Ruairí. The Goddess said as much, and I believe her."

His lips compressed as he gave her a helpless look.

"Sure, and I mean it," she said. "You'd better be believin' it too, or I'll lock you in this room."

"Well, the tides have certainly turned. A week ago you couldn't get rid of me fast enough, and today you want to keep me prisoner to service your every need."

His teasing grin never reached his eyes, but she went along with him.

"Yeah. Who'd have seen it coming besides little Sabrina

Dethridge?" Bridget snuggled into his chest, resting the top of her head under his chin. Keeping their conversation light was more than she could manage, though, and she shifted to face him. "I wish I hadn't wasted all these years with you."

He brushed noses with her. "Now you're just sounding maudlin. I'm about to weep, I am." With a wink, he helped her stand and gave her a friendly pat on the arse. "If it's my last night on earth, I'll be takin' my jollies where I can get them."

She laughed at his ridiculousness and tugged him to his feet. "And if it's my last night on earth, I'll be lettin' ya."

Curling a hand around her neck, he drew her close, and when his lips were but a breath away, he said, "I do love you, *mo ghrá*. That's never wavered, and it never will."

"'Tis the same for me, Ruairí. I've never wavered in that love, even when I was angry or disappointed and couldn't see a future for us. I'll not waver in the future, I promise."

His kiss was the balm her soul needed. Before things grew heated, he drew back and nodded toward something a few feet away. "I'm feelin' judged by your cat."

She turned her head to see Lucky watching them, and she had to admit he did indeed appear judgy. When she held out her arms to him, the cat leapt up and settled firmly within her embrace. "What is it, my little love? What has you vexed?"

"Him."

Bridget nearly dropped her familiar on his head. "Jaysus! He spoke!"

"What?"

"He spoke!"

"I thought. You hear with your mind."

"He did it again," she choked out, unsure whether to be terrified or fascinated or elated. "Lucky responds when I speak."

If a feline could smile, Lucky would have. Bridget was certain she saw a distinct upward curl of his mouth.

"Jaysus, you really speak." She laughed and kissed between his ears, happy to hear him purr. The sound was as loud as a motorboat engine in a cavern.

Ruairí attempted to pet him, only to draw back with a scratch on the back of his hand. "I don't think he likes me."

"O'Connor."

"But a good O'Connor, Lucky. You'll have to learn to get along with Ruairí, yeah?"

"No."

She bit one corner of her lip and gave Ruairí an apologetic look. "It may take time."

Her cat gave one long blink in his direction, then leapt from her arms to trot off, tail in the air, twitching in irritation.

"A lot of time."

With a light laugh, he drew her close and gave her a light buss on her lips. "Let's figure out how to duplicate your sword, *mo ghrá.*"

A SMALL SURGE OF WHAT FELT TO BE HIS POWER, SIZZLED ALONG Ruairí's veins. Not strong enough to burn, but enough to make itself known.

All was not lost.

Unlike the O'Malleys, the O'Connor clan wasn't part of the Six originating families. Their magic was born unto them through the centuries as the main families split off and married others. Ruairí had always expected his power would diminish should Bridget and her siblings restore theirs, and he'd always been fine with the thought. But here, in the moment, he knew real fear. Never before had he worried about being too weak to defend himself, but this sensation of being a newborn foal on wobbly legs disturbed him. He had little time to learn to walk again, so to speak.

And he had no idea which of his abilities were gone and

which remained. He certainly didn't know if he could conjure a sword. But then, Sabrina didn't say he *had* to do it. Only that he had to *help* Bridget do it.

"We're going to need a piece of rebar or a wheel wrench," he told Cian. "Where can we get one?"

"The boot of my car," Carrick said. "But it's next door, and it might take me a few minutes to get there and back."

Cian shook his head. "No, I'll go. You stay here."

"I'll go." Bridget gave him a no-nonsense glare when he began to object. "Goibhniu gave me the amulet for a reason. I've faith in his gift."

As much as Ruairí hated to admit it, she was right. She would be the best candidate to go, and it galled him to be unable to protect her. "Sure, and I'll go with ya."

"No!"

"Bridg, it's not open to negotiation. You don't have eyes in the back of your head, and you need someone to keep lookout." He shrugged. "And I believe your grand new necklace will protect whoever you want it to, but we don't know how it works yet."

"Before you go, I think you both should read what's in the book," Roisin inserted from her spot at the altar. "You're likely to need this one, to be sure."

They gathered around and read what was written, and as it dawned on Ruairí exactly what the spell contained, he laughed. "A glamour spell! We don't need to make a duplicate at all. We only need to glamour the metal so everyone believes it's the original sword."

"Should we shape it? At least give the impression it's the same weight in case someone is familiar with the original?"

"Yeah, and that's a brilliant idea, Bridg." Cian nodded, his pride for Bridget clear in the admiration on his face.

She bumped her shoulder into his and turned to address

Roisin. "As a whole, we've never cast a spell. Would you walk us through what needs to be done?"

"First, you need to set out the candles stored in the altar. You'll put them on the five points within the circle. Since you're all new to casting, I'd use salt and sage for added precaution on the perimeter of the ring."

They hurried to do her bidding, and Roisin took an extra minute to show them how to light a candle using only their finger and a gentle push of power. "You'll want to let the magic flow through you, yeah? Don't shove it out, don't pulse it. Visualize a golden ball forming from the nucleus of your body's cells." She touched her index finger to a candle wick. "Watch."

With minimal effort, she created a spark and softly blew on it to stoke the flame, thereby lighting the candle. They each took a turn underneath her eagle eye.

The act itself wasn't huge on the magical scale, but Bridget was over the moon in her excitement that her first spell worked. "Ruairí! I did it! Did ya see, love? I did it!" His pleasure in her success expanded her heart, and she hugged him tightly. "Thank you."

"For what?"

"For being selfless enough to give my family the sword. Even knowing you could lose your gifts, you did the proper thing, and I have no words to describe this feeling of gratitude."

"You already did, *mo ghrá.*"

"Since you all seem to have caught on quickly, let's get on with the sword issue," Roisin suggested then bent over the last candle, preparing to light it.

Footsteps down the stairwell caught their attention, and Ruairí silently directed them off to the side to hide as he went to see who it was.

Fearing for him, Bridget peered around the corner. The visitor she hadn't expected to see was Knox Carlyle, husband to Spring Thorne, Alastair's treasured niece.

Before Ruairí could challenge him, she ran by him and straight into Knox's open arms.

"Yeah, and I'd like to know why you're runnin' to hug every stranger the minute he arrives, I would," Ruairí muttered from behind her.

She laughed, grabbed Knox's hand, and dragged him into the expansive ceremony room. "What are you doing here, love, and where's your wife?"

"Sure and I feel better," Ruairí said. "Welcome, friend." After they shook hands, he faced her. "And I'd like to know why all the male company you keep look like they were molded by the gods."

"Because they are. Quentin, anyway." She looked up at Knox. "You?"

"No. Just the power of one." He ran a hand down the side of his face and revealed a scar that ran from the edge of his eye to the corner of his mouth.

Bridget sucked in a breath, never having known he had been so badly injured.

"It's not a big deal, Bridget. It happened when I was a child." An instant later, his face was restored to the perfect mask he showed the world. "Quentin thought you might need backup down here."

"Where is he?"

"Up there somewhere." He gestured overhead. "Assisting Alastair's security team in rounding up stragglers who work for Loman O'Connor."

"They'll turn on him soon enough when they realize he can't pay them," Ruairí said with a shrug.

Cian shook Knox's hand. "Good to see you again, man."

"You, too." After a nod to Carrick and Roisin, he turned smiled at Ruairí. "So I hear we're family, so to speak."

"I don't understand."

"You're Quentin's cousin, which means you are a Thorne by marriage, like me. We protect our own. It's why I'm here."

"Your timing couldn't be better, man. I've lost the bulk of my magic, and they gained theirs. But they're like baby birds learning to fly and in need of instruction." Ruairí grinned at Roisin. "She was doing a grand job, but the O'Malleys are hard headed, so we've no idea what will take."

Cian slapped him upside the head as Carrick shoved him and Bridget pinched his side.

"Ya see the abuse I suffer here? It's a wonder I stay."

"Stop whinging on," Bridget scolded as she stood on her tiptoes to give him a peck on the lips.

"It looks like a real hardship," Knox said dryly. Taking his time, he turned in a circle, his eyes missing nothing of the room. Glowing pentagram, the altar with the temperamental spellbook, torches on the walls, and tapestry map of *Éire*. "I can also see you have a ceremony started, though why you left a protective circle in the middle of a spell is beyond me. You'll need to rework it."

"We hadn't gotten that far." Roisin pointed to four of the five lit candles. "We were about to step things up a bit."

His expression turned grim. "No time. Things are pretty serious up there. Tell me what you need, and I'll conjure it."

"Ruairí suggested rebar or some type of metal to shape a sword." Bridget looked at the others and shrugged. "Why risk getting hurt when he can conjure what we need?"

"Why, indeed," Knox replied. "How long?"

"Roughly eighty centimeters in length, and the weight should be about nine-hundred grams." When Knox gave Ruairí a blank look, he laughed and said, "About thirty-one inches long and weighing two pounds."

"Thanks for the conversion. I'll remember to install an app on my phone for next time. What about color?"

"Have you ever seen a two-handed sword? This would be

steel, silver in color, with a black metal handle. Engraved on the handle there is a Celtic knot, similar to the pattern on Bridget's amulet with jewels encrusted in the design."

Knox chuckled. "That's pretty specific."

"It's an unforgettable sword, to be sure."

"Do you have it with you? I'd like to see and weigh it to conjure a duplicate."

Bridget retrieved the weapon, handing it over to Knox. "Can you do it?"

"I believe so," he said at length as he closely studied the Sword of Goibhniu from every angle. "Have you thought to summon the god who made this and ask for a duplicate?"

Cian shook his head. "We wouldn't dare insult him. Two hundred and fifty years is a long time for a god like Goibhniu to be patient over the loss of one of his prized weapons."

"I'm a metal elemental and can manipulate all forms, but I need something to work with. Might I use one of the rods holding the torches?"

"Aye."

Stepping up to the wall, Knox jerked one of the torches down with an effortless display of strength, turned it sideways, and ran his hand down the entire length of the handle. The flame followed the path of his hand, molding and shaping the metal until it began to resemble a sword.

"Deflammo."

The fire went out completely without a single sputter, and Bridget made a mental note to remember the word for the next time someone decided to blow up her home or business.

In another two minutes, the replica sword was ready with the exception of the jewels.

"What do we use to create them?" she asked.

"It's not my area of expertise, but I imagine if we can get glass, I can make a passable stone."

"I'm on it." She gave Ruairí a kiss for luck and jogged up the stairs, careful to listen for sounds of activity before inching open what remained of the hidden bookcase. Making short work of her glass-finding mission, she grabbed a large vase off the floor where it had fallen and darted back down the stairs. With a triumphant grin, she handed it off to Knox.

CHAPTER 29

*I*t didn't take Knox long to break the glass and reshape the pieces into the four stones he needed—a ten-carat diamond and three fifteen-carat emeralds. By the time he was done, the swords were identical.

"How are we ever going to be able to tell them apart?" Carrick examined one, then the other, and shook his head. "It's feckin' unbelievable, it is."

"Does yours hold magic?" Ruairí asked. "Do we need to worry about Loman getting his hands on it?"

"Not at all. The magic was in the making." Knox grinned, and Ruairí found himself liking the guy. "All Loman will get is metal and glass with a dull-edged blade."

"Yeah, and that suits me just fine. The fewer items he has at his disposal to harm another, the better." He gave Bridget a steady look. "Are we ready to join the fray, *mo ghrá*?"

"As we'll ever be." Her expression showed her nervousness, but it was outweighed by her sheer determination.

Ruairí drew her into a tight embrace, and she returned his hug with a fierceness of her own. She would be protected, and he would be a target, but he'd have it no other way. "Let's go murder my uncle."

Knox released a short bark of laughter. "That sounds dramatic. Are you sure you aren't related to Alastair by blood?"

"Alexander Castor."

"Of course. That explains it."

Bridget hesitated to leave, casting a concerned glance back at her brothers and Roisin. "Will you stay with them, Knox? Protect them?"

"He's needed elsewhere, Bridg." Carrick smiled his understanding, created a fiery blue ball and balanced it on one finger, spinning it with his other hand in a move similar to a professional basketball player showing off. "Sure, and we'll be all right. Cian knows the cloaking spell, and we'll do as the book instructed, yeah?"

When she bit her lip, undecided, Ruairí clasped her hand in his. "Trust your siblings, *mo ghrá*. You'd want them to trust you."

She allowed him to draw her away, but she ran back to hug each of the others. "I'll be cross with ya if you get hurt. You stay hidden."

"Jaysus, Bridg!" Cian shoved her toward the stairs. "We're not *weens*. We've made it to the ripe old ages we have without magic and no luck to call our own. Now we have both. We'll be grand."

"You'd test the patience of a saint, ya eejit." She smiled to soften the comment. "But yeah, I love you, all the same."

They had one foot on the steps when Bridget's cellphone rang. When she ignored it, Ruairí stopped her with a hand on her arm. A little voice inside told him she needed to take that call.

"Answer it, *mo ghrá*."

"It's Eoin," she said with a frown. "He usually leaves the callin' to Dubheasa."

"Answer it."

With a tap of the button, she said, "Eoin?"

"Bridget O'Malley, I have a proposition for you, I do."

Ruairí recognized the voice immediately, took the phone from her shaking hand, and hit the speaker option. "Hello, Da," he said with a calmness he didn't feel.

All the color left Bridget's lovely face, and she sat down heavily on the step. He touched a hand to her shoulder and silently vowed he'd kill his father for whatever evil he'd stirred up this time.

"Ruairí, my boy. Sure, and why doesn't it surprise me you're with the bitch?"

"Don't know which bitch you might be referring to, I don't. You're current wife isn't here."

A muffled curse sounded through the speaker, and he instantly regretted taunting Shane O'Connor. Eoin O'Malley had just paid for Ruairí's snide comment.

"Want to try again, boyo?" Shane's oily voice asked with glee. "The painter has more fingers for me to break. Eight and a dislocated thumb."

"Go to the devil, you fucking bastard!" Eoin hollered in the background. "Bridg, don't give into his deman—mmph."

"I had to gag him. The lad never shuts up, he doesn't."

Ruairí ran back for the altar, gesturing for everyone to move. He snatched up a bowl from inside the cabinet, put the phone on mute, and said, "Knox, water." Then he unmuted the phone.

Roisin jumped to find a scrying crystal and a stick pin, understanding what he was about.

"What do you want from Bridget, Da?" he infused his voice with resignation as he pricked his finger and added exactly three drops of his blood to the water in the scrying bowl. Once again, he muted the phone to quickly say, *"Goddess Anu, hear my plea, assist me in this time of need. Show me where me father be."*

He unmuted the phone so Shane would hear any background noises and not get suspicious.

"Don't bother trying to scry, boyo. I'll be long gone by the time you get here." Gloating was thick in his father's voice, and Ruairí suspected Shane spoke true.

Cian had whipped out his phone and was frantically scrolling through pictures the entire conversation. He showed one to Ruairí and Knox.

"Well, look who's decided to join us. And you brought me exactly what I was planning to ask you for, ya did." Shane's comment was loaded with triumph. "You learned to teleport faster than most, Bridget O'Malley."

As one, they turned toward the stairs, but Ruairí already knew what he'd see... or rather who he'd not see—Bridget. In her place was the Sword of Goibhniu, glowing golden in the firelight. The desire to vomit gripped him so hard he fell to his knees and bowed his head. Finally, he had her complete trust. But while giving him this gift, she'd put herself in Shane's clutches to save her baby brother, knowing it might cost her own life.

"I've no need of you now, boyo!" Shane cackled. "Give Loman my regards when he comes for you."

BRIDGET'S HEART WAS HAMMERING OUT OF HER CHEST, AND SHE almost missed Shane's last taunt to Ruairí before he hung up the phone.

"I knew ya were stupid girl, but this... Sure, and this takes the cake, it does." Shane tossed Eoin's phone away and stalked toward her. "You realize I'll not let you walk out of here alive, yeah? I mean, what better way to punish my son for his disloyalty?"

A quick glance to her right showed Eoin, sweaty and

covered in blood, or perhaps red paint, it was hard to tell, considering he was an artist. An armed guard was beside him with a gun to his head, and Dubheasa was nowhere to be seen.

His weary, pain-filled eyes met hers, and he shook his head, somehow understanding what she wasn't asking aloud.

Her relief was palpable, but she didn't let it show as she faced Ruairí's father.

"I don't think I'll let you kill me today, Shane O'Connor. Neither will Goibhniu. He's no longer cross since we've recovered what your family stole from us."

Shane's pale gray eyes narrowed in his displeasure. "Then we'll kill your brother and be done with it." His sneer was the stuff of nightmares. Full of hate and rage and everything twisted. They had all believed Loman was the worst brother of the two, but perhaps they'd dismissed Shane too soon.

"Sure, and you could, but then you'd have nothing to trade for your own life," she said matter-of-factly.

Reluctant amusement removed the hatred from his expression. "You tryin' to bargain with me, girl? *You?*"

"This sword for my brother's life. Simple and fair."

"Not your own?"

"No.

As Shane stared at her, no doubt trying to figure out the catch, a bead of sweat worked its way down Bridget's back. The urge to squirm was strong, but she managed to stand still. Not removing her gaze from her enemy, she said, "Eoin, love. I know you're temperamental and prone to vapors—" her brother snorted his disbelief, and she choked back an inappropriate laugh "—but just close your eyes, yeah? Dream of home. Of the fields beyond our house. Let the sun warm your face as you picture it in your mind."

Jaysus, she hoped he understood what she was telling him. Explaining exactly how to teleport, so he could get the feck out of there. The glow of their ancient magic was about him, and all he had to do was learn to use it.

She sent him a meaningful glare when he didn't immediately get it. A small, secretive smile curled his lips, and in a blink, he was gone. Just as she was about to follow him, Shane lunged toward her, screaming, "Kill her!"

Blinding viridescent light shot out from the stone of her amulet, encircling her and creating a glowing green dome, just as the first shot was fired. The bullet ricocheted off her protective barrier and found its way into the forehead of the man who'd fired it.

As the guard's eyes turned flat and his body dropped to the floor with a hard thud, Shane reached her, his expression rabid as he raised his fists to beat on the dome.

"Yeah, and I'm sorry about your bad luck, O'Connor. Don't ya hate it when your plans fall to shite?" Goddess, was that her taunting him so coolly?

"Make no mistake, Bridget O'Malley. I'll slit your throat with the Sword of Goibhniu one day soon," he promised, and the fire of his fury looked to be burning him alive.

Behind him, Ruairí and Knox appeared, but she didn't give them away with look or deed. Instead, she laughed. Loud and braying and intended to annoy the devil out of Shane as well as cover any sound the men made. In Ruairí's hand was the true Sword of Goibhniu, and she wanted to give him the chance he needed to take another playing piece off the O'Malley-O'Connor chess board.

The crackle of Knox's building energy ball gave them away, and Shane turned just as Ruairí was thrusting his weapon. The blade slid straight into his black heart, exactly as expected when wielded by one with pure intentions—the precise reason she'd left the sword for Ruairí to begin with.

He withdrew the sword and looked down at it in wonder.

Bridget was curious what he thought. Was he expecting to

see black ooze in place of the violet-red blood on the metal? Was he horrified he was the one to kill his own father?

Her magical forcefield faded away, and she dove for him, needing to touch him and reassure herself they were both alive and well. He appeared to have a similar urge, and he flung the sword, not caring when it clanked against the chrome stool by Eoin's counter.

Wrapping his arms around her, he hugged her, tighter than he ever had before. Crushing her, really. "*Mo ghrá. Mo ghrá.*" He gripped her face between his hands and moved her head away to create space and meet her tearful gaze. "I thought I'd lost ya. I thought…"

"I'm sorry, Ruairí. He had my brother. I couldn't not come."

"I know, *mo ghrá*. I know." He lowered his mouth to hers, and she felt everything he'd gone through in the last seven minutes. His disbelief, his determination to save her, his crushing fear that he wouldn't be in time. They were all there in his frantic kiss.

"I hate to cut this short, but we need to get the fuck out of here," Knox said, causing them to break apart. "Grab whatever you need and let's go before your father's reinforcements come through that door."

She nodded, unable to speak from the thick emotion clogging her throat. A shaky caress of Ruairí's face was all she could manage now that reality had set in and her adrenaline had worn off.

"It's all right, Bridg," he said hoarsely. "We're all right."

Again, she nodded mutely. After one last quick kiss, she bent and picked up the true Sword of Goibhniu, coldly wiping the blade across the clean part of Shane's shirt. "If I could stab him in place of you, take away the horror of killing your father from you, I'd do it, Ruairí," she said. "You shouldn't have to bear that burden, love."

"He had to die either way. And he had it coming, all the same."

"But it didn't have to be you," she argued.

With a smiled that didn't reach his eyes, he tenderly pushed the hair back from her temple. "I think it did, *mo ghrá.* Life always comes full circle. You and I know that, yeah?"

CHAPTER 30

*E*oin O'Malley landed with a thud and a savage curse as his injured hand hit the tree trunk next to him. The lush landscape behind the Black Cat Inn had grown and changed since he'd been gone these two years past. He hadn't realized until he saw his sister, appearing out of thin air like a warrior goddess, how homesick for *Éire* he'd been.

It had gone against his instincts to leave her, but the purpose in her eyes told him she'd had a plan, and anything he'd have done in an attempt to help might've spoiled it. Still, he felt like a fecking coward for abandoning her as he had.

Taking stock of the inn and pub, he leaned back against the oak tree in shock. Had that happened before or after Bridget appeared in his apartment?

Panic set in, superseding his shock.

His family might be under all that rubble!

Running for all he was worth, he closed the distance between the forest and the inn in less than a minute.

"Cian! Carrick!" He tore through the rubble, shoving drywall, wood, and furniture out of his way. "Roisin! Aeden!"

"They're safe, son."

He whirled around to see Alastair Thorne step through an opening in the outer wall. The man looked pristine, not a hair out of place, and almost exactly as Eoin remembered him from ten years before when the senior Thorne had attended his first gallery showing.

"Where are they, Alastair? My brothers, where?"

"Likely in your family's magic room, yeah? Why don't you show me where it is, my boy-oh, um, my boy?"

A chill encouraged his neck hair to stand on end. "Sure, and I can do that," he lied with a smooth, practiced smile, the one he reserved for handsy art patrons. "But would ya be doing me a solid and healing my hand first?"

Silver-blue eyes narrowed, but he smiled in return. "And what happened to your hand?"

"That gobshite Shane O'Connor thought he'd get the better of me, he did." Eoin lost his smile. "But he was wrong. *Dead* wrong." In truth, he had no idea if Bridget succeeded in whatever she'd concocted, or if Shane was even now standing over her broken body and gloating like the madman he was. However, if it was truly Alastair Thorne in front of him and not an impostor as he truly suspected, the man would be able to read the truth from Eoin's energy and internal conflict, as only a real empath could.

"Dead?" Rage curled the upper lip of the man in front of him.

With a casual scratch of his neck and a look around their destroyed home, Eoin nodded. "Aye."

And because he anticipated the strike, he reacted accordingly, diving behind the overturned sofa just as the fake Alastair tried to firebomb him.

"*Deflammo!*" Cian's sharp command echoed throughout the room, and dust particles fell down on Eoin from above. The inferno was snuffed out in an instant, and he peered over the smoking edge to see his brothers, shoulder to shoulder, in a fighting stance Cian had learned from his spy days.

"You can drop the act, whoever ya are. If you're Alastair Thorne, I'll be eating me feckin' left boot," Carrick said, edging in front of the sofa.

Eoin rose to his feet and stepped in the gap between his brothers. "Timely save."

"You always were dramatic," Cian said with a light laugh.

Carrick didn't bother to shush them, instead taking a step forward to confront the stranger. "We know you're not Loman—"

"Or Shane," Eoin inserted.

"—or Shane," Carrick added with a nod. "How about you tell us who you are before we kick the shite out of ya?"

"You, O'Malley? *You* think you have what it takes to fight *me*?" The stranger laughed, and his disguise faded away. The three of them shared a look, no closer to figuring out who the man was than they were ten seconds before.

"Sure, and I'd give it a go."

Cian laughed at Carrick's flippant reply, and Eoin was hard pressed not to chuckle himself. Being Irish, and pub owners to boot, his brothers were always up for a good tussle.

"Doyle."

Cian's face lost every trace of humor, and he edged closer to Eoin. "Get out, and take Carrick with you," he said in a low voice.

"Not going to happen. I—"

Bridget burst through the opening, accompanied by Ruairí O'Connor and some Loreal-blond, supermodel-type dude Eoin had never seen before. Ruairí stopped short, and based on his slack-jawed expression, he was thoroughly shocked.

"Fuck!"

"Does your father know you're a turncoat?" Doyle spat on the scarred wood floorboards.

"Aye, Madden, he did know." He gestured to the ground with a tilt of his chin. "You've still got the manners of a barnyard animal, I see."

Eoin inched closer to Cian. "How did he get past the wards?"

"If you take a good look around, you'll notice the wards didn't hold up."

It took everything he had not to laugh at his brother's response. Cian was seldom serious when it came to confrontation. He employed humor in every aspect of his life and gained great pleasure if his quick quips could disorient and anger an opponent into making a costly mistake. Cian had a charm all his own.

"A cornered animal," the blond man beside Bridget said. "Never a good combination."

Mr. Loreal lifted his arms, palms upward, and Eoin could swear he felt an atmospheric change. An instant later, electricity crackled between the guy's fingertips.

"I hope he's on our side," Eoin said in an aside to Cian.

"Aye. And be grateful he is. Knox is feckin' lethal."

"You've one real choice here, friend," Knox said casually, as if discussing the weather. "You can allow yourself to be arrested on behalf of the Witches' Council, or I'll kill you where you stand."

The cool delivery of the ultimatum caused Eoin's stomach to flip. Sure, he'd always known of the feud between the O'Connors and the O'Malleys, but it hadn't truly touched him. Happily creating away in his studio in New York, he was far removed from any drama. Or at least he had been until tonight.

Shite got real when Shane O'Connor had shown up with his thug in tow, and Eoin was still worried for his sister, Dubheasa. Her last text to him had been to say she needed a vacation and was going off with her girlfriends for the weekend. No amount of trying on Shane's part had gotten her to respond to the inquiring messages he'd sent as he tried to lure her to Eoin's place.

Dubheasa was brilliant, and she knew Eoin never asked about her personal life or whereabouts. He only ever told her to have fun, be safe, and call if she needed bail money. He certainly had never been pushy about details the way Shane had been. Eoin only hoped she understood and had gone into hiding for her own safety, especially considering Bridget's call the other day.

When Madden Doyle glared at Knox, raw hatred on his face, Eoin sensed what was coming. He didn't have long to wait.

"I'll never surrender to the likes of you! I've the blood of kings—"

Without a by-your-leave, Knox fried his arse.

Eoin's legs grew shaky when he saw Madden shudder from the electrocution and wet his pants. When the second bolt hit him, the smell of burnt flesh filled the room, and Eoin dashed for the door, afraid he was going to toss up his last meal on Bridget's not-so-pristine floors.

She gave him a concerned look as he passed her, but he kept going until he was breathing fresh air again. When had his family become embroiled in murderous games? Had he been so oblivious to the goings-on of his siblings, so willfully ignorant of the dangers?

He ran a hand across his buzzed hair and winced in pain. The beating he'd taken at the hands of Shane's hired mercenary came back to haunt him in the form of his bruised scalp and broken finger. His ribs didn't feel all that grand either, now that he was moving around.

"Eoin?"

Alastair Thorne turned the corner, and Eoin had a moment of panic. Was this a ploy, then? Were all the O'Conner family members going to show up as Alastair and try to hurt his family in sneak attacks?

"Calm down, son. Your emotions are all over the place, and you're making it hard to concentrate."

One look into Alastair's concerned sapphire eyes, and Eoin breathed a sigh of relief. "Sorry, sir. There was another—" he pointed toward his home "—another you that wasn't you. I'm a little on edge, to be sure."

"Another me?" Alastair's dark-blond brows snapped together, and the air around them grew overcast and dark as he tugged first one cuff, then the other.

The changing weather and approaching storm clouds told Eoin all he needed to know. This was, indeed, Alastair Thorne, one of the most powerful warlocks to ever walk the earth, and the type who didn't suffer fools lightly.

"You can remain calm. A hair model named Knox took care of him for you, he did."

As quickly as Alastair's temper flared to life, it disappeared in the face of Eoin's comment. "Hair model?" he choked out on a laugh.

"It's all those flowing Loreal-blond locks of his. I'm sure I saw that exact shade on a shelf in the supermarket."

Alastair nearly bent double laughing, and Eoin joined him. Maybe it was the relief of knowing his family was unhurt, or perhaps the punch to the head had sent him over the edge, but suddenly, the entire situation seemed hilarious.

After they both sobered, Alastair's gaze swept him from head to toe. "Do you need a healer, son?"

"For my broken hand, yeah. This hard head of mine likely wasn't damaged."

Lips twitching in an effort to suppress his grin, Alastair held out his hand. "Then let's get those broken bones repaired."

AFTER LEAVING WORK WITH ALL HER BELONGINGS IN A BOX, Dubheasa climbed in the back of a cab and texted Eoin she was going away for a long weekend. With a sigh, she shut off her phone and tossed it into her Coach shoulder bag. Lost in thought, it didn't register right away that her cabbie had made a wrong turn.

"Hey!" She leaned forward, prepared to give him a tongue lashing, when she caught sight of the man driving. *"You!"*

"Dovie, I need you to hear me out."

"Stop the fucking car."

She tried the handle, uncaring that she was in the middle of rush-hour traffic or that she'd need to leave her box of personal items behind, prepared to jump if she had to.

"Listen, love, I'm not going to hurt ya. We just need to talk."

"I said, *Stop. The. Fucking. Car!*"

"No." He winced when she screeched. "Jaysus, woman! You like to deafen me!"

"I'd like to cut off your bollocks and shove them—"

He turned up the radio to drown her out.

"I swear by all that is holy, I will gut you!"

When he began whistling as if he didn't have a care in the world, she lost her temper completely and banged on the glass partition. "This is kidnapping, and a punishable offense here in the States, you tool. I'll see you locked away for life, I will."

With raised brows, he turned down the music. "Did ya say somethin', love?"

Slipping a hand inside her purse, she felt around and withdrew pepper spray, surreptitiously setting it in her lap, then reached inside for her phone.

"I wouldn't do that, Dovie."

"I'm not talkin' to you. And my feckin' name is Dubheasa."

He sighed heavily. "You'll always be me Dovie."

"I'm not your anything, you delusional toad."

Minutes ticked by, and he remained silent, not trying to talk to her again. And as they approached the Lincoln Tunnel, heading toward New Jersey, her nerves went on high alert. In the city, she might've stood a chance of getting away, but whatever destination he had in mind was too far out for her comfort zone.

"What's your name?" She'd read somewhere that it might work to make yourself seem human to an attacker. Perhaps it worked similarly with an abductor. "Your *real* name, not the one you gave me when you first showed up at Lamda," she added quickly.

"Ronan O'Connor."

One of them was going to die.

CHAPTER 31

"We need to find Dubheasa," Bridget said without preamble. They were all gathered in the Aether's English home, looking like a bunch of dirty, homeless waifs, which they essentially were. Alastair had arrived at the inn to say they were to wait at the Dethridge estate, until Damian, Castor, and Ronan returned. But that was three hours ago, and Bridget was getting nervous.

"We'll find her," Cian promised. "I have all my contacts on it."

"Why isn't a simple scry working? It should've worked, yeah? Unless… unless…" She couldn't bring herself to say it. If Dubheasa had fallen victim to Loman or one of his mercenaries, Bridget would never forgive herself for not insisting she come home.

"Don't borrow trouble, my dear. We'll find your sister."

She tried to tamp down the urge to rail at Alastair, but he'd been good to her family and her, and he didn't deserve the lash of her temper. Not to mention, he was showing great restraint in the face of the riot of emotions they were all experiencing and he must be feeling as a result.

The endless hours, they'd been unable to reach her. No amount of scrying with her personal items or the O'Malley blood could locate her, and Bridget was slowly losing her mind.

"Ruairí, your da said something on the phone earlier. He said he'd be gone long before you got there. How could he disappear that quickly?"

"In our family, we were trained to leave small footprints behind where no one would find us. A strand of hair here, a drop of blood there, jumping from one place to the next so it would take a long time to find us. While someone was hunting, we could be in and out and safely behind wards before they'd catch us."

"So it's possible he set up a decoy and misdirected us away from Dubheasa?"

"It's possible, *mo ghrá*, but not probable. If my father got to Eoin first and was unable to reach her by text, it's more likely he never found her. Just why she's gone silent is concerning, as is her ability to hide her tracks."

She jumped up. "I can't sit and wait anymore. Dubheasa could be out there, hurt and helpless and unable to get home."

"Yes, or she might be fine." Alastair rose and poured her a drink from the sideboard. "Here. But go slowly this time until you're used to the alcohol-magic mix on your system. Things were done and said when you were socializing with Goibhniu that you probably would like to forget."

She froze, glass halfway to her mouth. "What did I do or say?"

When he chuckled, Bridget blushed. "It was bad?"

"No, it was adorable," he assured her with a wide smile. "I promise you."

The truth, painful as it might be, meant a lot to Alastair. He wasn't likely to lie to save her feelings, so she took his comment at face value. With a silent toast, she sipped her scotch.

"When do you think the others are likely to return?"

He shrugged. "I'd have thought they'd be here by now. A death match shouldn't last this long."

"But you don't seem concerned. Will ya be telling me why?"

"Even if Loman should defeat Castor, which is doubtful, no amount of power or abilities will allow him to get the better of Damian or Ronan. Both are levels above Castor."

Taking a closer look at him, she realized he wasn't as unaffected as he appeared. "But you *are* concerned because Castor's your friend."

"Yes." Alastair sighed. "He's one of few allowed into my circle of trust. For years, we thought he was deceased, but it turns out he was hiding from the very man his brother worked for."

"Why did he return?"

"To help us fight an evil entity taking over the Otherworld." He poured himself a drink and took a sip. "His intelligence and magical talents turned the tide and helped us contain the Evil in the Netherworld."

Bridget turned to look at Ruairí, who had his head resting against the sofa back as he watched her through lids that were half-mast. Love and concern were displayed, the two things she always saw in his beautiful blue eyes, usually for her. "I wish Castor was his da. He deserves better than what he got, to be sure."

"Castor wasn't great father material, my dear. Remember, he was on the run. Quentin was adopted at a young age by a couple in North Carolina."

"Maybe your Alexander Castor feared turning into his brother and left Quentin for his own good, yeah?" When Alastair didn't respond, she turned back around. He was smiling at her. "What?"

"I don't know why I never thought of it. You're exceedingly insightful, Bridget O'Malley. And an excellent person to have on one's team."

The compliment warmed her from the inside out. Alastair Thorne wasn't judgmental, but he was selective about the people he associated with. His words were high praise, indeed.

"Thank you." She downed the rest of her drink and held out the glass. "Now let's find my sister, yeah?"

Ronan strolled through the door, looking harried and out of sorts. "Your sister is fine and a pain in me arse."

"Are those scratches on your face?" Bridget's voice rose two octaves. "And why are your eyes bloodshot? Did Loman do that?"

"No, Dov—er, Dubheasa. And it's the last time I try to save her ungrateful arse, it is." He swiped the empty glass out of Alastair's hand and went straight to the bottles on the sideboard. "Yeah, and she refuses to listen to reason."

"Because your reasons are shite, like you!"

Bridget laughed and ran to hug her sister. "How are ya here?"

"The overgrown man-baby," Dubheasa said in disgust after they separated. "It was only a little bit of pepper spray, and he acts like—"

"Don't say it," Ronan warned with a growl. "I swear, you'd test the patience of a saint, Dubheasa O'Malley."

She flipped him double-fisted birds and set Alastair off into the throes of hilarity.

Bridget was hard pressed not to laugh.

Eoin was the first to hug their sister as she joined the others. Side by side, the twins were a beautiful sight. Her siblings made Bridget consider the dynamic between Castor and Loman. They were the only twins she knew who outright despised one another. One evil, one good, if a little unorthodox with questionable tendencies. How did two

T.M. CROMER

babies share a womb, a crib, first steps, and still hate each other as much as those two did? One would think the bond would help them grow stronger under the abuses heaped on them from their parents in their family's madness over the sword.

Ruairí drew Bridget down onto his lap and snuggled her close. "What has you thinkin' so hard, *mo ghrá?*"

"Your uncles."

"Ah, yeah, well, they aren't worth your worry. I say we go up to bed and give that brain of yours a rest."

"What'll we do about Loman?"

"There's nothing that can be done that Castor and the Aether aren't already doing, Bridg. You can't control everything."

She sighed her frustration. Glancing up, she met Ronan's impenetrable stare. She got the distinct impression he, too, was upset there wasn't any news. Would there come a time when father and son would need to square off like Ruairí and Shane had? If so, how would it affect Ronan without someone for him to confide in and care about him?

His gaze cut to Dubheasa, and he watched her with a hunger that stole Bridget's breath away.

"My sister's the one," she said softly.

"I believe so, *mo ghrá.* Ronan's emotions are never so close to the surface, but he seems to hold a fascination for Dubheasa, all the same."

"She hates him." And the thought somehow made Bridget sad for him.

"Sure, and I don't think she does. She can't stop checkin' his whereabouts," Ruairí replied in a low voice, careful not to be overheard. "If she isn't the next Guardian, I'd be surprised, I would."

The more she watched the two of them, the more Bridget realized they actually worked as a couple. Dubheasa was

234

fiercely independent and highly intelligent, the perfect foil for Ronan with his reluctant hero ways.

A smile curled Bridget's lips, and she leaned back within the circle of Ruairí's arms. "Sure, and she'll make a badass Guardian. Better than I ever would."

"I doubt anyone could be better than you, *mo ghrá*. But your sister would be a close second."

Eoin was quiet as Dubheasa told her tale of being abducted by Ronan to be brought back here, and her brother meandered over to the set of French doors to stare out absently over the landscaped lawn.

"He's the one I worry about," Bridget said. "He's lonely, I think. I wish I knew how to make him happy."

"We'll figure it out, Bridg. Together."

"Together."

He scooted her off his lap, stood, then clasped her hand tightly in his. "Let's go to bed, yeah? It's been a long day, and my arms ache to hold you while we sleep."

Rising up on her toes, she looped her arms around his neck, drawing his head down for a taste of his lips. She sighed her pleasure. "Aye, it's time for you to remind me how truly lucky I am, Ruairí O'Connor."

"What are ya waitin' for, woman? Take me to bed."

With a light laugh, she visualized the room Damian's wife had shown them earlier and teleported them with little effort. Sure, and she was going to love the gift of her magic. It remained to be seen what type of elemental she would be, but she didn't care at the moment. Learning how to be a proper witch was for another day. Right now, she wanted to shag her forever man.

"IT'S DONE."

Anu watched the earthly proceedings in Isis's favorite pond and nodded. "Aye. Loman O'Connor will live to fight another day. More's the pity."

"The Three believe it will mold Ronan into a better Guardian."

With a dismissive scoff, Anu turned her back on the scene, a frown marring her normally smooth forehead. "There are other ways. The Fates can be brutal in their tasks, and I believe they enjoy it. Ronan has proved at every turn he's worthy and shouldn't need to suffer another test."

Isis touched her shoulder. "Believe in the process, dear Anu. It will work out. It always does."

"You are too optimistic."

"Perhaps." They shared a wry smile. "So, who's next?"

"The easier of the two. Eoin O'Malley."

Isis laughed. "He's a temperamental artist. Do you truly believe he'll be easier than his sister? Especially after the way she took on our new Guardian?"

"That's exactly why," Anu said with a laugh. "It will take twice as long for Dubheasa to forgive Ronan's treachery. She was attached to her mortal job. As an artist, Eoin is ruled by his emotions. He'll save the girl from the drudgery of her life."

"Poor Brenna Sullivan won't know what hit her."

"Aye, her life is about to be upturned, but you have to shake a few trees to get the best fruit down. And Odessa Sullivan is the one bad apple spoiling the lot, but I believe Eoin O'Malley is clever enough to defeat her."

EPILOGUE

"*I*t's done."

Castor lay on his back, unblinking eyes staring at the sky.

"Are you going to lie there all day, or are you going to get up so we can return home?" Damian asked him.

"Shut up, Dethridge. I almost got my ass handed to me. I don't need you to mock me at a time like this."

"My bad."

Alex laughed. His friend was always the height of sophistication, and phrases like *my bad* spilling from his lips were humorous.

He held his hand up, and Damian helped him to his feet, dusting any stray blades of grass from Alex's back.

"Ouch, be gentle. Everything aches." Alex touched two fingers to his bloody lower lip and hissed out a breath.

"Don't be such a crybaby, Castor. It wouldn't have taken so long if you hadn't been the cat to his mouse." Damian smirked. "Although, I do understand the desire to toy with him. He was an easy man to hate."

Forty-five years ago, when the Aether had caught him

trying to steal his wallet, he'd taken one look at the scrawny boy Alex was and bought him a meal. The entire time Alex shoveled food into his mouth, Damian and Alastair had questioned him. And by the time he was full, he had the presence of mind to wonder why two men, so elegant and beautiful as his intended victims, would bother with a young boy.

But the men hadn't wanted anything from him. Damian had simply written an address and phone number on a business card, handed it over, and told the boy if he wanted to learn the craft of magic, he was willing to train him, but he expected Alex to work hard and leave off his thieving ways.

So began his rigorous training in all things. Magic, fighting, schooling.

It was Alastair Thorne who had taught him how to play the stock market and build his portfolio, and it was also Al who had convinced him to change his name so that Alex didn't have to continually look over his shoulder, waiting for his loathsome family to find him.

Those two outstanding men had not only become his mentors, they became his best friends, and he'd lay down his life for either, just as they would lay down theirs for him.

"Perhaps it's because I'm facing my twilight years, or perhaps it's the fact I barely escaped death this time, but I find myself getting sentimental, Dethridge." He shoved away the embarrassment he always experienced when revealing his innermost feelings and continued. "I owe you a debt of gratitude that I can never repay. You saved my life when you caught me stealing from you. Thank you, my friend."

"Stop it. You'll have me tearing up, and how will that look? The formidable Aether bawling like a toddler?" Damian mock shuddered. When he saw Alex wasn't wavering and wouldn't laugh off the moment, he smiled. "I couldn't have been prouder of you if you were my own son, Castor. You took every tool we gave you and expanded on it, making yourself great. But at your core was a kind heart." He glanced down at Loman's inert body. "Something your brother was severely lacking."

Alex followed his gaze and stared down at his twin. "I see other siblings and wish we could've had that kind of relationship."

"He was too filled with hate. Some people are simply bad seeds, Alex. Remember that."

"What should we do with him?"

"I'll make a call to the Council. They can dispose of the body."

"It feels strange walking away. Leaving him to rot."

Damian dropped a hand on his shoulder and squeezed. "That's your kind heart again. But I think you know better in this case."

"I do." Expelling a heavy sigh for the innocent childhood he wished he'd had and the family that was never going to let that happen, he turned his back on the past. "I need a drink."

"I've got that covered. But first, we have a debrief with the Witches' Council."

"Fuck."

LOMAN SPENT EXACTLY ONE CELESTIAL HOUR IN THE HOLDING area of the Otherworld, waiting for judgment to come down. Or that was his best estimate based on the alignment of the sun through the trees. He was under no delusions as to where he would be sent when he faced the Goddess. As a mere boy, he'd secured his place in hell by killing one of her favored creatures. Of all things, a stupid cat. But at the time, he was arrogant enough to believe he'd displace the Devil himself and take the throne for his own.

He chuckled at his own foolishness.

Bored out of his mind, he leaned back against the rough

bark of a large oak and caught sight of the sunlight as it sparkled off a barely discernible symbol floating in the air in front of him. Had he not been in that precise spot at that exact moment, he might've missed it. He reached to trace it and got a nasty burn for his troubles. With a hiss and a vicious curse, he looked around for something he could use. A fallen branch looked to be perfect for his needs.

"Yeah, and here goes nothin'," he muttered.

To his surprise, he didn't get burned, electrocuted, or punished in any way for tracing the symbol. Words he'd never before seen or spoken came to him, and he chanted them three times as he continually traced the sigil.

Fire flared to life, burning away the invisible shield covering the tree's opening, and Loman laughed at the discovery. If he wasn't mistaken, it was the portal to another dimension. He had a moment's indecision at the thought he might end up in the Underworld, but he recalled a word in the spell he'd spoken, *terra*, which was Latin for *earth*.

"Watch out, feckers, here I come!" he shouted as he stepped into the opening at the base of the tree.

He experienced a rush in his veins, similar to when he fired up to teleport from one location to another. The burning in his cells was on the brink of being unbearable, and he opened his mouth to scream, but the sound remained locked in his throat. In another instant, he was at the base of another oak tree on a property he'd never seen before.

With a dismissive look at the expansive gardens with their hedge maze, he closed his eyes and thought of his estate. Nothing happened. No warming of the cells, no instantaneous travel home. Nothing.

His magic was gone.

Furious beyond measure and determined to rectify the problem, he began walking.

THANK YOU FOR READING BRIDGET AND RUAIRÍ'S STORY. IF YOU want more of the O'Malley family, Thank you for reading Bridget and Ruairí's story. If you want more of the O'Malley family, be sure to look for *Cocktails & Cauldrons*, book 4 in *The Unlucky Charms* series, around mid-December 2022!

ALSO, IF YOU HAVEN'T ALREADY SUBSCRIBED TO MY NEWSLETTER, tmcromer.com/newsletter, or joined my Facebook reader group, tmcromer.me/vip-readers, I encourage you to do so. It's the best way for you to stay current on upcoming stories. After I'm done with the O'Malleys, I'll be introducing the Aether and friends, and you won't want to miss it.

Books in The Thorne Witches Series:
SUMMER MAGIC
AUTUMN MAGIC
WINTER MAGIC

T.M. CROMER

SPRING MAGIC
REKINDLED MAGIC
LONG LOST MAGIC
FOREVER MAGIC
ESSENTIAL MAGIC
MOONLIT MAGIC
ENCHANTED MAGIC
CELESTIAL MAGIC

Books in The Unlucky Charms Series:
PINTS & POTIONS
WHISKEY & WITCHES
BEER & BROOMSTICKS
COCKTAILS & CAULDRONS (Dec 2022)
WINE & WARLOCKS (Mar 2023)

Books in The Holt Family Series:
FINDING YOU
THIS TIME YOU
INCLUDING YOU
AFTER YOU (Jul 2023)

Printed in the USA
CPSIA information can be obtained
at www.ICGtesting.com
LVHW010732061023
760132LV00049B/1162

9 781956 941135